"To read Brenda Cooper's work is to experience the natural world in your bones: sea, sky, river, forest, and the miraculous creatures that inhabit our land and waters. Despite the beauty of the surroundings, Cooper respects her readers enough not to serve up easy answers to the ecological perils we humans have created. Her stories grapple with the consequences through various lenses—personal to political to technical to magical—as her characters come to terms with our impact on the planet."
　　— Tara Campbell, author of *City of Dancing Gargoyles*

"*When Mothers Dream* is a beautiful, colorful, exhilarating, and terrifying collection. These stories and poems are infused with the energy of the divine feminine, and solidly based on its wisdom. Cooper is one of our best short story writers, and it's a rare treat to see hard science fiction handled with such an artistic touch."
　　—Louisa Morgan, author of *The Age of Witches*

"Brenda Cooper's *When Mother's Dream* is a must read book. This often poetic, compassionately prophetic collection of stories shows us our possible futures measured by the breadth and depth of a mother's love. It haunts me like the best of our genre's work."
　　—Ken Scholes, author of the Psalms of Isaak series

WHEN MOTHERS DREAM

STORIES

OTHER BOOKS BY BRENDA COOPER

WHEN MOTHERS DREAM

STORIES

BRENDA COOPER

FAIRWOOD
PRESS
Bonney Lake, WA

For J:35 — Tahlequah

CONTENTS

FOREWORD

This is a time for the power of women. It's the time for our soft power, our brilliant intellect, our anger, our political power. It is time for our family power. After I set out to collect my most recent work about climate and biodiversity, I realized my stories and poems on this topic are almost all about women. It's fitting. To find to a future where we can thrive, we need to grow up. When I watch us wrestle with each other on social media or in the news, or even in the halls of power, I am reminded of schoolyard bullies and high school cliches. If only, I think, if only we cared enough to give each other love and empathy. Women can help with this. The many faces of the feminine include power and mystery and advice, afternoon tea and cookies, and hope. Women can help us grow up.

This collection is not just for women. A world filled with only women would not be as beautiful as a world with all the myriad expressions of family and gender that enjoy the world today. These stories do center on women, on mothers and daughters and grandmothers. But they are written for all of us. I am a woman, and here, I'm exploring what women can bring to the future.

In other ways, these stories are quite diverse.

I'm a futurist; I know that there are many possibilities. Some are good, some are perhaps less hopeful. Some possible futures exclude others.

I am a technologist, and so there are stories in here about using technology to solve problems.

I'm a poet. I snuck in a few poems.

There are rather a lot of stories and poems about Orcas. I live in the Pacific Northwest, and we have a heartbreaking story: three pods of beautiful, local, Southern Resident Killer Whales live in our waters. They are struggling to stay alive. As I write this, a mother orca, Tahlequah, carries a dead baby for the second time, her mourning either consuming her or meant for us to see. Who is to say? These whales do not have enough food. Whale watching boats fill their immediate area with sound that blocks their ability to find prey and even to speak to each other. An entire generation is missing; babies were taken to water parks to jump over ropes for money. The few fantasy stories I've included here are about *these* whales. It might take magic to save them.

The cover image is a perfect artistic rendering of the feminine call of the wild. It was not commissioned for this book. I found the picture online and it stopped me cold. So I found the artist, Rachel Byler, who gives money to help save the whales and creates art that depicts whales of all kinds (and much more). Consider obtaining a piece of her art.

Even though I included hope, these stories do not pull their punches. There will be pain and heartbreak, guilt and damage between now and whatever future we choose to create. Some hard emotions crept into these stories. Of necessity.

I hope you enjoy this work.

—Brenda Cooper

ICE-FREE FUTURE

In a white-linen restaurant, summer sun fought through a shade-screen.
A friend lifted his iced tea and told me he was speaking to a fellow
futurist who told him some words, right there in the middle of normal sentence:

Now that we have committed to an ice-free future

Now, on this perfect day in a normal spring when snow falls on the
glacial tops of Mt. Rainier and frosts the Olympic range, in this time
we keep setting and resetting treaties about climate in motion, making
stuttering progress as the world remains beautiful and the birds sing.

We—Germans, Americans, Chinese, Mexicans, South Africans, Indians,
Brazilians—the people of the developed and developing world, the only ones
with the means to stop or even slow the melt, we sit here
in a shady outdoor patio and eat sage-lemon flan and talk of words.

I choose to buy clothes—manicures—steaks—and trips I do not need. Surely there
will be more tomorrow, even though each flight across the sea commits
the bears and butterflies, the sedge-grass and the mosquitos to go with us
(they who gain nothing from our travel or our heating or our decorating)

to an ice-free, stop and hear that, ice-free future. That's the new phrase. Three
words that will bury medical waste dumps under the ocean. Images fit to cut
away land and return it to the sea, to paint white mountaintops brown, to
kill our weak and young with novel diseases. The words that change it all.

Future, a time we are moving toward, a time we will arrive at and live in,
a time when this ice-free phrase has changed everything we know. We will
decorate our souls with guilt and small triumphs, we will adapt to higher
waters and drier land, to fire and thirst, and

we alone will make all the ice.

SOLASALGIA MEETS THE ALPS

July 26, 2053, 10am Seattle.

Good morning, Mom." Lia mumbles this, sprawled across the kitchen bench in a boneless pose. She gazes at her feet. "Where are you going this time?"

I keep my voice light. "To where the air is thin and clear, and water runs uphill."

Her face turns to me, sadness making her appear older than her 22 years. "Are you reading science fiction again?" She shuts her eyes, thinking. "Uphill? No pollution? Underground?" Then she's certain. "You're going underground." Her eyes open, wide and blue. The dregs of yesterday's mascara stain her cheeks. "To look at empty aquifers?"

"There are as many aquifers with too much water in them as there are without enough," I respond, automatically countering her overstatement. "Switzerland."

Lia stands up, taller than me by almost a foot and yet thinner, her height a gift of her long-dead dad. "You love your safe geography." Her tone makes the words sharp little darts meant to shred hope. She hates hope. Before I can reply, she stumbles toward our shared bathroom, clutching her tea to her chest like a lifeline.

"Remember to feed the cat," I say, then, "I'll call." I call often when I travel. We have each other, and Buster, the orange tabby. I have my job. There's not much else, not yet. Neither Lia nor I know anyone in Seattle. Not well, anyway. We moved here from Cleveland three months ago, and I've been gone two of the three months. She leaves the door open and calls down the narrow hallway. "What time zone?"

"Central European. I'll be nine hours before you."

"So, call in your morning."

"Yes, your highness." I am laughing. That's how we get through our days. She laughs to hide fear and bitterness. I laugh to conceal how much I fret about her, and for her. I hate leaving. But I am a climate reporter and a futurist, and my job keeps me sane. It helps me give people hope, feel like I'm adding more than I'm taking from the world. The young and depressed, like Lia, are hard to reach. If only I had help with her. If only I were a better parent. If wishes were stars.

I drain my coffee cup—tea doesn't do it for me—strap on a face filter, pick up my suitcase and backpack, and step out into the toxic air of Seattle's wildfire season. A month of skies the hue of sockeye salmon has me second-guessing our decision to move here.

Eighteen hours later, I land in Geneva and suck in a lungful of clear air. Here I am, ready to witness to the world. The client (I have many; this one a power company) will use what I see to plan investments and tell big stories—or small fictions.

My hotel room is hot, the thermostat locked by the front desk. Opening the window doesn't help. The rich, Swiss coffee has barely hit my blood as I brace myself and tap my phone. Lia answers my call with a flat "Hello, Mom." She's outside; I hear wind and the buzz of a crowd. Lia's camera points away from her, streetlights illuminating the sienna fog of wildfire haze.

"Hi, Sweetie. Here's Geneva." I turn my head so that the camera in my glasses displays the busy street five stories below, the sharp-angled red roofs, a sliver of blue Lake Geneva. "I'm only here for a day, so this is our chance to see it." Then I switch to the phone camera and show my sleepy face, hoping she'll do the same. She doesn't.

"Are you okay?"

"Sure."

So, no. I swallow guilt. She's a young adult. She'll starve if I stay home and do nothing. Besides, who knows whether my staying home would help her broken soul? She has been depressed since puberty. So have many of her friends. Her generation seems to split between angry activists and children who can't hold up the weight of the world they inherited. "Geneva is one of the cleanest cities in Europe."

Lia pans her phone over to a trash can overflowing with food wrappers and compostable cups.

I wince but keep my voice cheerful. "I'm going to see a giant water battery and a restored glacier."

"Will you also tour the damage from the floods last summer?"

She's been doing her research. I wonder if 22-year-old women in Geneva are as depressed as my daughter. They call it solastalgia. Grief over the state of the world, the climate, the loss of species, the plastic pollution. All the hard problems. She hates it when I offer her hope, looks at me as if I were lying to her. I'm running out of ideas.

As if my unvoiced thought has sparked some curiosity, she asks, "What's a water battery?"

"You know how hydropower works, right? Flowing water spins turbines, which then generate electricity, like the brakes in our EV."

"Mmmmmm . . ." she says, her camera still focused on the trash. A symbol of the hell she believes the world has gone to?

I ignore the view she's given me. "OK, well during windy, sunny weeks the grid gets too much power, but during dark, still months there's often too little, right?"

"I did graduate high school."

I smile, hoping Lia can see my face even if I can't see hers. "At Nant de Drance, they've hollowed out the heart of one of the Alps and dug tunnels that connect the cavern to a high Alpine reservoir and to a big lake down in the valley. When there's excess energy, pumps inside the mountain lift water from the lake up to the reservoir. Then the next time the grid is short of energy, they release water from the Alpine dam, and it falls back down to the lake, spinning turbines and making power along the way."

She's quiet. I take a breath and ask, "See? Like a battery—but as powerful as a big nuclear plant. And it doesn't need anything precious dug out of the ground. No strip mining. No exploitation."

"Okay, you win." I hear a faint smile in her voice. Her camera flips back to the smoke hanging over Puget Sound. "Got any ideas to clean up the air?"

"From wildfire smoke? Quit starting fires." My response is flippant, but she laughs, finally. Not a single comment on the Swiss scheme to help stabilize their grid.

Then again, it's not exactly news. My client is looking into building a water battery in and on Mount Rainier. With snow-pack dwindling, they can charge farmers and cities premium prices for summer water releases. Seasonal water arbitrage, as in-dustry analysts call it, is now the fastest growing profit center for private utilities that serve mountain states.

"Look, Mom," Lia mutters, the laugh gone. "I've got to go. There's a show at the Neptune starting in a few minutes."

She loves live music. I need to meet my minder for the day, anyway. Here in Geneva, it will be all business and putting a good face on everything. Tomorrow, the Mont-Blanc express to Canton Valais and the Alps. "I'll talk to you tomorrow."

Her screen is already dark.

Worry weakens my knees, and I sink into the soft, gray chair by the window. Our children have been infected with our fears. My mother worked for a plastics company. I may have inherited her guilt, and then passed it on. I take a deep breath and stand, reminding myself that I can bear this, and even if hope isn't inher-ited, it can grow and spread. Even to Lia. Most importantly, to Lia.

My driver calls up the hallway. "Doctor Bear? Dr. Pauline Bear?"

"Coming," I call out.

*

Lia's call four days later is so early it startles me. I'm out of bed, coffee brewing, running warm wash water. My heart beats a worry-tone. "Are you okay?"

"There's a storm coming." Her voice sounds tight, strained.

I turn the water off and sit down. Her camera displays a screen with a red warning ribbon and white words I can't read. "What kind?"

"A windstorm. In fire season. I don't how I'll breathe."

I make sure my camera points at me, shows me smiling reassurance. "We have air filters."

Her voice quavers. "I can't stand breathing dead trees."

I feel a stab of guilt for being in the still-beautiful Alps while she is there. Seattle is doing well compared to places like India and Mexico. But July through October keep getting hotter and drier and browner. Dying trees are tinder. There is nothing good to say about the trees. "I saw the Nant de Drance plant yesterday. It's impressive."

"I got your pictures. Didn't the tram frighten you?"

"No. It was steep, but there were ibex, standing on a sheer cliff. Exotic and magnificent. I missed getting them with my camera, sorry." I take a breath, seeing the ibex again. Four feet close together hugging a rugged rock, curved horns, wide eyes. "And the scale of the plant . . . really amazing. The two tunnels span 17 kilometers and are wide enough to hold a highway. The cavern for the turbines is as long as a football stadium—"

"Mom!" Lia cuts me off. "Good for the Swiss. But there aren't enough mountains to water the whole world, and it's hot and miserable here."

"We have mountains. Rainier and Baker, Adams. I'm going up into the Alps with an ice engineer who restores glaciers. Floka Lagman. We're starting on her farm. I may not be able to call. We'll see."

"I can't breathe, Mom."

Damn it. "You can, sweetheart. Just don't panic. Go find someone to help. Take some air filters to the homeless shelter."

Her camera turns off. I can hear her breathe, in and out. In and out. A little fast but not panting. She isn't having a panic attack—not yet. I close my eyes and repeat myself. "Go help someone."

If I were her, I would detest me. But what else can I do? I can't join her despair, or even feed it. "I'll call you when I can. Tell you about Floka then. I hear she has dogs." Lia loves dogs. "I'll send you a video of her border collies. And the mountains. I hear everything is in bloom."

"Okay. I'm going back to breathing dead trees."

"Pray for them."

Laughter, finally. "I will."

I laugh with her, bitter and sweet and just a little desperate. But we laugh.

Outside my tent, cross-legged on a flat boulder, the air smells of water, grass, and damp rocks. I can't remember the last time I shivered. It's cold in August.

Lia answers on the first ring, maybe the first half-ring. "Hello."

Just hearing her voice makes me smile. "Hi. How's your air?"

"Better. The windstorm. Remember? Yours?"

"So clear I can see peaks in France." I angle my camera toward the black-faced sheep in the high meadow near me, and the collie, which is nothing more than a still, dark head with one white ear peeking up above the grass.

"Oh! That's so pretty."

"It is." I have to admit this pasture in front of me—alpage, Floka calls it—so steeply sloped and utterly green, punctuated with yellow buttercups and pink Himalayan balsam, is even prettier than the Olympic mountains near Seattle. I want to hold on to this place, this moment, carry it with me like a shield. If only Lia were here, could see and feel and smell this . . .

"Tell me about your day?" Lia asks.

I heave a deep sigh, trying to think of how to start. "Right now, we're on a common grazing area that's way up at 6,200 feet, but early this morning, we took a helicopter up to 9,000 feet, where they make temporary glaciers."

"Doesn't it take millennia to make glaciers? Or at least decades?"

"Yes." I stand up, stretch, pan the camera across the wild hay fields sloping above us. "We landed near a crevasse about a third of the way up. Floka introduced me to the Minister of Climate, a Dr. Rutger, who has been working on saving and growing glaciers for years. He's famous. Ancient, too. He was here in the twenties when the Himalayan monks came to show them their techniques for building ice stupas—artificial ice hills they make in India.

In front of me, the dog, Tess, circles and stops 10 meters closer to me, tucking two sheep back into the fold.

"Himalayan Monks?" Her voice is almost drowned out by the sheep.

"They helped Dr. Rutger learn what parts of the glaciers to cover. You can't cover the whole thing, you know."

"I thought Floka *makes* glaciers."

"More like conserves them? They spread tarps that reflect the sun away. They kind of look like emergency blankets—remember the ones we used last winter? When the windstorm blew the power out?"

"I used them day before yesterday."

"Oh." I should have asked about the windstorm. "Well, it's very cold up there and we have to wear special gloves and shoes with spikes that stick to ice. There are places you can walk under the cover and see the new ice and the old ice."

"How do you tell which is which?"

"The new ice is clean. The artificial sleet builds up the ice in cold pockets—ravines and remnant glaciers and shaded spots below bluffs. Then the covers help them stay colder so that ice doesn't start melting until most of the snowpack is gone."

"What happens downstream? To the plants and animals that don't get the water?"

I sigh. Lia, always looking for the sour apple. "Look around here. It's green *because* they've done this right above us. Some of the ice I walked on yesterday is only a year old. Meltwater streams last until late summer, like they did before the mountains got so warm. Without the extra months of water, these meadows would die."

"So, who suffers?"

I try not to sound offended. "Who says anyone suffers?"

"Aren't you supposed to be the great searcher after truth?"

"Maybe the truth is that something works." I don't like my tone of voice. She is getting to me, the way only kids can get to parents.

"Prove it."

I'm tempted to just hang up on her. But even when she's hard to love, I love her. So instead of hanging up or saying the wrong thing, I make my voice deliberately light. "I'll call you back."

It takes me half an hour to find Floka on the alpage. A few hundred feet of elevation above the tents, she is walking through summer-dry grass still green-gold at the bottom, tangled with flowers. Black-necked and red goats surround her, grazing, hemmed in by three guard dogs. One of her granddaughters, a girl of maybe seven, is with Floka's six-foot tall grandson. They glance at me as I approach but quickly return their focus to the goats.

I'm a little in awe of Floka, who looks like a blonde supermodel in braids. She is strong enough to climb mountains all day, sweet enough to be loved by goats and grandchildren, and a successful scientist. I come up behind her and clear my throat, "Will you help me?"

Maybe she hears the desperation I'm trying to hide. She cocks her head, as if listening to the soft, cool wind. Then she and the grandson exchange glances. She shrugs. "Sure. I was going to come down to you at lunch anyway."

She sounds philosophical rather than frustrated, and I start to tell her about Lia. "My daughter is angry. She's trying to find the parts that don't work, the reasons we can't possibly win."

Floka smiles. "We will all die."

This answer shocks me into a stumble. I scramble down the steep slope and slide 15 feet, and almost a lot more. Floka puts a hand up and laughs, loud and sweet. "I wasn't suggesting you die today."

"No!" I laugh, too, as I struggle up. We go more slowly the rest of the way, Floka herding me as if I were one of her sheep. We talk of cutting the highest, steepest hay. She ends on a positive note. "Winter is sometimes worse now. Storms and floods. But it's shorter. So, we don't need to store as much hay."

Floka steps inside a warming hut on the slope. "Let's stop here and talk to your daughter. It's out of the wind."

"Thank you." Relief that she will help makes my knees weak.

"I have a son who refused to have any children because he thinks we are killing the planet."

I feel a sudden kinship with her, relief that I am not alone, and the sadness for her, for me, for our children. I breathe the feeling away.

Inside, the weathered wood hut, we rest on a stone bench next to a shelf of dust-covered jars. It's almost 11:30 p.m. in Seattle. Nevertheless, Lia picks up right away and shows her face. She has combed her hair. The cat is snuggled on her lap.

We do introductions. When I ask Floka to tell her story, she has an elevator version ready. "My mother left a business career to farm, and I left the farm to become a scientist. I took a month off every year to help with the herding." She smiles. "And to escape stress. Now two of my children run the farm, and I oversee the glacier work from here. I visit each project once a month, whenever weather allows flight." She pauses a second, waiting for Lia to ask a question, and then continues when she doesn't. "We make snow starting in late October, or as soon as it gets cold enough. Our robots pack it down through the early winter. I feed the goats during the worst months. In spring, robots help us blanket the lowest parts of the snow fields. When there is too much rain, we pump excess water up to the reservoir and high lakes during the day. Then at night, we spray very cold water from those stores onto the ice, and it freezes. So now the high places we graze in summer get watered."

Lia's brows are drawn together. "So, you do all this to water your farm?"

"No." Floka shakes her head and takes a deep breath. "The alpage is commons. We chose glaciers based on how easy they are to make snow for, or to cover." Her smile shows fine wrinkles I hadn't noticed from a distance. "Even the Swiss cannot climb every mountain with machines. We also chose places near people who need water. In two cases, we moved people to the right places."

To my secret relief, Lia is polite as she asks, "What does all that engineering do to the environment?"

Floka smiles. It is a question she has heard before. "We direct water's path. Where it goes," she gestures toward the steep, grassy slope just above us. I make sure Lia can see it well. "We are able to maintain some of what we had. Not everything. There is heat and fire to contend with. But trees and people and animals can all drink, and that is necessary for life. But we also cost *some* places below the glaciers *some* water. They would have lost it anyway, but maybe not for decades. Those are drier now, and some are dying." She glances down, frowns briefly, and returns a calm gaze to the screen. "We are being good engineers, Lia, but even when the only engineer was nature, there was death. Water is life and death."

Lia. "Death by lack of?"

Floka purses her lips, takes another deep breath. "Last year, overhanging ice on two glaciers broke off and fell into snow fields, triggering avalanches. One of the avalanches destroyed a farm. Another one killed a group of schoolchildren hiking on the French side of this mountain range."

Lia does not look as shocked as I feel, but she has an edge in her voice. "Were you engineering those glaciers?"

Ouch. I watch Floka's face. Her jaw has tightened, but her expression remains pleasant, her voice even. "Not my project, but it could have been. I oversaw the investigation. There were small mistakes made."

Lia scratches the cat, who stretches languidly in response. "So, why do you do it? Pretend to be a god?"

"We had the power to destroy the climate. Accidental gods. Bad gods." She glances down at the sheep and dog below us. "We did this, and my sheep cannot undo it."

We all fall silent for a moment. Above us, a vulture circles high over something. It makes me shiver, although it is also beautiful. I watch it to avoid looking at the screen or staring too hard at Floka's face. Will this help?

Lia asks, "How do you know you aren't making it worse?"

"Because people I serve can drink water. And we had twenty-seven lambs this year." Floka turns to face me, a question in her gaze.

I hesitate, then nod. I can't speak right now. I'm sure I'd say the wrong thing. I make a go-on gesture with my fingers, and Floka asks Lia, "What is your purpose? What higher objective do you serve?"

There is a long silence, and I think maybe something damp glistens on my daughter's round cheeks. She keeps her gaze on Floka. "My mom serves truth. Maybe I should start with that."

"What would that mean?"

More silence. "Maybe it's not all bad."

"Maybe not," Floka says.

I close my eyes to hide sudden tears, let my breath out in a long, silent sigh. And then the conversation moves on to smoke in Seattle, and I learn that Lia can see stars for the first time in a week.

IN THEIR GARDEN

I'm running back through the desiccated woods, going too fast to keep the sticks and branches that have fallen from the trees from cracking under my weight. My skin and mouth are dry The afternoon sun has sucked all the water from me, and I haven't stopped to drink. The sole of my right boot is thin enough a stone bumps the ball of my foot, and I want to swear, but I keep going even though I don't hear anyone behind me. Not anymore.

I realize I haven't for a while; I got away again. I saw ten friendly travelers this time before I met one who meant me trouble. I know better than to go out alone, and if I get back in one piece, Kelley is gonna kill me.

It's not far now, I can see the wall rise like a cracked egg, dirty white with gray, the top edges jagged.

I trip over a log, going down sharp on my right knee and catch myself on my hands, scraping the pads of my palm. I can see the black soil line from the fire ten years ago, the one that saved us from burning up when everything else around caught fire. The dry trees around me are saplings that tried to grow back and made it for three or four years before they died of thirst. They're as tall as me.

My breath breaks the silence, and I sound like a rabbit before a thin coyote kills it, scared and breathing too hard. I make myself slow down, try to remember what Oskar taught me. Breathe through your nose. Breathe deep in your belly, so you can feel it going out and in.

Slowly.

S l o w l y.

I'm getting there. A hot breeze blows back my hair and helps me feel better.

"Paulie."

I hate it when Kelley calls me that. My name's Paulette. I hate it that she moves so quiet and I'm so loud and clumsy.

She extends her left hand but doesn't help me up. There's dirt ground into the creases of her hand and stuck under her nails, and it smells wetter and stronger than the dry, cracked earth under my hands. A year or two ago, I would have apologized first, but I manage not to do that this time. I'm almost as tall as her now, and I can look down on the graying dark hair she's pulled back and tied with a strip of bark, as if we didn't have anything better. She holds her taser in her right hand, a black oblong that she protects as if it means her life. She leaves it out as we walk back, swinging in her hand, the arc of its movement precise.

My knee is bleeding, but we both ignore that.

Between here and the wall, all the dead woods have been cleared, and we walk on gray and green grass, stuff Kelley had us plant in the moat of cleared ground around our walled garden. The grass thrives out here in spite of the dry, thirsty ground. I don't like to admit it, but she picked well; the spiky, low growth has been alive for two years now, and it creeps back into the forest as we clear it further away.

She doesn't say anything, but I make up her feelings and words in my head anyway. *The walls are safe. You aren't old enough to leave them yet; you might bring people here. You might get hurt, or raped, and die all by yourself. There's men that would take you in and make you trade your body for water and food. It only takes three days without water.* If she was lecturing me instead of staring off, lost in her head, she'd look down at that point and see I have a small canteen clipped to my belt, one of the old ones where the metal's all banged up. *Well, maybe you'd live a week.* She'd look disgusted. *We have all the people we can water now. You might get lost and not come back, and then what? We'd lose all the training we spent on you.*

The biggest problem with a lecture in your head is you can't fight it. Kelley knows that, and it makes me even madder at her, but it's not like I'm going to be able to explain to the others why I picked a fight with someone who doesn't say anything to me. The other problem is that she's right. I shouldn't want to argue with her in the first place. But I hate that we live like the world isn't all screwed up when it really is, or maybe we're living like it is all screwed up, and it's starting to not be so bad. That's what I'm beginning to believe. Whichever it is, I'll never amount to anything if I stay inside my whole life and work on little things that don't matter with little people who will die behind a wall. The wet, verdant world we live in is a bubble, and I want the real world.

Right before we get to the wall, she turns and looks at me. I expect her to be yelling angry, but what I see in her dark blue eyes is just sadness.

I wonder which one of her plants died this time.

I'm sorry she's sad, but I don't tell her that; I can't show weakness.

The door in the wall is big enough for an army and there's a whiter spot in the wall where Kelley's old boss, James, ripped the sign off in the second year of the first drought, and also the second year after I was born. The door opens to let us in, and the two of us are much smaller than an army even though there's a war between us.

Inside, it smells like home and it smells like jail. Like dirt and water and frogs, and faintly, of flowers. Later, in the summer, it will smell more like flowers, but the spring is showier than it is smelly. We pass magenta azaleas whose bloom is just starting to wilt, and in spite of myself I smile when I see three bees on the one plant. Kelley and Oskar both taught me to see the little things, and I can't help but watch out for the plants.

I stop smiling when I notice that the Board of Directors is waiting. All of them. They're sitting in their formal place, on benches in a circle under the sign that used to be above the doors. "Oregon Botanical Gardens." The Board has run us since the first years of climate collapse, and the half who are still the original members are gray and wrinkled.

There's four Board members, and Kelley makes five. She says, "Paulie, please sit," and gestures to the hot seat—the one for people who are in trouble. I've been here before. The Board's all as old as Kelley; they all remember the world I only see in movies, and they all remember my dad, who's dead now, and they all remember they're the ones who made all the rules and I'm the girl who keeps breaking them.

I wait for them to ask me questions.

They don't. Kelley clears her throat, and keeps her chin up and her voice is as sad as her eyes. "Paulie, we've done everything we know how to do to keep you in here. I can't keep putting us at risk by letting you in and out the door. I've told it not to open for you anymore. So if you sneak out again, you will never be allowed back in."

She can't mean it. She's the one had the most hand in raising me, teaching me. I'm her hope for the future. She wouldn't kick me out.

Tim and Li are the two old men of the Board. Li nods, telling me he supports Kelley. Tim is impassive, but he would miss me. We play chess sometimes in the hour between dawn and the breakfast. Sometimes I win, and he likes that. He would never kick me out.

Kay and Shell are the two women on the Board. They're both stone-faced, too, but they might mean it. They're scarier than Tim and Li.

Kelley holds my eyes, and she still looks sad. Usually when she's getting me in trouble she just looks frustrated. "Do you understand?"

"Yes."

"Tell me what will happen if you leave again without permission."

"The door will not let me back in."

"And we will not let you back in," she adds.

Maybe she does mean it. Now her eyes are all wet, even though she isn't really crying yet. Kelley isn't done. I know because no one is moving, and I feel like they're all watching me, probably because they are. Kelley says, "Just so you don't do anything rash, you're confined to the Japanese Garden for a week. Report to Oskar in ten minutes."

She does mean this, except maybe the ten minutes part.

I nod at them all and walk away, keeping my head up. I hate it that they've made me feel small again. In my room, I sweep my journal and two changes of clothes into an old bag, and I brush my hair and my teeth, and put those brushes in the bag, too. I sit on the bed and wait, determined not to be early or even on time.

But Oskar doesn't notice. I walk in the glass box and close the outer door, wait a moment, then open the inner door. I wonder if these doors are now locked electronically, too, but I don't test them to find out how strict my sentence is. I am inside walls, some glass, and under a plastic sheet roof. The air is heavy with water, although cool. Oskar is nowhere to be seen. When it was finished, the Japanese garden was billed as one of the largest on the west coast. The designers wanted the roof to keep the delicate pines from drowning. It does. But most days, it holds in moisture.

I negotiate the stepping-stone path, walking through pillows of pearlwort. The cinnamon fern that lines the right wall still has some tender, brownish fiddleheads so I pick them. Maybe it's a form of penance.

The very first of the wisteria blooms are showing purple. Oskar is on the other side of the flowers, between me and the waterfall.

He doesn't turn around for the space of two breaths. He's squatting, bent over, clipping the leaves of a Japanese holly. He is a small man, his skin pallid from the damp air he lives in, his long red hair caught back in a braid that falls down a freckled, white back. The top of his braid is gray. He is only wearing shorts; he likes to garden as naked as the Board will let him. Even his feet are bare. I have always suspected that at night, he goes out with his flashlight and gardens more naked than that. Even though he is almost sixty years old, I think I would garden beside him, with my nipples exposed to the cool night air.

He wouldn't let me, of course. They all treat me like glass.

He stands up and turns toward me. Even though the light is starting to gray to dusk, I can see that his eyes look like Kelley's did. "Why do you run away?"

I lean back against the big cedar column that holds up the wisteria arbor, breathing in the sweet air. "Why don't you ever leave this garden?"

I've never asked him this. Instead of looking startled, he smiles. "Because I am saving the world." He is lying. He is, at best, saving a tiny part of the world that I can walk across in five minutes. Everyone here thinks small. I hold out my hand, the one with the fiddleheads in it, and he takes them and says, "See?"

I don't see at all.

He leads me to the kitchen, which is the only room here with walls that aren't made of waxed paper or bamboo. When we get in, he hands me back the fiddleheads, and I wash them in a bowl full of water and then pour the water into a bin so it can go into the waterfall, where it will be scrubbed clean by the filter plants.

We have everything ready, but before we start to cook, Oskar takes me up to the top of the rock wall that the center of the stroll garden, and we look out toward the ocean. It's too far away to see or hear, but the sun will set over it. He has made a hole in the roof by overlapping the layers of water-capturing plastic so we can see the sunset directly. There are enough clouds to catch the gold and orange a little, but most of the last rays leak up like spilled paint and fade into the blackening sky.

I try to decide whether or not I can use the hole in the roof to climb out of.

After the color starts to fade, there is a hole in time between night and day. Oskar speaks quietly. "I answered you. Will you answer me?"

So that's what he has been waiting for. I guess when you are sixty you have a lot of patience. "We live in a bubble."

He laughs and pokes the plastic, which he can just barely reach from up here. It answers him by rippling, as if it were up-side-down water.

I frown. "We do!" I wave my hand at all the roads and people we can't see from here. "In the real world out there, people are travelling and learning and meeting each other. They're struggling. They're taking back the world. This time . . ." I haven't really told anyone about this trip yet—I mean, no one had asked. Should I? "I walked the interstate and talked to people on it. Like always. I have my escape routes. They work."

He cocks an eyebrow at me but doesn't say anything.

"Eugene's coming back. There's five thousand people there now—they dug a well deep enough for water and they think they can irrigate. I met two families who were on their way there."

He clears his throat. "A year ago, you told me it had all gone to desert. Not even any grass."

"That's what I heard. But this time I heard different." I paused. "I don't *know* anything. How could I?"

When he doesn't say anything else, I just keep talking. "A band of singing priests went through last night. They saw five jet airplanes in a day over Portland."

He can't say anything to that. We saw a plane fly over the gardens a few weeks ago, and everybody came out and watched. We hadn't been able to hear its engines, and Kelley had told me it was shaped different that the old jets. What Oskar does say is, "They don't have the right plants. That's what I'm saving for your generation. The bamboo and the bearberry, the astilbe and the peony."

He says the names of plants like a prayer, and I imagine him naming the others in his head. *The wisteria and the wild fuchsia, the fiddlehead and the mountain fern . . .*

"I know what you're saving. You keep telling me about it." It's an old story, how we're saving the genome of the native plants in case the weather ever goes native again. "It's good. I'm glad you're saving it. But that's your dream."

He pretends not to notice my tone of voice. "What your travelers see is the Mediterranean weeds that killed the right plants in California when Father Serra brought them on his donkey. Now that it's warm enough, dry enough, they come here and invade Oregon like they invaded California a long time ago." His face wears a stubborn look that makes him more handsome, wiping some of the wrinkles away with anger. He starts down the rock face as all of the colors of the garden began to fade, and I hear him tell me, "It is your duty to the planet to help."

I sit on the stone until stars swim above the plastic roof, diffused by the beads of water that start gathering there as the evening cools. After my eyes adjust enough to the dark, I come carefully to ground and Oskar and I share cinnamon fern fiddleheads and cattail roots and some jerky from a thin bobcat that had the good grace to jump into our garden before it died of starvation and fed us.

That night, I lie in my bed, separated from Oskar by waxy paper and bamboo, and listen to the roof crinkle in the wind. I'm too young to save the lives of doomed plants for a people that might be doomed, too. The world has changed, and we'll all die if we try to stand still in its current. We have to adapt to the new climate and the new ways, or die here in Oskar's Japanese stroll garden, walking the stone paths until there's not enough water left for the wisteria.

They've taught me the things I need to know to help, and now they want to keep me in a box. But I don't hate them. Oskar's breathing gets even and deep, and it's a comfort.

But not enough. I toss and turn. I can't sleep. I pack my things in a blanket roll I can swing over my shoulder. I write Oskar and Kelley a note. I tell them I love them and I'm going to go save the world, and I'm sorry they won't ever let me back in.

I find Kelley waiting by the door, a thin stick of a shadow that only moves when I open the door, like she's been waiting for that one moment. I'm caught.

Oskar comes up behind me.

He leans forward and gives me a hug and he whispers in my ear. He says, "Good luck."

I blink at them both, stupid with surprise.

He says, "Me and Kelley both knew you'd go. It's time. The Board told us to keep you, because we need young backs and young eyes. But you don't need us. Go find out what they fly those planes with and where they go."

I feel like, thick in the throat and watery. I say, "I'll come back someday."

He says, "If you take long enough, we'll even let you back in."

I go before we all cry and wake the Board up. The stars look clearer out beyond the wall, and the moat of grass muffles my footsteps.

CALLME AND MINK

J ulie stepped outside into the first light of morning and opened
the door of the chicken coop. She tossed left-over white rice
onto the ground. The chickens scurried for breakfast, throwing
thin and busy shadows across the grass. She scooped the nearest
hen and took it to the side of the house, snapped its neck with a
flick of her wrist, and plucked the colorful feathers into a bin by
the garage door. Back inside, she gutted the bird and boiled the
meat free of the bones.

Julie prepared breakfast. This morning's bottom layer was
stale, dry cereal from a cupboard four houses away and a fist of
last night's rice. She added the heart and liver, and then white, soft
meat from the chicken's breast.

Callme curled with her back to the corner and watched Julie's
every precise move. The old border collie often knew more about
their surroundings than Julie, and so Julie trusted her to help
guard. This morning, Callme's ears pricked forward in benign interest as she focused on the younger dog, Mink, a two-year-old
male golden retriever. Mink sat straight and pretty, his nose up,
his ears alert to every flick of Julie's knife.

She ordered each dog to its food spot: Callme to the corner
by the fireplace and Mink to the bottom of the stairs. It took two
minutes for Mink to settle, tail thumping.

Julie bent at the knees to set the dishes down so that each
hit the stone floor at the same moment. While the dogs' rough
tongues and eager noses scraped the metal bowls lightly across
the floor, Julie peered out the kitchen window at the chicken

coop, and beyond it, toward the beach. Her weather app suggested ninety-two degrees with a soft wind, low tide in an hour and three minutes. A perfect day for the dogs.

Ten minutes later, Julie set the dogs' clean, dry dishes on the counter, ready for dinner.

She closed her clothing over her joints to keep the sand out and braided her silky hair into two long braids to keep the wind from wrecking it. When she opened the door, Mink bounded out. Callme followed, then turned, swirling this way and that as she did her best to watch both Julie and Mink.

Julie dropped to all fours. The three of them raced toward the waves. Mink plunged directly into the surge, but Julie went no further than the seafoam at the edge. Callme pranced beside her while Mink bounded joyously into waves almost as tall as he was. Drops of salt spray on his fur sparkled with mid-morning light.

Julie watched him duck in and out of the waves, throwing his head up, prancing. She and Callme circled each other, raced up and down the sand, and circled again. They glanced at Mink regularly, ready to go in if he faltered. But he knew the water now, no longer stumbling with excitement or turning his back to the sea.

When Callme looked exhausted, Julie whistled Mink back. All three loped along the beach, disturbing raucous crowds of seabirds. Julie avoided empty glass bottles and bright green and blue shards of plastic and broken shells. They alone shared the vast expanse of warming sand until they reached the pier. There, a simple non-gendered carebot wheeled an old woman down the wooden boards, her face turned into the sun and breeze. Below the old woman, two repair bots scuttled along the sand, taking advantage of the low tide to scrape barnacles away from the pier's supports.

Julie stood, ordering the dogs to heel as she walked down the old main street toward Jack's Ice Cream. The building sagged on one side, and two of the windows needed paint and fresh panes of glass. When Jack could get milk from one of the town's fifteen cows, it opened. Yesterday, it had been closed. Today, the swinging half-door hung open. Jack stuck his head out and gestured her toward him. He was small, slightly hunched, an old man with wheeled prosthetics. His face had been splotched red from years of sun. His broad smile elicited a return smile from her, a casual note in her programming. *If a human smiles at you, and is no threat, then smile back.*

The dogs raced to the side of the building and lapped water from the bowl he kept in there for them.

"I found a family for you to consider." Jack filled two tiny cups with ice cubes and frozen cream for the dogs. "They can use the help."

Julie took the cups from him, knelt and placed them as carefully as she had the dog's breakfast. "When will they come to me?"

"This afternoon. After lunch. Only the mom knows the dogs exist."

"Thank you." She had come to Jack's every day the weather allowed the dogs out. During that time, Mink had grown into a stable, well-trained two-year-old. He had been ready for six months, but no one suitable had come to town. The gates and loops of logic inside Julie's head should be settling into a pleased relief, and the beginnings of new programming designed to let him go should be gating open. She didn't feel that yet. Instead, she watched her own reaction with something like puzzlement. *Must it be time?*

As if he heard her, Jack said, "It's time, you know."

Some humans seemed to react to her thoughts as well as her facial expressions. This was especially true when she saw humans often, and she had seen Jack one-hundred and fifty-two times in the last three years and eighteen months. He had found good humans for her twice.

Julie watched Mink finish his treat while Callme's pink tongue flicked around the edges of her half-empty cup. She knew Jack required a verbal response from her. "Yes." It was time, but she still did not feel settled about the conclusion. Her programming learned. It had to. She would never have survived four decades since her release without adaptation. What made it stutter? "I don't want to learn attachment."

Jack laughed. "Is there anything else I can help you with?"

She turned around and lifted one of her braids. "Behind my ear."

Jack opened the bottom door and rolled out. He bent down to examine her neck. The tips of his fingers felt warm. He fished in his pockets for a multi-tool and then used the tweezers to pluck something from behind her ear. "How did you get a splinter there?"

"Was that it? Maybe fixing the door on the chicken coop yesterday." She swiveled her neck back and forth. "That's better. I guess I'll go home and wait."

Jack scooped up the dogs' bowls, stopped, looking right at her. "What are you trying to say?"

"I hope you don't move on yet. You told me you might."

"It took four hours to forage yesterday." *Do not ally yourself with a single human. To do so is to weaken your gift to all mankind.*

He cocked his head at her. "I know your programming has nothing much to do with me, except that I'm a resource." He reached down to pet Mink. "But I also know you won't hurt me, and I like you in the neighborhood." He hesitated. "I feel safer with you here."

She had long ago calculated that Jack was trustworthy. He had been here when she arrived, an old man with health problems and a store he'd owned for fifty-seven years. "You are a resource. Who else would have found that splinter?" *When a human helps you, help them.*

He smiled, his eyes a little sad.

Not lying to him meant she didn't signal emotions she didn't believe were appropriate. She could signal most feelings back to humans, but they were always a lie. She acted. She did not feel. She chose a patient configuration for her face. "I will do as I must."

There was only a little bitterness to his laugh.

"Who am I watching for?"

"A woman and two children. A boy and a girl. The girl is about seven."

"One adult?"

He hesitated. "That was all I talked to. They came for ice

cream three times before I spoke to the mom about what you do."

"Thank you." She called the dogs to her, dropped back to all fours, and led them in a bouncing chase up the beach. Outside, she cleaned off the bench by the front door. She blew the sand from her feet and her clothes, making sure no small tear or puncture had let any of it inside of her. Then she blew the dogs clean, sand flying away from the air hose and losing itself in the grass. Satisfied, she led them all in. Each dog curled up for a post-play nap. Mink's fur smelled of salt and ocean, Callme's of sand and crabs.

The chickens scratched contentedly in the yard. She had between one and two hours, by her estimate, before the people Jack had spoken of arrived. She started her daily code review, looking for mistakes, following branches and tidying up stray instruction strings that had created themselves overnight but went nowhere. She reviewed and snipped files that did not matter. The color of the plastic cap she had accidentally stepped on halfway between here and Jack's. The creaky hinge on Jack's top door. Then she reached back and removed more details from the previous week.

She reviewed her interaction with Jack closely. He liked the family. He wanted them to succeed. Everything in his micro-expressions calculated as factual, truth in which he believed.

Still, her algorithms flashed a fifteen percent risk. High. She had less information than usual.

She had done this twelve times in twenty-two years. The first family had been brought to her by her trainers. She had found the rest on her own, except the three Jack had helped with. He had also told her where to find Mink, behind a broken tractor-trailer with three other puppies. She had chosen Mink and left the others; she could only raise and feed one. She hadn't gone back to see if they lived.

Julie moved to the front porch and watched. She spotted the three humans approaching before they found the house but stayed completely still. Observation time was valuable.

The woman was easily as tall as many men. She wore long green pants, black boots, and an orange tank top. Her skin glowed a burnished brown. A wide black pony band kept her hair from her dark eyes, allowing it to spill down to her broad shoulders. The boy, almost her height, still sported the skinny shoulders and awkward gait of a young teen. He was also some form of mixed-blood dark, but the girl he carried on his hip had fine red hair and freckles. Her long legs dangled down past his knees, too long for her worn jeans. They spoke in low tones, peering at houses but sensibly not approaching.

They looked more confident than a small group should, especially weighed down with the girl, but Julie's analysis suggested competence rather than bravado. The boy whispered in the girl's ear often. Twice, she laughed.

Julie stepped out into the middle of the street.

The dogs woke at her movement, but the first thing she taught any of her dogs was silence. She could hear their toenails on the floor and Mink's slight panting, but both would be inaudible to the family.

The girl saw her first, stopping and pointing. She whispered at her brother. "She isn't a robot."

He narrowed his eyes, peering at Julie. "She might be. See how straight she's standing?"

Before the girl could reply, the mother stopped them all with a wave of her hand.

They obeyed, as silent as the dogs.

Good. "I'm Julie."

"Jack sent me," the woman said. "I'm Maria, and these are my children, Tom and Belinda."

Julie calculated the chances that Tom was her physical son as close to seventy percent, but the girl was not hers by birth. Older than Jack had reported, maybe ten. Old to be carried.

Julie gestured toward the house she and dogs occupied. "Would you like to sit a moment and tell me about yourself?"

Maria nodded. "Of course."

Julie waited as they splayed across her front steps, and then she leaned on the wall beside them, her posture calm and ready. *If a human is new, then let them know you are strong and peaceful.*

"Why do you want a dog?" she asked.

"For Belinda. She wants a dog more than anything, and she is wasting."

"I see that."

"She has a few years left. I would have her be happy."

Jack had decided not to tell her that the girl was sick. "How do you know her?"

Maria raised an eyebrow. "I found her. Someone had left her by the road with a sign. Free." She laughed. "Free like a puppy used to be."

Julie would not charge for Mink. *If a human wants an animal, then find out if they can keep it safe.* "Where are you going?"

"South."

"North is reported to be safer."

Maria took a breath, and the boy clutched his sister. She snuggled in close to him, her eyes shining with her illness. "We came from New York," Maria said. "I don't know what 'safer' is, but it's not safe." She hesitated, her eyes drawn a little tight and mouth pursing. Signs of human thinking. "How long have you been here?" she asked Julie.

"Two years and nine months and one day and three hours."

Maria laughed. "And not a minute more or a minute less." The joy of her laughter left her face. "Your information is old. Many people have gone north, some with guns. We will keep heading south. I am a good forager, and Lou has enhanced hearing. This has kept us safe."

Julie glanced at the boy, clicking her teeth together very softly. "How many clicks did I just make?"

"Seven," he answered quickly, a sly but friendly smile on his face.

She glanced at Maria. "Enhanced?"

"As soon as he hit puberty. Some of the clinics still run, and we used to have resources. He can also see farther than me, but he can't smell as well as a dog." She blew out a breath, glancing at the girl. "Belinda wants one very, very much."

Belinda's wide green eyes blinked up at her, but she said nothing. Another sign of competence.

Jack had not mentioned the competence or the illness. The enhancements. But humans often told robots things they would never tell another human. Jack might not know about the enhancement.

Maria watched the front door, as if hoping that it would open and show a puppy waiting inside.

Julie told her, "The south has been foraged almost empty. We have moved north every few years."

Maria cocked her head. "We?"

"One of the dogs had been with me for eight years. She stays."

The woman nodded. "What do you need to know?"

Julie's algorithms decided Maria was sincere. *When a human has told you all they want to, then watch how they act.*

Julie pushed herself away from the wall and opened the door. She went in first, checking that the dogs were in their places, Callme against the wall and Mink in front of the wood stove. They were, each curled up, noses resting on paws.

They watched her quietly.

"Come in," she called to Maria.

Tom pushed through the door, his sister leaning on him but shuffling on her own feet. Good to know she could stand, even with help.

Callme raised her head, ears pricked forward.

Julie gestured a release to Mink, who stood, head lifted, tail flipping back and forth.

The boy set Belinda to the ground beside him and sank to his knees.

Maria's bulk blocked some of the sun, her shadow covering her children.

The two dogs stayed still.

The only sound was the swishing tail and the slight excited breath of dogs and humans. Julie whispered, "His name is Mink. Call him."

Belinda whispered, "Mink." The single word sounded like prayer.

Mink glided over to Belinda, whining softly, and Belinda whispered, "You are beautiful."

Tom spoke over her head. "Gently."

"Yes!" Belinda buried both her hands in Mink's fur.

Julie stood and faced Maria. "I will have to teach you to care for him."

Maria nodded. "Someone told me that."

"Who?"

"Jack. But before him . . ." Her voice trailed off, her face lost in a memory. "One evening we met a man with a dog at his heels, and I had tea and a rabbit and he had skillet cornbread. He told me that you existed, that you raised dogs to be companions. We could have found a stray, but Belinda . . ." She shrugged. "Belinda will never be stronger than she is today. I can't take the risk or time to tame a stray. This man's dog was beautiful, and strong, and guarded our camp for a night before we parted."

"What dog?"

"A black and white one. Big. Charlie."

Two dogs before Mink. "What was the man's name?"

"Joel."

She had liked Joel. A steady man, middle aged, stout, and afraid of most people. *Verify your work when you can. Evaluate how well you do.* "Thank you for telling me about Joel and Charlie."

Maria watched her children stroke Mink while he stretched out, relaxed, tail thumping. "Has anyone failed?"

"Once. I had to take a dog back from a woman who couldn't feed him." When Marie said nothing in response, Julie asked, "Can you kill a chicken?"

Maria's eyes widened. "I suppose."

"Then we should start the dogs' dinner."

"Where will we stay?"

"There are four bedrooms here. Unless you want a neighboring house. The one next door has beds and linens."

Maria smiled. "Here will be fine. How long?"

"Until you learn." She glanced at the children, who clearly could not move very fast. "But I will exercise the dogs every day."

"Whatever you want."

"And you will have to feed yourselves. I do not eat."

"We will forage during the day."

"Come outside. I will introduce you to the chickens." She glanced once more at the two dogs and two children. Callme watched, unperturbed, her ears relaxed. "They'll be okay."

By the end of the third day, Maria was making the dogs' food and both of the children had demonstrated success in giving Mink orders. More importantly, Mink had started to follow the children's orders. Maria began to sing from time to time.

Mink would make the family happy and bark if anyone neared them while they slept. He wouldn't fight for them like Charlie might for Joel; it wasn't his nature. But Charlie would never have allowed Belinda to brush him for hours.

It would be time soon.

Julie watched them all settle into bed and then took her place by the door, sorting through the synapses in her head. Five of ten evaluation flags had flipped to green. If two more flipped, she would watch the family walk away. It was likely.

She didn't like the direction they were going. *If a human reaches a different conclusion than you do, find another opinion.*

A robot would be good, but the only three other robots she had seen in this town for months were low-level senior-care bots; they would provide no help. Very few mobile humans had settled here.

No matter which direction they went, the girl would not survive. The woman and the boy might, and if so, Mink would love them and protect them. She slapped her thigh softly, signaling Callme to her, and then dropped to all fours, leading the border collie outside.

The night air smelled of sea salt and overripe apples from a tree in the back yard of an empty house. No threats. Her eyes showed the heat of squirrels and rabbits, of a solitary and slow cat, and of birds roosting in the darkness. She and Callme walked side by side, slow, circling the block. Julie's head ran through the routines of snipping what she didn't need, what no one needed.

She caught herself with an image of Mink that she had trouble de ciding about. Mink as a puppy, two days after she found him. He looked round and soft and vulnerable. Maybe ten weeks old. The little sharp baby teeth had just been pushed free by his adult teeth, and his smile was still slightly lopsided. *Do not become attached to more than one animal. Dogs are to help human hearts.*

What a strange phrase to be in her programming. She had always had it. One of the five mantras. *Dogs are to help human hearts.* Even though she was still far taller than Callme when moving on all fours, she could look the border in the eye far more easily than when she stood on two legs. Callme had learned over three hundred and seventy words. She said none of them. Here in the wild, Julie had no devices that allowed Callme to use human words. But she reacted to them, and Julie's core programming knew how to read dogs.

Dogs are to help human hearts.

Julie had no human heart. Neither, by definition, did the dog beside her. But Callme had helped her raise three pups. She chose to save the image of Mink as a pup, but the next three she deleted. She had only saved a hundred images of Charlie, and a hundred of Grace, and a hundred of each of the others. Of Max, Gandalf, SusieQ, Sasha, Odin, Whisper, Buddy, Nixie, Thomas, and Pearl.

Callme stopped in the middle of the road, so Julie stopped beside her. Two young ground squirrels raced across the road. The dark shadow of dark wings slid though a patch of moonlight. One of the squirrels gave a sharp cry as the hawk's talons pierced its neck, and the other kept going until it reached a tree-trunk. There, it stood on its haunches and screamed at the sky, then stilled and watched.

Attachment. A futile gesture for the squirrel.

She had to delete a hundred more memories of Mink before the red flag for attachment flipped to green.

Julie led Callme home and quietly entered the house, where the dog curled into a ball and Julie sat and mentally flipped through pictures of the dogs she had sent to protect humans.

In the morning, she took Callme and Mink to town while

Maria and the children foraged for food. She allowed Mink his hour in the waves, which were low and soft, and she and Callme lay side by side on the warm sand.

It was impossible to tell whether or not Callme knew she was saying goodbye to Mink. Likely. After all, some humans like Jack seemed to guess her thoughts. Callme was nearly as smart and spent every day with Julie. Familiarity bred knowledge.

Jack's Ice Cream was closed. A few old people and their minder-bots wandered down the main street with no apparent direction. No one unknown appeared to be in town. Her algorithms insisted on more about the difference between north and south, driving her to look for information all day before they petered out, the last of the looping calls to find more data stilled by the utter absence of information.

She walked back fully wearing her human form, ambling on two legs. A woman and her dogs.

Maria, Tom, and Belinda sat on the front stoop watching for them. Belinda brightened as they neared, and Tom carried her to meet them, setting her in the middle of the street so that Mink could nose her and lick her cheek. Belinda's thin fingers stroked his side.

Maria stood, keeping some distance, watching. When Julie, the children, and the dogs neared, she said, "I found three cans that are still good. Kidney beans. And dug up an onion from an old garden. There were more, but most were rotting. We need to leave soon."

Julie sat beside the woman, relaxing into a human-coded pose, her legs crossed and her spine soft. "I taught Mink to catch rabbits."

Tom brightened. "I'm a very good hunter."

Marie was silent a moment, her eyes on Belinda, who gazed at Mink as if nothing else mattered in the world. Maria's eyes shone in the evening light, filling with tears she didn't allow to run down her cheek. Her voice was soft. "Thank you."

"He will be a guard dog as well as a friend."

"You can come with us."

Do not ally yourself with a single human.

"I cannot. But you can take a few chickens if you like. I will help you make a cage for them using a wagon. You can take it with you. I'll have it ready by the morning."

"I'll cook the beans."

Julie stood up and brushed the dirt from her pants. There was extra chicken wire in a garage four houses down. She signaled for Callme to join her and headed down the street.

She and Callme reached Jack's at noon the next day. The door hung open and he rolled out to greet them, carrying a single bowl of frozen cream.

"Thank you," she told him. "They took Mink."

He set the cream down for Callme and waited for her to start lapping at the white treat before he stood up and looked at her. "Will you be going?"

"Can I help you fix the walls?"

"Are you going?"

"Not until spring. Not if you let me help you fix the walls."

He smiled.

If a human smiles at you, and is no threat, then smile back.

ELEPHANT ANGELS

Francine cracked open her window, filling her tiny apartment with damp cold that slapped her cheeks and helped her blink awake. She smelled coffee from the breakfast food-truck below and breathed in the slightest hint of Puget Sound salt. People scurried through the bare gray of early morning, fleece coats pulled tight around them, gloved hands clutching purses and briefcases.

She watched until she spotted her granddaughter's face, brown and round, with dark eyes and a long fall of black hair that ended just above bright yellow sweats.

A few minutes later, Araceli herself burst through the door wearing her smile of hiding. She produced a small cloth bag from behind her back. "I brought you something."

"And how are you?" Francine took the bag and fumbled it open. She pulled out a sky-blue shirt with a photo of an elephant on it. She stared, awed. It signified an approval she hadn't expected.

"You're one of us, now. They took your application." Araceli practically jumped up and down with enthusiasm, a bounciness reserved for excited nineteen-year-old girls. She had helped Francine fill out forms online and spent hours teaching her how to be elsewhere, had run her through the training simulations twice before Francine took the real test.

The elephant on the shirt was a savanna matriarch, which Francine wouldn't have known a month earlier. The words *Elephant Angel* had been hand-embroidered along the hem of the right sleeve.

"Try it on."

Francine went into her bedroom and pulled on the shirt, which fit her far better than she deserved. It looked good.

She found Araceli in the kitchen, stirring the special tea into a hotcup. She looked up and smiled. "Now. Your first shift is now."

"Really?" Francine's mouth dried and she felt dizzy.

"Drink your tea."

Francine took the cup to her easy chair and sat down. Araceli had mounted tiny speakers around the headrest, since earbuds tickled Francine's hearing aids. A small table held her teacup, her VR glasses, a pad of paper, and a blue pen.

Araceli perched on an old love seat across the room, her long legs draped over the arms and her flimsy open and glowing on her lap as the screen powered up. Araceli would see what Francine saw and hear what she heard, but would have no control. It would be in 2-D, like a movie. Part of the training had put Francine in that position, the watcher of the watcher, and it reminded her of the days when movies were flat.

After the first few sips, the bitter tea began to brighten Francine's senses, accentuating the tickle of the slender wires that rode her jaw and hooked behind her ears.

The last step was to drop her glasses down in front of her face and sip the dregs of the tea.

"Hello," a human voice whispered. "All clear."

"Thank you." The other pilot winked away as soon as the exchange ended, the transition instant so that the two pilots wouldn't crash in moments of confusion. As she'd been taught, she left well enough alone for a breath, trusting the expertise of the person she replaced to have left the craft on a stable trajectory.

While she couldn't feel the hot summer sun, it forced her to squint, delighting her, as if Africa kissed the Northwest. Cicadas. Always the first thing she noticed, the sound so foreign to Seattle and so embedded in Africa. Wind sighed through trees, barely louder than the swish of the elephant's feet through grass. She had entered close-in, her view almost that of the mahout. She snapped her fingers wide and flat and drove her hands up, telling the tiny machine half a world away to rise.

Flying delighted Francine. It was as simple as the video games she'd grown up with, where her movements told cartoon characters on the screen what to do.

The tiny drone gained height.

The matriarch marched in front of a family group of six—four females and two calves, one about two years old and the other one younger. Only the matriarch hosted a rider, long limbed and dark skinned and almost naked, swaying with the elephant's steps. The girl had a slender waist, long legs, and barely formed round breasts. She wore long feathered earrings and looked relaxed even though she rode an animal big enough to crush her with a single step.

Francine did her job and spun the drone three hundred and sixty degrees. This gave her a slightly jerky view in all directions. Far off, a herd of giraffe walked with awkward grace. A kite wheeled through a dusty blue and cloudless sky. Nothing else obvious moved except for the elephants, although there were enough trees to hide all manner of birds, buzzing insects, and sleeping prey.

Other Angels watched the satsites and evaluated data flowing from swarms of sensors as thick as the cicadas. Francine watched for the glint of sun on metal and listened for conversation or the interrupted call of any wild thing.

The elephants meandered. Twice they worked together to push over acacia trees and nibble at the tender, sweet tops. The rider stayed on the matriarch easily even as the big beast bent into the trees and strained. Even though Francine could hear and see the savanna, the only feeling she had was the sense of movement that came from the drone's feed, sort of a vague up and down and sideways that felt like an echo in her bones, and a very slight sickness on her middle.

These were her elephants. Would be her elephants. This was so frightening that Francine shivered briefly. She had not been responsible for anything outside of herself for at least twenty years. Or jointly responsible, she reminded herself. Each herd had help on the ground, in the air, and remotely. A circle of Elephant Angels.

She hovered above the girl's right shoulder, just behind the dangling feathers that touched her deep brown shoulders. Francine remembered the feel of skin that supple, of joints that flexed and moved easily.

The matriarch watched the next biggest elephant lean forward to push against a tree as thick as her leg.

It exploded.

Not the tree itself, she realized. The ground around it.

It took a moment to recognize an attack. A rare thing, but the reason she flew a drone in Africa.

The drone sped away, up and back, a reaction to Francine's unintended jerks of surprise. The elephant's images grew small as the drone receded. Smoke from the explosion created a thin smudged line of white and black that rode the wind. Francine twisted her right hand and lifted her left, overcorrecting so that her cameras pointed at the sky and the ground and the far horizon in the wrong direction. She took a deep breath, and then tried again twice before the drone cameras yielded her the elephants.

The matriarch's head swung back and forth, her wide ears flapping. She held her tail out away from her body. Her shoulders twitched.

Her rider clung to the neck strap.

The wounded elephant lay on her side, trunk writhing, the skin on her chest and front legs peeled away as if she has been flayed with giant knives. Pink flesh glistened in the cuts.

Francine realized she had been hearing squeals and trumpets, had failed to pay attention to sounds with the sight below her so awful and the drone barely under control.

She flew close to the fallen elephant, who struggled to stand, failing.

Messages blossomed across Francine's glasses, and voices chattered with each other in her ears.

The elephants trumpeted again, the matriarch the loudest.

Pain. It was a sound of pain.

Or anger.

Francine felt what she heard in the animal's voices, anger

and dismay and the sharp shock of going from a placid afternoon to death.

Thinking was hard. This was nothing like the simulated attack from training, which had been a man with a gun and a jeep
she had been able to see coming. She tried to ignore the chaos for
a moment, to let her brain breathe and review.

Poachers would know their trap had sprung.

The elephants were in mortal danger. She had been taught
they would want to stay with the injured.

One of the babies approached the elephant on the ground,
touched her with its trunk. Probably *her* baby. A cry strangled in
Francine's throat. Not now. No time to mourn. She sent her drone
up high, spotted the dust blossoms of at least three vehicles.

The mahout struggled atop the matriarch, holding on to an
ear with one hand and twisting to stay in the saddle as the elephant screamed a complexity of emotions.

Francine took the drone as close as she dared, using the
smallest of movements so as not to startle anything or anyone. It
took three tries before she got close enough to whisper, "Wasps,"
into the girl's right ear.

The girl turned and nodded, dark eyes wide. Francine flew
higher and watched the rider touch a button on her belt. A swarm
of autonomous drones the size of fingernails spread out behind
the girl. The drones created sounds too low for humans to hear
and harried the elephant.

Her rider hunkered down.

The matriarch trumpeted, stamped her feet, swayed, and
stamped again.

Francine fretted.

The elephant began to lope. When the others—even the
calves—caught up, she sped up.

Francine remembered her training and begun to rotate the
drone in all directions, watching the plumes of dust resolve into
dusty jeeps. She recorded who came, and watched, still and horrified, as five men in shimmering active camouflage severed the
elephant's wide trunk near its eyes and used carbon saws and

chains to force the long, curved tusks free of the flesh.

She witnessed the moment the life left the elephant's eyes and was skewered by it.

Three more plumes of smoke appeared. A fourth. Angels, the drone indicated. They would already have her recordings.

She could go.

Francine hovered for a moment, torn. She wanted to know what happened next, but every delay opened more distance between her and her herd. Still, she hesitated. Would the poachers get away? Would there be a fight?

The world exploded.

A lens of one camera remained intact and fed her glasses, tumbling fast through blue on blue sky to green grass and resting near the bloody, gray body. Francine had barely registered the new point of view, barely comprehended that she had been shot from the sky, when the last of whatever powered the camera flashed away.

Araceli lifted the glasses from Francine's head and turned them off.

Francine blinked away the silent dark of the drone's death and stared at her granddaughter, flinching at the tears streaming down her cheeks. Araceli had seen what she saw. Francine's hand shook as she extended it and took her granddaughter's slender hand in hers. "I lost my herd."

Araceli nodded. "Fucking poachers," she said.

"Don't use that word with me."

"Even now?" Araceli grimaced and wiped her cheek dry. "Let's get you some food."

Francine had been immersed in late afternoon, in summer. It shocked her to return to a winter morning. She shivered and pulled her blanket closer. She had failed her herd, failed in her new job.

Lost a drone.

Francine's body demanded attention, shaking softly with sorrow and post adrenaline crash.

Her granddaughter bathed her face and brought her oatmeal

and half a slice of toast. The warmth infused Francine so she felt strong enough to ask, "What happens now?"

Araceli glanced at the lights on the body monitor Francine wore on her wrist. She was more adept at reading them instantly than Francine, and she said, "You rest. I'll stay with you today. You have another shift tomorrow."

"I need to know about the poachers. Did they catch them? What about the little mahout?"

Araceli nodded. "I'll find out while you rest."

"I want to know now."

Araceli obliged her by looking through the Elephant Angels webmesh until she found information. "The other elephants are safe. There is a fresh observation drone flying in now. They caught one poacher but not the others. There's a watch on the ivory through all local ports."

Makena turned onto her belly and slithered down behind Delba's ear, clutching the neck rope until she could push off and scissor out away from her charge's huge side. She landed lightly on the calloused balls of her feet and regarded the herd. Delba seemed undecided. The matriarch stared back the way they had come. If a look could undo the past, hers would. Then she turned toward the calves, let out a long, low rumble, and trundled into the watering hole Makena had led them to. The other two adults waited for the calves and then followed.

Makena turned into the grasslands to find a place to pee while there was no drone to record it. There would still be watchers via satellite, but she would be small to them. She had insisted on seeing what the Elephant Angel watchers saw after she took the job and passed her six months' probation. Mostly they saw things in big pictures, on maps with moving dots that identified various individual animals. They saw weather and monitored the location of safari tourists from a distance. The drone was the only constant nag on her own privacy. She hated it even though it had saved her and the elephants at least three times.

A new person flew the drone today. She had been told that at the start of her shift. The pilot hadn't been clever enough to give a warning, although she *had* reminded Makena to loose the wasps.

She shouldn't have panicked. She stepped over the bones of a rhinoceros, long since picked clean, and looked back at the herd. The adults' trunks roamed the calves' sides.

Makena did not remember explosives ever being buried so close to trees. The area had looked normal and smelled good to Flower, which didn't seem right. Elephants could smell storms a day ahead.

The poachers had been clever.

She returned to the water and washed her body and her face carefully and slowly in the watering hole. The water barely felt cleansing.

Luis's voice in her ear. "Makena?"

"Catch them."

"I will. Are you okay?"

"After you catch these people, I will be fine," she told him.

"I'm sorry this happened."

"Stop talking to me and catch the poachers."

He broke off. Good. She didn't want to talk to anybody, not even handsome Angels from foreign lands. Not even sexy Angels, maybe especially not those.

Usually the watering hole was a happy place where the herd played and relaxed. Not this afternoon. They had run far, and their movements were as slow and unhappy as Makena's own.

They mourned.

Flower was dead. Makena had hated the name, bestowed by some fat American a decade ago. Donors bid big money to name African elephants, and in her few bitter moments, Makena supposed she was lucky none of them had paid to name *her*.

She had not hated Flower herself. Only her name. Flower had been strong and willing, and good at looking out for the babies.

Makena walked out into the water and stroked Bee's back. Flower's small son had nearly stopped nursing. He might live even after losing his dam. If he didn't die of a broken heart. She slopped water over his leathery skin and found herself crying. She had not cried since her mother died of AIDS a year ago, and the tears surprised her and then overtook her, so that she leaned on Bee with half of her weight and spilled her tears over his back.

He curled his trunk and touched her shoulder softly with the tip.

Before they came out of the water, Makena climbed back onto Delba and shimmied to her spot on the elephant's neck, her legs spread wide behind Delba's huge ears. She signaled the matriarch forward. Delba led the little band out of water and toward the closest stand of acacias.

Cicadas hummed and birds called back and forth to each other in the not-yet-cooling afternoon.

Makena used her wrist-phone to call Saad. "Be careful," she told him. "The elephants are restless and there is one less. Flower was killed." She told him the rest of it, and he asked her if she had a video and she told him no, even though she was sure she could find one if he wanted it. She did not want to see it again. "You are bloodthirsty," she said.

"No," he said. "But I am sorry."

Mollified, she settled into worrying about whether or not it would be safe for him to come.

The slanted early-evening sun had started to edge the savanna's grasses and trees with gold. Flower would not see another sunset, and so Makena found it hard to drink in the normal peace of this last moment before the evening hunting started.

The sun hung just barely above the horizon when Makena's little brother sent her a message. "I am near."

She chewed her lower lip, watching the way the elephants walked and held their ears and trunks and how close they were to one another. She had no wasps left, but Delba was under as much control as the matriarch ever granted her. Generally, Delba did Makena's bidding, but she never gave up veto power. She seemed docile enough now. "Okay," she said. "Come out."

Saad stood where the herd could see him and where the wind would bring his scent to them.

Makena stopped Delba and waited until she was sure the elephant saw her little brother, now only a head shorter than her, but still clothed in the slenderness of boyhood. She helped him climb up onto Delba's back and seat himself right behind her. He handed her a bag of antelope jerky. "Poaching?" she asked him.

"Harry Paulson is."

She grunted but took the meat, which was tough and salty and tasted like heaven.

"I am an Angel," he teased her.

"Not yet."

"I will be."

"Maybe." Saad had been accepted as a courier for the Angels, allowed to bring Makena parts or supplies from time to time. He wasn't supposed to ride, or even touch, the elephants, but they took advantage of any times the drone wasn't around. "If you are taking jerky from poachers, how do I know you won't succumb to bribes for ivory?"

"I will not."

"You should stop talking to any poachers about anything."

"You are eating the jerky."

She wished she hadn't taken it, but it tasted fabulous.

"I will ride elephants when you go to the city."

"Maybe."

He stuck his lower lip out and she laughed softly at him. "I love you, little brother. When I have earned enough to go to Pretoria, I will tell them you should take my place. But that will not be until you are older. I'll have to wait."

"You can do that for me. Then you can be my Angel, too."

"I am already your Angel," she said.

"Truth, that."

Much later, Makena and her grandfather sat on their wooden verandah. The dusky time of hunting animals had passed, and the evening quiet had settled around their small house. Her grandfather had raised her and had taught her of elephants and zebras and lions and hyenas and white rhinoceros. He had been a ranger at Dzanga-Ndoki before he retired, and she hoped he would understand more than Saad had. "They took an elephant from me today," she told him. "I have never lost one."

The faint and flickering light of a low lantern illuminated deep wrinkles around his dark eyes. "Tell me."

She did.

"You are lucky *Delba* did not step on the IED. You might have lost the most important elephant."

His way of saying she could have been hurt herself. "I failed. It's unthinkable to lose even one."

"I lost a whole herd once. We let a monster storm drive us all inside, and the poachers were not so afraid of floods as we were. Rain and wind kept us inside for a day and a half. The tractor flooded and wouldn't start. We had to patrol on foot the next day. I found seven dead elephants. Two of their babies died over the next two weeks. We were only able to save the oldest." He sighed and stared off into space for a moment, as if he could still see the dead elephants. "All that because we did not want to be wet."

She spoke softly. "How were they killed?"

"Elephant guns. In my day we fought poachers with guns, not eyes and websites and satellites. They don't even give you a gun."

"I know." He had encouraged her to take his, but she had told him no. She would be fired if she were caught with a personal weapon.

He sipped his nightcap, a mix of tea and brandy that smelled so sour it made Makena's stomach light. "There are twice as many elephants now. Maybe more." He smiled at her. "There is more land for them, and more of them. There is progress."

"I know." She drank her water. "I still feel sad."

"Look up," he told her.

"Why?" But she did and drank in the deepness of stars over head, like carpet of pinpricks in the nearly moonless night.

"My grandmother lived in the first bush, the wild bush. She told me that when an elephant dies, a star falls. Perhaps if we watch, we will see Flower's star."

Makena wrapped her arms around her knees and kept staring upward. The sky looked close enough to touch even through the mosquito nets. "What would your grandmother say if she knew the wildest elephants were ridden every day?"

"As long as she knew you were doing it she would be pleased."

"You're lying," Makena said.

He stood up and kissed her forehead with his cool, thin lips. "She would be proud that you are caring for the family. Are you coming to bed?"

"Not until I see Flower's star."

Saad smelled of elephants. He lay on his bed and watched a Chinese professor with passable English stalk the stage back and forth, using expressive hands to illustrate the economy of the commons. The class itself was *in* the commons and he could pay a little bit and take a test if he wanted the credit. An Oxford class. He expected to get an A even though he was only thirteen and living in resettled Africa. The commons was easier for him to understand than international trade or the physics of space elevators.

His sister, Makena, made a living sufficient for all three of them, riding a beast that had become the apex herbivore of the most famous commons of all: the wilds. The same commons had been stolen from his people long ago, and now it was a different place. Still, he almost expected Makena to show up in Professor Jiang's presentation.

Maybe he should send the man a picture of his sister.

He didn't. He took careful notes in longhand. When the class ended, he placed the paper in his lockable drawer and put the key on a string around his neck.

He'd learned to do classes with paper notes, to stay away from his gaming devices and just focus. For some classes, he locked his bedroom door and locked all of his extra machines on the far side of the door. That way, he'd have to take an extra step and that would make him stop and remember how much the classes mattered.

He wasn't allowed to ask the professor questions since he wasn't formally enrolled, but he wrote down the questions he wanted answered.

He retrieved his phone and opened a chat window. He called up an Angel Makena had connected him up with as a tutor, Luis Castanova. Luis had led him to these classes.

Luis lived and breathed international data and data synthesis, and Saad had never failed to find him online. "Luis," he typed. "Ask why the commons was so hard to sell into the middle of America."

Luis typed back. "Because commons had no value in a greedy, capitalistic society. How about if I ask why they're gaining in value?"

"Okay." Saad stared out of the window, and then typed, "If the commons are gaining value, does that mean Makena gets a raise?"

"It means more people get hired."

"We lost Flower today."

"We all know," Luis responded. "I'm chasing her ivories."

"What?"

"I'll show you. We'll go together and you can be my witness."

Saad pushed the right buttons to slave part of his computer to Luis's and open a verbal window as well. Luis's image showed up on his screen. He looked as Hispanic as his name suggested, with wide lips, an easy smile, and long dark hair. Slight. Saad was pretty sure Makena had a crush on him, but his sister was too imperious to say anything when Saad asked.

Luis stared at something so intently it looked like he might fall into his screen, but then he noticed the completed connection and smiled.

"Take me away," Saad said.

"Okay. We're going to Cotonou. I'm looking for a ship there."

Saad pursed his lips. "Twelve hours since Flower died. Would the ivory have gotten there so fast?"

A map flashed up on the screen. A red X showed the place Flower had died, maybe twenty miles from Saad and Makena's grandfather's house. Luis's thick Spanish accent forced Saad to turn up the volume and stay as still as possible. "The drone pilot got footage of the three jeeps, but they shot the drone down before we could tell which one they put the ivory in. We caught one, and it didn't have the ivory. The other two went in almost opposite directions, one south and one west."

"Did they split the ivory up?" Saad asked.

"The jeeps were stealthed moments after Flower died. We could see where they went as long as they made dust, but no details. They disappeared completely once they hit pavement. We couldn't even tell how any people were in them. They both ended up in towns, where they stopped in a few places and could have transferred the cargo. Or maybe they wrapped it up in invisible cloth . . . I don't know. No one reported any ivory and none of our Angels actually saw any." Luis raised an eyebrow. "But we did get a clue."

Luis was playing with him, stringing him along, having fun. But Saad was okay with that. He learned every time Luis talked with him. He played his part of the game and asked, "What's the clue?"

"We know who is planning to buy the ivory."

"Who?"

"A madame in Charleston caters to Chinese clients. They will pay well. She also has a deal to sell some ivory to a priest in Chicago."

"How did you find that out?"

"The priest's secretary likes elephants more than ivory rosaries."

"We are lucky."

Luis laughed. "Yes, Saad, we are very lucky. She told us about this six months ago, and about where the money is. She said to watch the money. It moved fifteen minutes after Flower died."

Wow. "Okay, so her tusks are being shipped to the United States. But there are a lot of ports in the United States," Saad said. Even a kid from Africa knew that.

"So how do you think I figured it out?" Luis asked.

"I don't know."

"Think about it. You tell me that, and I'll tell you the rest of the story."

Saad pursed his lips. Luis had never done this before, tested him this way. Maybe if he succeeded, he could get a job as an Angel investigator like Luis. If he worked for Luis, he would miss the elephants. Still, this might be a chance. A good chance. "Let me work it out for a minute."

"Okay, I'll go check on our question." His screen darkened.

Surely there wouldn't be an answer that fast. Maybe Luis would stop and call a girl. The thought of that made Saad shiver, but then he forced his mind away from girls and back to the problem at hand.

Twenty minutes later, he sent a text giving fair warning and reconnected to Luis. "I think I have the answer."

"Tell me."

"I used globenet to track every ship going to America from Africa by port. I used a time window that allowed the ivory to be driven to possible ports. That narrowed it down to thirty-seven ships."

Luis was smiling.

Feeling more confident, Saad continued. "Twenty are the wrong kind of ships—cruise ships or tankers. The tusks are probably in a container. So that left five ships. One of those was from South Africa. It goes to Miami. I think it's the best bet."

Luis was grinning from ear to ear and laughing. "Not right. But you are thinking really well. What if I told you ivory can be detected in containers now?"

"Then I would say it must be on one of the tankers." He imagined Flower's tusks tied down to the flat top of a supertanker and covered with blue tarps that blew in the wind.

Luis still shook his head. "Most-regulated ships in the world."

"Then what?"

"What's left?"

"A cruise ship? Isn't that really busy?"

Luis had stopped laughing. "Did you notice the *Ruby Sea*?"

Saad drew his brows together. "No. I just set all the cruise ships aside."

"You were right to set aside commercial cruise ships. It's possible, but it would take more than one crewman acting together to hide something so big. I think the ivory is on the *Ruby*. She's private—only a few hundred cabins, and all of them bigger than your house. The cost of ten days on her would buy your house. There's stealthed stuff everywhere aboard her, from money to the daughters of sheiks."

"Where does she get in?"

"It doesn't matter. We're going to get the ivory before it leaves Africa."

"You'll come here?"

"No. But we have rangers we trust. I'll tell you about it after it happens."

"I hope you find the ivory."

"We will."

"Someone from here is going to be your mule?"

"You need to be older."

"That's not fair! You're barely older than Makena, and Makena is barely older than me."

Luis laughed. "There's two times two years in there."

"I can do math." But then he didn't want Luis to think he whined. "Did you get an answer?"

"The commons are getting more expensive because they are getting more beautiful as they become more protected. Even strips in cities."

"I want to do what you do," Saad reminded Luis.

"Graduate."

"One more year."

"Well, you have to be at least sixteen, too."

"Maybe I'll have my master's degree by then."

"Maybe you will."

"You said I could follow you to the port."

Luis grinned and then shut off his camera. "I'll slave the right window."

This wasn't as good as going with Luis in a drone. He'd have no view he could control.

"Watch," Luis said.

They were on a small dock. The *Ruby Sea* filled a berth. Brightly painted gangplanks spilled out over the sides. Music played from a band on the deck.

Swarthy men and veiled and covered women boarded, and occasionally he spotted a more nordic face on a man or woman or a couple.

Security guards waited at the foot of every entrance, checking ID casually, chatting, and here and there holding the hands of people boarding or kissing them on the cheek.

Saad loved the flowing robes and colorful belts and scarves worn by both men and women.

His and Luis's twinned point of view wandered through three different people. Saad kept trying to guess who they were, but they were professionals, and whenever he looked at where he thought he just been standing virtually, the place was empty. He didn't dare talk since he had no idea if the sound would come out on the scene.

He could hear the band and the conversations, mostly in lan guages he didn't speak. His guess was that the people were Arab and Egyptian and perhaps American.

After an hour, everyone had boarded the ship.

"Did you learn anything?" Saad asked.

"I think it's there," Luis said. "I'm almost a hundred percent sure. But there was no sign."

"So now what?"

"I watch it sail, I watch it while it sails, and I watch it land."

"Thanks for taking me along."

"Anytime."

Saad dropped his connection and wandered out to see his sister. "How was class?" she asked.

"Great. We studied African literature." He struggled to remember that class, which he had actually passed months ago. "We studied Chinua Achebe."

"I didn't like his work."

"I like it that he was smart." *Like me,* he thought. *You don't see it yet, but my light will be very bright one day.* He never said this out loud, but it was his way of reminding himself he would surpass Makena in many things when he grew up. He had to bide his time, but some day he would please her by becoming greater than she could imagine, just like he was helping her to buy him an education far greater than any of them had imagined. "I talked to Luis. He may know where the ivory is."

"I heard." A slight blush touched her cheeks. She had showered. Even though she smelled more of slick shampoo now than of beast, he felt Delba looking over her shoulder at him.

Luis sat on a bench and sipped black coffee as the *Ruby Sea* approached Charleston harbor. The open water between him and the dock she'd pull alongside reflected a nearly cloudless dawn sky and the wheeling forms of seabirds.

He'd been in Charleston for three days reporting what he knew to every agency that might care.

He wore dockhand work blues: jeans and a short-sleeved shirt with a light coat he'd buttoned against the cool and then unbuttoned over and over. Even this early in the winter, the air felt sticky. Thankfully, it wasn't hot—just thick and damp and full of the promise of heat.

Whatever he saw streamed back through his glasses to his watchers in five points of the world. "The boat's here," he told them.

He picked out Saad's voice. "Lucky day."

Makena chimed in from the top of Delba. "Get them. Delba knows something's happening. She's got her trunk up in the air and she's waving at you."

Luis fed a sat shot of the beautiful and brilliant Makena into the left window of his glasses and left it there so he could watch her. Delba's trunk was in fact up, and she trotted slowly around, the closest thing an elephant could manage to prancing. "For you," he whispered, talking to the elephant and her rider.

Makena sat like a queen of the savanna upon her massive gray throne. Her beauty always made his throat swell up and catch his breath. He had never met her in person, and probably never would. But still, she had become his icon for the whole project. She and her brother, who was perhaps even more brilliant than Makena.

"I want these men," a new voice piped up. "For my grandmother."

"Hi, Araceli." Luis checked on the *Ruby Sea*'s progress. She hadn't touched the dock yet, but now she loomed close. "How's your grandmother doing?"

"She still has nightmares. She saw them cut out the tusks. She's taken two more shifts, and nothing happened on those. They haven't cleared her yet, though. The dumb Angel monitors think she might not hold together under stress, and they want me to babysit her through two more trips."

"That's two more times you both get paid," he reminded her.

"Just get these guys."

"I either did or I didn't," he said. "The work's already done." Still, he fingered a handgun in his pocket. He did know how to use it—he'd spent a few years on the drug-soaked and bloody border between the United States and Mexico when he was in his early teens. A friend here had loaned it to him.

Hopefully he wouldn't need it.

He had a knife with him, too. In his boot, the hilt scratched at his calf.

Both seemed like bad ideas.

"Quiet now," he said to all of his lurkers. In addition to the three, he was being ridden by two senior Elephant Angels and a lawyer. It made him feel heavy for no logical reason.

As the *Ruby Sea* turned to present her broad side to the dock, her engines turned deep and throaty. Dockhands caught silver snakes of ropes and started the dance of tying her up, calling to each other.

Seabirds dipped above the *Ruby*'s decks, calling mournfully and looking for scraps of food.

The cruise ship dock was a city-block-sized square of walkways. He stood onshore. Two sides of the dock went straight out to meet a thick white immensity of concrete with cleats as big as Luis's arms. The *Ruby Sea* tied up just in front of an even bigger boat. Temporary fences served as security, each manned by armed, uniformed men in formal poses.

A few passengers and crew stared out over the rails on the second and third decks. This would be a port of call only, but it was also the first few hours the passengers had onshore since the *Ruby* left Africa.

Doors opened and bright orange gangways started to roll out.

"Can you get closer?" Saad asked.

"I'll kick you out if you're not quiet."

"Beast," Makena teased in a hushed whisper. She had the last word—his watchers all shut up and watched like they were supposed to.

A group of ten mixed Coast Guard and uniformed Port Authority police marched out onto the dock. Luis recognized some of the faces from agencies he'd been asking for help. He smiled.

They left a human barrier five people wide on the far side of the fence. The other five walked through the gate and past the watcher and up to one of the pursers. A policeman showed the purser a set of papers.

The purser shook his head.

Words were exchanged. Luis couldn't make them out, but they sounded determined.

The purser called two others over. Apparently, he wanted them to watch the police, since the purser then disappeared into the bowels of the *Ruby Sea*.

The scene looked tense.

The gangways were all out now, bobbing from almost flat to slightly canted as the *Ruby Sea* reacted to slight and periodic jerks of her engines.

People started down the closest gangway. The guards by the fence let them through with no questions, but the five on the dock stopped them. Hushed but heated voices talked over one another in multiple languages.

News bots started arriving, many no bigger than his hand, a few even smaller. A mix of drones and UAVs jostled for position. One knocked another out of the air and it fell into the sea and floated.

The standoff continued for ten tense minutes.

Four huge men in suits came out of the *Ruby Sea*. Two stopped to talk to the authorities right outside and the other two moved toward the blocking police, talking the crowds out of the way.

Luis narrated as best he could. "These will be bodyguards, and maybe also lawyers." To his surprise, they only said about three sentences to the officers, and then the officers turned and left the dock, followed by a string of passengers.

"Anyone know what happened?" Luis whispered to his watchers.

The lawyer spoke. "Diplomatic immunity."

"Damn." Luis gave out a slow whistle. "On what grounds?"

The lawyer again, bitterly. "One of the women on the dock is the new ambassador from Benin."

"But we can still search the cargo areas, right?" Luis asked.

"If they've pasted a diplomatic seal on them, then, no. Otherwise, maybe. Watch."

The rest of the passengers disembarked. Some looked sleepy, some excited. Only a few had young children with them. Women carried purses and men and children backpacks, but none wheeled luggage.

The tusks weren't escaping this way.

He was even more certain they were here. Diplomatic immunity might succeed, too, darn it all. There had been nothing about it on globenet, but names and nationalities and bank accounts of passengers could be hidden by international law.

A bus and two cabs pulled up and collected the passengers. The newsbots floated slowly away. Nothing to see here.

He would wait until the ship left if he needed to. It was only here until nine in the evening. He had brought an apple and cheese in his bag, and although he was hungry, he decided he might be hungrier later. He thought of talking to Makena, but she liked her privacy. So he settled for waiting, staying as meditative as possible while watching statistics for the other Angel programs. Tigers and rhinos were doing well, but the world had lost four whales to three separate incidents—two to the Japanese whaling fleet, one that beached itself off Baja California, and a legal traditional hunt by Native Americans off the Washington coast.

He had applied for whales, but there were no openings there yet. He might not go now, even if they offered him a job. The elephants needed him.

On the dock, all but one of the gangways pulled back in.

The early morning wasn't yet spilling light into Francine's window. Almost. While she watched her flimsy screen at the kitchen table, Araceli glanced at her grandmother from time to time. Francine flew the drone smoothly now, with a sense of grace in the flutter of her hands. She knew the elephants by name, too.

Araceli watched Makena through the drone's cameras. Spears of sunset bathed the elephants in hot orange light while Araceli shivered in a navy-blue hoodie and fuzzy slippers.

The animal tracking maps showed impala near the herd, and a family grouping of wildebeest, but no lion or tiger or human to threaten the scene.

Araceli noticed movement in her window to Luis. It was already midmorning in Charleston, and the shift in point of view as Luis stood up clued her that something had changed. A boat slid through the water from behind the *Ruby Sea*.

"Makena," she whispered. "Watch Luis."

"Yes," Makena said softly. "I already am. Two more boats are coming."

It was hard to see—her point of view was slaved to Luis, who appeared to be running; the scene in front of her jerked up and down. Then she heard a loudspeaker proclaim, "Stop! Coast Guard."

Two larger boats chased the medium-sized boat that had come from behind the cruise ship.

They weren't far from the dock. Too far to jump, but close enough to swim.

"Shit."

She had never heard Luis curse.

Men in black uniforms boiled up out of the center of the boat, shooting. At least six of them.

Shots came back from the Coast Guard boats.

Figures and guns fell into the water.

Newsbots zoomed over Luis's head.

Araceli's heart pounded in her chest as if she were there. She wanted Luis to back away so he couldn't be hurt, but she had no control of him.

The muzzle of a gun showed up in her viewpoint, looking like she was aiming. "Don't!" Araceli yelled. Luis could end up getting caught up in jail, or in trouble. Besides, how would he know who to shoot?

Makena's voice joined hers.

Luis's hand shook and then he breathed out, "You're right."

The gun disappeared.

There was no more gunfire anyway. Police and Coast Guard called back and forth to each other, coordinating. One of the two Coast Guard boats drifted away from them, but the other came up beside the smuggler and nudged it toward the dock. Luis's hand took a line and pulled, but then someone else took it from him. He let it happen and walked away. Araceli's view changed to the sidewalk in front of him. After a long time, he turned back so they could all watch from a distance.

"Luis," she said. "They got them."

"Thank God and Mary," he whispered back.

Someone dragged a body onto the dock, wet and dripping sea and blood. Another. They way they were treating the bodies suggested they were the smugglers.

Police cars rolled up one after another with lights and sirens, and then two ambulances and a fire truck.

The newsbot swarm grew again.

Araceli flipped to a news channel, which might actually be able to see more than Luis could. Her instincts paid off: they already had pictures of the bottom of the boat lined with ivory. "They got them!" she shouted out loud. She checked on Francine, who wore a wide smile on her face. Makena stood on Delba's neck with an arm touching the sky, like a triumphant ancient warrior. But then, Araceli was grinning, too. It felt like their shared happiness had jumped distance and time and infected them all with lightness.

Francine blinked at her and then returned to her watch, tears filling her eyes, looking incongruous above her smile. Araceli felt as if she had expanded. "They did it," she repeated to Makena. "They got them!"

"It is a lucky day," Saad said to them all.

Araceli flipped to Makena, sitting again now, and to the elephants. The two babies were pushing at each other and touching trunks, flaring their ears and making short mock charges while Makena sat on Delba and watched the play with a great wide smile on her face.

Bits of summer sun from Africa kissed the cold Northwest.

ZOMBIES

A family of orcas swam through Prince William Sound
after the Exxon Valdez. They remain there. They play.
They call to one another underwater. They breach for tourist
boats. They have had zero children since the oil spill.

Two Northern White Rhinos still exist. Females. They live in Africa,
are owned by people in Czechoslovakia. In Africa, they remain
under armed guard, for any man could become so rich
from one horn that he could send all of his children to college.

It's possible
we are all
zombies.

WHEN MOTHERS DREAM

The campfire released embers that rose like tiny hot suns into the moonless sky. I leaned into the fire, thinking of the cold oceans below our camp near the tree line in the Olympic Mountains. Hot flames threatened to blister my face while the night threw cold at my back. My daughter, Nilian, poked the fire with a sharpened stick covered with marshmallow guts. The flames and sugar created pops of color when they met. "Tell me again Mommy."

Her small voice sounded so soft she seemed more like a seven-year-old than a ten-year-old. With only the two of us on watch tonight, it was a good time to bond. "Which story?"

"The whale story."

I grinned. "I have many whale stories."

"How you met the mother."

"Oh, *that* story." I stared at the dancing flames. An owl hooted above and behind me and another answered. "The water was cold, and a wicked cold wind blew across my cheeks."

Nilian sat back, the charred stick dangling from her fingers.

I closed my eyes, remembering the details of my mother's face. Tanned. Deep lines digging rivulets of age around her mouth and eyes, strands of gray in her dark, cropped hair. The strength of her gaze, her biceps, her back. Nothing about her had been frail.

She had died the day after Nilian was born, sick for a week and then gone.

I swallowed, pulling myself out of grief and remembering the most beautiful night I ever had with her. "It was a summer island evening. A full moon spread a river of light across the flat, dark water. I was fifteen, a strong swimmer used to rowing and running. Mom liked my company. I liked being out on the water where anger never lived long." I looked up. The Milky Way spread like pale mist behind the moonlight. "The town was angry. Mom and I were not, but we felt it like a thousand arrows slamming between people. You've never seen towns like they were when I was little.

"Mom slid all of our watches and phones and rings and flashlights into a float-bag that buried their signals. She tied it shut before we ever left the shore. She was taking us to find whales, but no one was supposed to find us. Whales were already rare. She did not want to help anyone else find them, not even the people who wanted to save them. Mom had a way of laughing at those people, of saying the whales did not need them. But then she would go looking, for she needed the whales." I let out a long breath at that realization. "Funny thing, daughter. Whenever I tell you a story about your grandmother, I learn more about her. She needed the whales even more than they needed her, but they were kind enough to include her in their world, and sometimes they took me, too." We were a line of women. Nilian would be as strong as my mother. "Your grandmother had layers."

Nilian grunted as she pulled her shoes away from the fire, rubbing them in the dirt to cool them. "Is she why we hide our watches?" A log fell in onto the embers, making a small red explosion in white ash.

"It's to keep you free. That's the hardest thing in the world to do. It takes stripping yourself from every electronic communications feed and feeling wild air. That's what Mom used to tell me, and I didn't like it, not then. Now I know she's right. The air over the sea or the mountains, or any empty place, is easier to pluck stories from.

"That night, mom hummed as we rowed away from shore. We caught an ebb current and rested as the water carried us. After twenty minutes, Mom pointed. We dug in and paddled to slow seas. When I looked back, Orcas Island's lights were small enough I could pretend they were stars resting on the ocean's back. Mom hummed and our paddles dipped and dipped and dipped. From time to time, we stopped to listen to the rocking buoy's that marked the places where currents moaned over rocks. Every sound popped—the edge of my oar sliding through the largely still water, a fish jumping far away, my mom humming.

Other scientists used speakers in the water to find whales. Mom hummed and listened to her heart.

We had been out long enough for my hands to stiffen, the curl of each palm against the oars aching with the effort expended to row quietly and confidently.

The whales rested with their backs and dorsal fins limned in moonlight. Scars from boat propellers showed up as shadows on their skin. Seven full-grown female orcas and two babies in a sleeping circle, nose to nose, their breathing as synchronous as a metronome. Three breaths all together, and then a long rest, then three, each outbreath sharp enough to travel over the still sea.

I whispered, "I've never seen whales sleep."

Mom whispered back, "They dream together."

I didn't ask how she knew. I simply understood that she did. I stared into her wide, wise eyes, and asked her, "What do whales dream about?"

"Let's see." She took my hand and started to hum again, the water lapping the boat. We floated with the whales, far enough away not to bump them, close enough to hear their breathing. I thought, perhaps, I saw one whale lift from the water, looking at us when mom began to hum, but I couldn't be sure.

In moments, the sound of Mom's humming closed my eyes. The water rocked me into place full of blue skies and sun-dappled water. Behind my closed eyes, I saw the whale's silhouettes and the moonlight on them and the water. Images shimmered slowly into view, starting like ghosts and glowing more brightly when I caught them from the periphery of my dreaming vision. Lines connected the dreaming cetaceans, part light, part sound, something I felt as well as I heard. They vibrated. A net encircled the babies. I felt the new lives reaching out to hold it, to breath into the parents, to send their thin, bright lines of energy into the water like the adult's thicker and slower connections.

I picked a line and followed it to a large salmon. The fish had lines of its own. Life flowed along these lines as the whales breathed, as the fish shimmied, as mother hummed, as my heart beat softly and rhythmically in tune with lines to seabirds resting in the rocks by the shore, to seals below them on the cold winter sand.

My mother's hand held mine, and her touch made the lines of whale dreams flutter and convulse for just a moment as we dreamed into the great web of lights and beating hearts.

The single salmon glittered in our dream, decorated with artsy colors as if its fins were feathers. As much art as fish. A whale swam behind it, flicking its great black tail, its fins and flukes also splashed with reds and blues. It opened its mouth and took the salmon into it. For a moment, both glowed. The dying dream-salmon exhaled, a satisfied sigh.

I struggled to open my eyes, but my mother's hand closed more tightly over mine, her thumb caressing my palm.

I curled into the bottom of the boat and sank into the dream, barely able to feel the wood under my head, the touch of my mother's hand. The lights of the dream grew brighter around the gathered whales. A thread ran from my dreaming heart to one of theirs and then to all of theirs. I felt that the lines of connection going from heart to heart and back in the circle of the world. I sensed the dream continuing forever, looping through all of the oceans and the forests and the rivers of the world and returning, but I chose to stay inside the circle of the whales. I felt like the salmon, like anything could happen to me and it would be all right.

My mother stayed beside me.

Lights pulsed brightly as the whales folded me into their anticipation. That's the only way I can describe the feeling. They looked forward to something. Mom and I floated in their dream. No words passed between us, only light and the knowledge of imminence.

We floated together in that dream for so long I felt the water around my body, the salt, the buoyancy. I breathed with whales.

The boat and the waves and the anticipation blended as if every part of the Salish Sea touched every other part.

One of the whales grew brighter than the others. All focus slid there. This was what we waited for, what the song and the sea and the bright dream demanded of us all.

A small form slid free of the bright mother, sending wisps of its own dream-light to be picked up by the other whales, to twine around the line between me and them.

Anticipation slid to soft rejoicing, and all of the focus of the Earth fell onto the dream baby. The whales circled it. I felt them with my dreaming and my physical body, knowing every shift they made, every slide down into the water, every touch one to another.

The baby floated in the water, and then it fell, the mothers—for they were all mothers—following it down and down, as if it and they were feathers instead of huge creatures. Their anticipation had slid into acceptance. Wisps of sadness grew, until the sorrow threatened to pull me down, out of the boat, into the same acceptance that the whales had of the baby's fall.

I felt free with it, pregnant with death and change, as if I could birth the entire world or simply fall into its dream and stay forever. I felt like the salmon, about the be consumed and resigned in a pleasant way, as if a new thing waited on the other side, close enough I felt its pull.

Darkness and warmth. Pure possibility.

Mom's hand tugged me back into my body, my shoulders tight with cold and tears falling down my cheeks.

The whales were gone, fallen after the vision-child they had made.

We cried the dream out of our blood as we paddled back, digging our oars into the soft tops of slow swells. A cold wind fluttered across our cheeks and mom sang a mournful song, her words sliding across the water.

I imagined the orcas heard her.

Nilian touched my hand, the heat of her fingers startling me back into my half-warm body, driving me to blink at the fire. "You're crying, Mom."

A finger to my check verified her claim, and I smiled. "Those orcas, the ones in the Islands, did not give birth again. Not once, not ever. They are all too old for it now. A poet I know calls them a ghost pod."

"But you had me. Why are humans making babies when orcas aren't?"

"Some orca pods *are* having babies. Those were from L Pod, and they chose not to have more babies."

Nilian's voice rose a little. "They chose?"

"Yes."

She poked at the fire in silence for a few minutes, kicking up showers of sparks. "Are we choosing?"

"I chose to have you."

A smile flirted with her lips, escaped, followed by a wise sigh that nearly broke me.

"What did it feel like? That dream? Do I have to be near the orcas to dream with them?"

"You have to start somewhere."

She furrowed her brows and set her stick down, scooting closer to me and placing her soft head on my shoulder. She seldom did this anymore, but perhaps the memory of the orca's dream caressed her like it did me. "Do trees dream?" she asked.

"Let's find out." I took her hand in mine, closed my eyes, and let the scent of cedars fill my nostrils.

SOUTHERN RESIDENTS

E ven though Julie Pol wanted to dance, her mouth was dry with anxiety. She stood beside at least twenty dignitaries. A blue and green Ocean Research Institute and Spa (ORIAS) sign undulated above their heads, driven to movement by powerful air-recirculating fans. Julie had spent every professional favor she had to make the institute real. New building materials had been developed and refined. Environmentalists had been alternately fought and partnered with. Sincere citizens had sworn that if money was wasted here, babies would die. Perhaps they had, or would. Julie had signed approvals for so much money she could have fed all of Washington State for a year. All that for one of the greatest environmental clichés: *Save the Whales*.

Julie's feet hurt from pacing all night. Nevertheless, she smiled as she shook hands and murmured thanks to current and former state legislators, the entire Whale Museum Board, the Chair of the Northwest Indian Fisheries Commission, a famous futurist who had been fighting for the orcas for six decades, two science fiction writers and four science writers who had written books about whales, the University of Washington President, and finally, the Governor of the State of Washington. Governor Mary Liu had been the final human brick that built ORIAS. It had even been in her campaign platform. Her voice sounded warm and full of humor as she said, "Thank you, Doctor Pol. We're grateful to you for all that your team has done to keep the Salish Sea clean." She reached a neat and bejeweled hand out toward Julie.

Julie smiled as she took the Governor's hand. "Thank you."

She didn't say that the Salish hadn't been *clean* for eighty years. But it was cleaner than it had been in 2040, and given ten more years, given ORIAS, it would be better yet. "Thank you."

The governor added, "I just heard that two more whales have been confirmed pregnant."

That was true, although the survival rate for orca calves was still less than fifty percent. But ORIAS had been built on hope, so she merely said, "Yes. Good news."

A beaming graduate student handed her the center of a blue ribbon decorated with sea shells and scissors the size of a brief-case. Two minutes later, she and the governor each used one side of the awkward scissors to snip the ribbon.

ORIAS was officially open.

Half an hour later, Julie went looking for a sink in which to dump the contents of a tiny flute of cheap champagne. In the closest lab, she noticed a young woman standing near the back, dressed in a bright blue jumpsuit that contrasted with her long dark hair and dark eyes. She had rigged up a camera and stood gesturing animatedly into it. Julie inched closer, listening. "— expensive waste of money that could be spent on feeding and housing us."

Julie cleared her throat and the woman looked over at her, startled, her mouth thinning into a grimace. "I'm—"

"Recording. I see that. I'm Dr. Julie Pol. I run the place. Do you have any questions I can answer for your audience?"

The young woman's cheeks flushed red, but she glanced back at the camera and gestured for it to swivel toward Julie. "I've been joined by Dr. Pol, who runs ORIAS. Doctor? Are you excited to see the first hotel rooms open?"

Julie fought a grimace. The girl reminded her of the unskilled citizen reporters who had lied as they attempted to stop the sanctions on whale-watching boats. "The hotel has been slept in for two weeks to train staff. I'm far more excited about the lab work. We're standing in the specimen analysis lab. Here, we'll examine everything from whale poop to ocean sediment to understand the health of the Southern Resident Killer Whales."

The girl's lips curled up in an oversized grimace meant for her audience. "Whale poop?"

"Whale poop. It can identify toxins in the water, tell us how well the whales have fed, and identify some diseases. We've been collecting whale poop for almost sixty years."

The young woman rolled her eyes before flashing a bright, impish smile and glancing at her camera. "I need to go learn about whale poop for a while. I'll see you all tomorrow!" She picked up the camera and flicked it off.

Julie held her hand out. "I presume you're one of the students who won the lottery?"

"Yes." The girl took her hand but then let go quickly and turned to dismantle her lightweight tripod. "I'm Amaria Nitel. From New Texas University. I'm a journalism major."

There was a journalism major in the lottery-winning class? "I'll be lecturing your group in the morning."

"I'll be broadcasting some of the lessons to my feed." The girl spoke with too much confidence, as if daring Julie to tell her no.

Julie stiffened, prepared to tell Amaria broadcasts would have to be pre-approved, but Amaria interrupted her before she could get a word out. "That's how I pay my rent and books. The college pays my tuition because so many people follow me, the admissions office says it boosts applications for on-campus work."

Julie closed her mouth. Her own daughter, Sarai, took every opportunity to remind her that she was utterly out of touch with survival outside of academia. *Life is hard*, Sarai had told her just last week. *You've never starved or been in debt. Have a heart!* Julie took a deep breath. "Pleased to meet you. See that you have researched whale poop and how we harvest it before tomorrow morning. I know there is a paper in your preparation packet. I put it there."

The girl glared at her and shoved the camera equipment into her bright blue bag. Her dark hair and eyes went well with high cheekbones and carefully crafted brows. Now that she wasn't staring into the camera, she looked lost.

Julie remembered Sarai's statements again and promised herself she'd think about the lost part of the girl rather than her edginess. She poured her champagne into a nearby lab sink, put the plasglas in the recycler, and turned toward the girl. "There will be a show out the observation windows in half an hour. I'm sure your class has been invited. I can escort you in and get you a good seat."

The girl's eyes widened.

Julie spoke a little softer. "The robots will be there."

"I think I should go find my classmates."

Her *classmates*. Not her friends? "I can put you with the press. You can record there. You won't be allowed to broadcast live—that's all licensed. But you can use it later."

Amaria's smile looked weak, but Julie took it for assent and led Amaria from the lab onto the observation deck. Julie had to thread through three groups of crucially important people with her head down to avoid getting trapped in a conversation. Joe Hui, the dour head of the ORIAS Press Corps, pressed his lips together in frustration when Julie said, "This is Amaria. She's studying Journalism. Please find her a place to record."

Joe mumbled, "There might be room in the back."

The relief that crossed Amaria's face made Julie pause. She had assumed any oceanography student would love being here. But Amaria looked a little queasy as she started to pull her camera gear back out.

No time to worry about it now.

Five minutes later, large curtains drew open, revealing a school of fish. Scales flashed in rainbow colors as they swam past the outside lab lights ORIAS used to augment the pale daylight that barely touched the ocean here, a hundred feet below the surface. The fish slowly revealed that they were robots; sort of a reverse fishy Turing test.

Reporters and VIPs applauded. Julie stood in front of the observation window and offered a summary of the science. "The Salish Sea is rich and diverse, ecologically significant and economically crucial. Because of our beloved Southern Resident Killer Whales, there have been microphones in Puget Sound for decades. They were valuable. They were also sparse point solutions."

Julie stopped to look around, catching eyes, hoping to convince the press ORIAS would help the world, that it was worth it. They lived in the real world, the one the frightened student had come from, the one where climate refugees fought over food scraps in tent cities. "ORIAS is more than a point solution. Far more. It is this building, and almost five-thousand stationary sensors. It is almost seven hundred different types of mobile data collectors, seventy-two of which you just saw perform for you. That number will grow: ORIAS has partnered with the State of Washington to send toxicity data to the robots dismantling drowned structures along old shorelines. All of this data gives us hope, it gives us knowledge, and it gives us a chance to understand." She took a deep breath, feeling the data pouring in all around her. It felt like the secrets of the sea were speaking to her. Most systems had been online for weeks in test, and today would start the collection of baseline data. "Many of you in this room helped us reach this dream. Thank you. It's your turn. What do you want to know?"

She and her principle scientists answered questions for an hour. By then the guests had consumed most of the food and seemed happy to catch elevators to the surface.

By the time Julie found Joe, the girl was gone. "How did our foundling journalist do?"

Joe frowned. "I had to ignore her at first. Busy with the pros. But when I got back to her, she was looking at the wall and pointing the camera at herself."

Interesting. "She was looking away from the ocean?"

"Either she's totally self-absorbed or she doesn't like crowds." He hesitated. "Or she's scared of being underwater."

The classroom was on the fourth level down, and thus below the observation deck where the opening party had been hosted. A twenty by five foot observation window occupied the upper half of the classroom wall. Living fish came up to the window and peered in from time to time. When other students laughed and pointed at the finned spies, Amaria sank deeper into her chair.

At the break, Julie pulled her aside and led her out of the classroom. "I watched a few of your videos this morning. You smile a lot in them, and you're outgoing."

The girl's features were closed, but Julie had dealt with hundreds of students. She felt anger lurking behind this one's hooded eyes, and under the anger something else. Fear?

Julie let the silence linger until Amaria couldn't take it anymore, and blurted out, "I took this class to graduate. I don't care about science. It sold us all up the river. Science made plastic and atomic bombs and gasoline. Science stole everything from my generation."

Such old, stale talking points. Julie sighed and started her rebuttal. "The bomb and plastic grocery bags were both feats of engineering which seemed useful at the time. I choose to believe the people who made those choices meant well."

Amaria snorted. "Oil companies? Tobacco companies?"

"Well, no. But we used science to bring them down and change their behavior."

"Fine." Amaria's tone suggested she didn't agree, or care. "But how can you possibly say that saving less than a hundred whales is worth millions of dollars?"

"Saving the whales requires saving the sea. Saving the sea saves us."

Amaria went quiet, again sullen. But the sour looks covered up something more, something Julie hadn't touched yet. Once more, Julie let silence work until Amaria said, "Saving the sea here doesn't stop the Texas drought or the storms."

Julie smiled. "Everything is connected. Everything. For example, the more trees you plant where streams start in the mountains, and along the banks all the way down to the sea, the more salmon you have."

"How do trees make salmon?"

"They make the streams richer with food for plankton which feed the sea creatures that eventually feed the salmon. If you have enough salmon, you feed both the orcas and the bears, and the bear poop feeds the trees."

"And this connects to Texas?"

"The food webs between your seas and your land are just as complex. I could lecture you for hours. But I have a better idea."

Amaria actually looked interested.

"There's an extra place in our submersible trip this evening. I'll add you to it, and you can use that as your extra-credit lab."

Amaria's eyes widened and she stiffened. She pointed toward the ocean, even though they stood in a hallway with no observation windows. "You want me to go out there?"

"Yes. Yes, I do." Clearly the girl had no idea how many classes had entered the lottery for the chance to be the first one on ORIAS, or how many grad students would give a year's tuition to have this week. "I'll see you at 3:00 P.M. I'll pick you up at the end of your afternoon lecture." She smiled. "It's on whale poop."

That elicited a brief smile before Amaria turned her head away.

Was Joe right about the girl being frightened? "Please come with me on the submersible. You can record the trip."

Still no answer.

"I'll let you broadcast live. The only condition is that you can't say anything bad about ORIAS while we're out there. I can't stop you after you leave at the end of this week, but for this week, you must be neutral or positive."

Amaria turned her face toward Julie's. She looked pale and her lower lip trembled. "I . . ."

"Surely some of your followers would love to be here? Aren't there almost a hundred thousand of them?" Julie had asked a graduate student to look the girl up on the most recent social platforms, which had names Julie had never heard of.

Amaria swallowed. "More on good days. I can do it."

"I'll meet you at three. For now, break's over. Come back to class in two minutes and I'll tell you about the crucial role of culverts under roads in Seattle."

*

Julie was surprised when Amaria showed up on time and in vaguely appropriate clothes: jeans, soft-soled tennis shoes, and a long-sleeved T-shirt. She already had her camera out, held in her hand, and she whispered into it as Julie handed her up into one of the front seats in the bright yellow sub. Julie took the seat next to her. The other two seats were stacked above them, as if the sub were an exaggerated theater. All four seats could control the sub, but at the moment control rested in the hands of Doctor Ian McDonald, a deep-water biologist. Sadhita Chopra served as copilot. She was a graduate student Julia had invited into the sub in hope that she'd connect with Amaria. Julie had briefed both Ian and Sadhita on her simple goal. *Help her enjoy the sea.*

The front and top of the sub were transparent, the back and sides a mixture of view screens for video, places where instruments attached, motors, and control surfaces.

As Julie strapped in, Amaria focused intently the camera in her hand. Julie patiently plucked it free and gave Amaria a verbal tour of the sub and the proper safety lecture. In spite of the fact that they were still docked with the lights off, Amaria's eyes slid away from the front window when Julie pointed toward it.

Julie leaned close to her and whispered, "We're safe. It will be okay," and more loudly to Ian, "Let's go."

He turned on one set of front lights, illuminating a school of mottled chinook salmon right in front of them.

A great sign. "That's whale food," Ian said.

Amaria gazed at her own lap.

Julie told the girl, "You can look through your camera, see if that helps."

Amaria nodded woodenly and held her small camera up toward her face, streaming it to her phone. She watched the video of her face on the phone, trying out fake smiles. Her hand shook, which made the video shaky.

"Point the camera at the window."

Amaria's current pretend smile failed. Still, she obeyed. Julie glanced down at the display and saw eel grass streaming by.

As the sub moved off, the salmon turned all at once and schooled away. "Ian?" Julie asked. "Can you show Amaria the outside of ORIAS? She has a following that might want to hear about it. I can narrate. When we get close to the surface, maybe fifteen feet, let's use the sensor webs to find some sea lions or dolphins."

He snapped a friendly, oversized salute at her. "Yes'm."

As Julie started talking, she found herself surprisingly conscious of Amaria's camera. No good reason—the sub had three cameras that were always on. But right now, this little camera mattered far more. "The outside surface is designed so that barnacles and other sea life will eventually grow on the parts of it that aren't window, and there will be one robot assigned just to keep the ORIAS windows clean. So this video might be one of the last ones where ORIAS looks quite so industrial and man-made."

When Julie stopped, Amaria spoke. "Hi guys. I see some of you are along for the ride. I'm in a sub. We're looking at ORIAS."

Julie narrated the various levels: maintenance, storage, and the robot shop on the bottom, which had fewer and smaller windows. Living quarters and offices, with a window in each office and bedroom. Two level of labs, including the one with the observation deck where the opening day party had been. She pointed, "You were looking out of that window yesterday. Today we're looking in." She waved at two students staring out of the windows and pointing at the sub. "The hotel has one level fully below the waterline and another at the mid-point. We've designed it to withstand up to three more meters of sea-level rise. We're hoping for less."

"Nine more feet?" Amaria sounded incredulous.

Finally. Some engagement. "Yes. Although as I said, we're hoping for less. Climate is complex. And the numbers are starting to move in the right direction. We've been cutting carbon emissions by more than five percent a year for ten years."

"But isn't it still getting worse?" Amaria asked.

"Not everywhere." A sudden warmth touched her. "Here, the balance is starting to . . . maybe . . . stabilize. We have saved a lot of sea life, and the ocean water here is some of the healthiest on the planet. We built this," she waved toward ORIAS, "to help it stay that way."

"I thought you built it to save the whales."

"We did." Julie really wanted to say *we built it to save you*, but she managed a more politic reply. "But to do that means healing the sea, designing quieter shipping engines, and protecting the places the whales feed. We need to help the salmon and the sea lions, and really, everything else." She looked at Amaria, who held her little camera up and pointed it Julie as she finished, "If the oceans die, we die. There was a point in my life when I thought we might lose them."

Amaria looked at her, her mouth a little open now, curiosity playing around the edges of her face. "Why don't you think that now?"

Julie gestured Ian towards the shore and paused to think as the sub shifted direction. "As I got older, I realized I could help. To help, you have to believe your choices matter. The decisions people made in the past don't matter. Humans have caused a lot of problems, but we've also solved a lot of them. I want to be a solver."

Ian clapped softly.

The waters at this height were full of light. Fish swam all around them.

Sadhita said, "Port, at four o'clock. There are three dolphins."

"Point your camera at them," Julie said.

"Where?"

"To your left. Can you look?"

The girl moved the camera around, missing the dolphins entirely. Julie wanted to tip her chin up and direct her gaze out of the main window.

Sadhita burst out in warm, good-natured laughter. "Now they're in front of you."

Ian struggled to keep the sub's front view centered on the dolphins.

Amaria finally got her camera pointed at the small school of dolphins, which had grown to five animals. She gasped and started babbling at her phone. "There are five dolphins in front of us.

They're bigger than I thought. They are *really* graceful."

The sub approached a rocky promontory. In silence, Julie pantomimed for Ian to point that way. He did, and Amaria sighed. "I wanted to keep looking at the dolphins!"

Ian said, "There's an octopus."

Julie spotted it right away, red tentacles moving against a background of grays and mossy greens, punctuated here and there with the purple of a sunflower sea star.

Amaria managed a furtive glance at the wall of sea life, looked away, and then back. She dropped the phone into her lap and watched directly through the camera for the first time, leaning slightly forward and pointing. "I see it! Look, gang, there's a big octopus! Its arms are longer than mine."

From behind Amaria, Ian told the girl, "You tell me where to point this thing. See what you can find."

Amaria whispered, "Can you go forward ten feet?"

Ian complied.

After three more sets of halting directions, Julie pointed. "That's a brown cat shark."

"A brown cat shark? It's really named a *cat* shark?"

Julie laughed. "Yes."

"What was the name of the octopus?"

Sadhita answered. "A giant Pacific Octopus. I wrote a paper about them once. They're almost as smart as humans."

Thousands of herring surrounded them, silvered finger-sized fish, scales flashing as they darted past on some mysterious errand. Amaria forgot to look through her camera. She simply sat entranced, one hand over her mouth.

Amaria's audience was missing the herring.

Julie smiled. She could stop worrying about ORIAS. It was already working.

TAHLEQUAH

The last time you carried
a dead baby through
the waters of
Puget Sound we wept
with you. We cried
and sang, followed your
salty tears with ours.

Something . . .
perhaps a line of light,
perhaps a dream,
perhaps a shared sorrow
connected you to us,
us to each other,
the world to itself.

Today, you carry a second
dead baby.
No warm salty tears
streak my cheeks.
No shock stops me.
Not even the enormity
of your sadness.

It is too great,
too lost in the sea
of all our losses.

We are designing intelligences to help us talk to whales.
If we succeed, what can you possibly say
that you are not telling us right now?

CURSE OF THE ORCAS

You stare over the rail with round astonished faces, pointing,
joy cloaking your cold hearts, smiles you wear like a veil of guilt.

Curse you for following us all day, curse
you for disrupting our speech with droning boats,
curse you for destroying our silences.

Half our babies die. Most are male. We lift them up from poison
water to breathe air that reeks of your boat engines.

Curse you for turning freshwater that runs to the sea
toxic, curse you for the poison in our blubber, curse you
for destroying our home like you destroy your air.

We hunger. We used to thrive on great runs of silver
chinook salmon that are simply gone now, the ocean empty.

Curse you for engineering dams and lakes, curse
you for feeding yourselves fat on our fish, curse
you for watching us to death. Curse you.

ANNALEE OF THE ORCAS

Annalee grew up in the dark and grumpy middle of the country. She knew she did not belong there. Something in her dreams told her this, over and over. It cajoled and called and whispered. It gave her a direction, and did so in a language that she could not have reproduced if she had to. Most important of all, it filled her with need. Greedy, insistent, demanding need.

Three days after her twenty-third birthday, she inherited her father's tiny fortune. She packed the few things she cared about into a big purse and walked for two days to Chicago. There, she boarded the Empire Builder train and went west, happily escaping her two unhelpful brothers and, less happily, leaving the family dog behind. She carried no electronics and wore no wearables. She chose to travel through the twenty-first century as if she were firmly a member of the nineteen-forties instead of the twenty-forties.

Annalee was small and sensitive, with skin as white as the bones of a fish and hair as dark as the night sky, her brilliant black eyes full of colored specks. Streaks of feeling shuddered through her body like meteors. Annalee painted her lips the deep red of vine maples in the fall, and her eyelids the gray blue of her dead mother's hydrangeas.

She disembarked as far west as the train would go, and wandered lost in Seattle for a time. One foggy early morning in July, Annalee found herself on the dock in Anacortes, Washington, staring toward the San Juan Islands and beyond them, at Canada. *They* were west. She felt her inner compass as a quivering string between herself and anything west, a force that she could not repudiate any more than she could deny her lungs air.

As she stood on the end of the creaking wooden dock, the sea washed over her. The scent of salt caused her nostrils to flare in pleasure. Morning fog spangled her eyelashes.

A harbor seal rose slowly out of the water and stared at her for a very long time, so still it looked as if it stood on the back of a log or a stone hidden under the water. It looked like it wanted to have a conversation. But Annalee could not speak seal, and after a time it sank under the smooth surface of the morning sea and disappeared.

A woman in a red wooden canoe paddled up near her. She was gray where Annalee was black and white, her lips pale and her eyes the washed-out color of a high summer sky. Wrinkles made rivers and hills in her cheeks and the skin on her arms sagged over strong biceps that held bright red paddles. "Are you looking for a ride?"

"Yes."

The woman brought the rocking canoe up to the still dock, and Annalee stepped carefully into the front seat, the woman's strong arm steadying her. When she could grasp both sides of the moving boat, she let out a long breath in relief.

The woman introduced herself as Paulette, and smiled when she heard Annalee's name. She asked for nothing else, no destination, no fee, no history. She paddled the canoe out through long swells and the mist enveloped them and then was gone.

The water's size frightened Annalee. It rose and fell as if it breathed. A long neck of it reached up toward Canada and out to the Asian countries, as if the sea went on forever. It hid wavy fronds of golden weed in its green darkness, and sometimes Paulette had to slide a paddle free of floating sea-garden and push them into open water. Anything could be below them: a squid large enough to pull the boat down, a shark with a great white fin and teeth as big as her fingers, a sunken ship full of ghostly sailors.

They stopped beside a boat that was four times the length

of the canoe. Paulette climbed on board and pulled Annalee up, pointing to the cushioned cockpit. Then she stood and waited until a wave lifted the canoe and she tugged it onto the boat and lashed it to the top of the deck with bungie cords. Paulette spoke for the first time since she picked Annalee up. "I will take you to San Juan Island, and you can stay with me."

"Why?"

"I speak harbor seal."

That shouldn't have explained anything, but Annalee felt the line of compass inside her twang and shudder, and then fade away. She swallowed, suddenly afraid. She didn't ask what the seal said, but went to sit on the deck in front of the canoe. Paulette pulled two anchors aboard and set them dripping near the wooden steering wheel. An engine coughed to life and small chugging sounds escaped the back of the boat until it began to move away from the dock, gliding on the rolling waves.

July sun pounded on Annalee's back and forced her to braid her long hair into a rope as thick as her arm. Salt filled her nose and dried on her skin. She leaned out over the railing and the wind on her face calmed her rocking stomach. A fish leapt up through the water's surface and landed with such a great splash that the salty spray kissed her cheek. She lifted a hand to wipe the water away. A pink mouth followed the fish, and then a great black head that glistened in the sun like a tire. A black fin rose and then fell beneath the water, followed by a tail as wide as Annalee stood tall.

The un-repeatable sound from her dreams vibrated through sky and sea and through her veins and nerves and set her skin tingling. The lines which had tugged her from her home to the sea came back to her, filling her bones and strengthening her muscles. She felt longer and taller. Like she should have always felt, as if right there on the boat her body had changed into its native form. Dizzy, she fell onto the surface of the boat, the hard painted wood slapping her cheek.

Her eyes closed and she floated free of all she knew, free of her braid and her fall-colored lips and the blood beating through her fingers and toes. She looked down on the boat and the sea and the black fins, and thought perhaps her body hadn't changed after all, although it looked very still there on the white fiberglass next to the red wooden canoe. The sound filled her and she followed it past her still form, past the boat and the canoe and Paulette and into the water, which closed over her like a child's blanket.

She rolled inside the water, mountains below her and a school of fish jerking and calling in the water-sky nearby. Five great whales spoke with sound-not-word to each other in close formation, mouths cleaving through the flying salmon, powerful flukes and tails rowing through the sky of the ocean.

The boat's engine puffed above her, as loud as ten beating drums, sending piercing and painful ripples into the three-dimensional sea-sky-sea-whales-fish-rocks-fish-whales vision that existed all around her.

The sounds of the orcas' conversation painted pictures in the empty places that had been full of her compass. She knew—always, instantly—where each animal swam, who they were, that they cared for each other and for her. She knew they were amazed that she had come.

She understood the hunger that drove them after the fish, and the joy they took in the hunt. She recognized sadness in the animals. Loss and under that something like hope. They did not feel as humans felt any more than the sound they had sent her sounded like humans sounded. Nonetheless, the emotions of whales surrounded her. The watery sky of the ocean surface seethed with family.

This was how she first came home, and how she became what she was ever-after, the witch-queen of the orcas, the black and white woman who came to the sea to save them. As she recognized the great cetaceans, they recognized her, and both knew each other as part of the great long history of life.

Orcas had swum inside these waters for fifty million years, and humans had joined with them five thousand years before. Annalee held a soul they knew of lifetimes and lifetimes ago, and in that first long and joint swim, they had taught her to see as much like them as humans are capable of seeing. They spun through water with her, the matriarch speaking to her, with her, weaving the story of lifetimes together in dancing images that filled the sea all around them, and which she could—miraculously—partake in, so far as it was possible to hold so much inside of a small human.

She grew as large as the waters of Puget Sound where the orcas lived, and her size startled her, her heart beating fast staccato and her head on fire.

She coughed and spit up water, her hands and breasts and braid all pressed against the hard wood of the boat. The engine had silenced, the boat drifting up and down on the swells like a slightly revolting lullaby. A voice whispered in her ear to *roll over* and she rolled. Paulette's strong hands picked her up so that she sat, staring out at the sea and feeling the breeze sweep the stray strands of escaped hair back from her forehead. "They're gone," Paulette said. "Chasing the chinook, for one of the older cows is pregnant and all of them are protecting her, driving the fish for her and into her mouth."

Human words sounded flat and loud in Annalee's head and she felt as empty as the surface of the sea in that moment. A tear fell down her cheek, and then another. "I did not cry when my father died," she told Paulette for no good reason at all.

Paulette answered, "The harbor seal told me the truth."

"What did it say?" Annalee licked a tear from her forefinger.

"It told me that you had come home."

"I could have told you that!"

"Before now?"

"No." She had stopped crying, but a great pain filled her chest, threatening to bring her back down to the surface of the boat, and her stomach felt light and thin. "No. They're dying. They were all starving."

"How do you know?"

"They are thin and frightened. I didn't know about the baby but that explains why they chose to move the way they did.

They spoke to me of the present and the past but perhaps . . ." She help her hands over her eyes. "Perhaps they were unable to talk of the future."

Paulette began to slide toward the back of the boat. "They have never told me of any future. They did not tell me you were coming. Only the seal knew, and that might have been after you came to the sea."

Annalee scooted after Paula, noting that she was no longer afraid of falling into the sea, and no longer thought she even might.

The engine sputtered back to life. "I will take you to the shore, to a place where you can sleep."

"I need to sleep now." Annalee lay in the bow of the boat, restless in the sweating heat and lulled by the waves, empty of her compass and full of her home, dreaming of whales and seals and salmon.

Deeper, sharper waves woke her just before the small wooden boat pulled up to a wooden dock beside a clean white expanse of motor yacht bigger than her father's house had been. A house the size of seven houses stood on a knoll facing the ocean. "You live here?"

"In the boathouse. You can stay on my couch for now."

Annalee did. She slept for three days and three nights, sweating and stinking and twisting, dreaming of the rich sky beneath the waves. As she slept, she gave away everything she no longer needed. She gave up her frustration and her fears and her angers. She dripped her past out in sweat and it evaporated into the air and left through the small boathouse windows covered with orange curtains.

On the fourth morning, Paulette brought her a cup of steaming stiff coffee and a plate of simple breads and blackberries. As she knelt before Annalee with her offerings, a thick respect filled her eyes and a smile escaped the wrinkles on her face. "They are calling for you."

Annalee swallowed and drank the coffee and ate the berries and one piece of bread. She went to the kitchen and cleaned away the scent of who she had been with sage oil soap. She dressed in gauzy pants and a thin white shirt with wide sleeves that she found hanging on the door.

Paulette met her by the door and they walked slowly down to end of the wide and sun-washed dock, the older woman's footsteps sliding gently behind her. A morning breeze plucked at the sleeves of Annalee's shirt. The water lay flat on the world, smooth as a mirror. Whales rose and fell through it. They left ripples that danced with the ripples of other whales and of diving cormorants. Birds hopped and chattered in the trees near the shore. A white ferry passed by so far away that it might be a toy.

The matriarch rose up so that Annalee recognized her. Annalee did not fall into the water-songs of the whales, but remained cross-legged on the edge of dock.

They nosed a baby in front of them. It floated, barely breathing, listing to the side. She sat on the edge of the dock alongside all of the whales in the matriline and watched the baby orca pass from the world. Its last breath silenced the shore birds.

The whales took the baby's carcass away with them, pushing it with their noses. Neither she nor the orcas nor Paulette spoke a word to each other in the entire exchange. After the place where the whales and the dead baby had been was rippled only by late morning breeze, Annalee turned to the older woman beside her. "I must find them tomorrow."

"We will get you ready."

Paulette picked up a great net that she stored in her boat and called out to the ocean, a high sweet call that sang respect and re-started the bird's songs and righted the small world of this part of the island's rocky edge. She held the net out in the water and a salmon a long as Annalee's braid leaped up into it, the fish's sides gleaming silver. Paulette stunned it and opened a gill, placing the fish back in the water to swish its tail and empty itself of blood. The two women carried the fish to the kitchen and cleaned it, hanging long strips to smoke and only eating late that night, after the sacrifice had been properly cared for. The sweet flesh strengthened Annalee and she ate more than she remembered ever eating.

That night, she dreamed of the loss of children, of her sister who had died in a car wreck when Annalee was still small, of a puppy they had lost to an eagle one summer, of the barn kittens that almost all died. Right before she woke, she dreamed of the baby orca, and when her eyes opened, they were full of warm water and salt.

She sipped coffee while Paulette brushed and braided her hair. Neither she nor Paulette spoke while they readied the canoe together. This time, Paulette did not have to help her settle onto the seat in the canoe. They practiced turning and paddling before they pulled around the spit that protected the big house and big boat from nearly everything. The sea, the sky and the cedar and fir forests on the island seemed bright and full of color and life. The place that held her purpose beat against the inside of her chest. Maybe today.

They passed through kayaks and other canoes, small boats with low, soft motors and a fisherperson or two, and big sailing boats with white sails barely puffing out in the late morning. It was one of the last moments before the mainland children went back to school, and the water was full of noise and energy.

She worried.

How could she even hear the whales? Loud music and boat horns and the engine of a big boat that spit up a tail of water behind it on the horizon filled the air. Children called across the water. A little girl with yellow hair saw a seal and squealed. Five small boats surrounded the spot where it had been, children calling happily to each other and flashing cameras and taking pictures.

Still, the two women did not speak.

The sun beat down on them. Annalee's arms grew tired. She kept going, paddling and paddling and thinking and worrying.

Paulette began to hum.

As the sound flowed through Annalee, her arms had less trouble pulling the oars through the blue-green water.

A small white lighthouse squatted on the beach to their right. The whales came around them, rising and falling close to them, so close she could touch them if they asked. One had a scar all down its side and another had a smaller, deeper scar near its fin.

Annalee felt dizzy. She set her paddles down in the boat and held onto the sides. Her head heavy with sleep.

"Head for the shore," Paulette told her.

"I need to dream."

"You need to paddle to the shore."

She picked her paddles back up. They felt like someone had coated them with iron. She could barely hold them when the boat scraped bottom. An old man came and whispered in Paulette's ear. She whispered back, and he took the boat, but only after he handed them a blanket.

Paulette took Annalee to a small ledge and took off her coat, wrapping the wet-part inside so it made a dry pillow and letting Annalee lie down. She covered her with the blanket.

Annalee's eyes closed. Again, she fell into the strange dream-world of orcas. She flew through a sky full of wriggling, flashing fish. Orcas ate. The waves and the shallow sea folded around her and them, and they swam near the surface and snacked on salmon. A starfish walked on shallow rocks and an octopus swirled her many feet and moved like wind in the sea-sky. A small shark searched for its own fish.

She rose to breathe as if she herself were a whale instead of a woman.

Again, they were happy to see her, and again the matriarch reminded her how they caught many of their fish in this part of the sea as current swept them near the rocks and the lighthouse, and of how once there were many more, and that once they were almost always here. Once, all days were like this day, fat and full of fish.

A deep-throated thrumming burst across her and the picture of the world shuddered and broke up. Fish escaped through the holes in the picture. The whales called to each other, tails rising and falling and sweeping them away from the noise, and from the food.

She felt pulled like taffy and kicked in her sleeping body, trying to follow them.

A hand covered her forehead, cool and soothing. She gulped

for three deep breaths and fell back into a cacophony of sound that kicked her out and awake again and made her retch bile onto the rocks.

She opened her eyes. Not one, but three, boats ran alongside the whales. Children leaned over the edge and pointed. The wind whipped the words from loudspeakers into mush. She stared, thinking, and after a while she mused to Paulette. "I can hear the people, but I could not hear them clearly when I was under water. I can barely hear the engines from here, but they sounded like sea-rockets there."

"Whales see with their ears."

The hunger of the orcas and the reasons for it settled clearly over Annalee and she glared at the boats. "I see." Annalee stood and led the way back down to the beach.

The harbor seal had told Paulette that Annalee could help the whales, but how could one small woman with a long black braid take on three boats of whale watchers and their burly crew?

Annalee did not want to admit that she couldn't think of a way to help, and so she kept all of her words tucked inside of her as she paddled back with Paulette equally silent behind her. This island had become home. The task of stopping the whales from starving in an ocean full of fish was hers to do.

The whales came two mornings a week. Her body lay on the dock as if dead while Paula watched over it. She swam with her pod, re-learning the language of whales, which did not have sentences or single ideas, and which was both concrete and full of philosophy. For everything she learned, there were three other things to learn, and some uncounted number that she could never learn.

One morning in the late fall when the vine maples were the color of her lips, she put on a wetsuit the color of orca skin and dove into the water. She swam out a ways and the great mother whale of the matriline swam near and looked her in the eye and bumped her up to the surface and then dove. Annalee followed, swimming into the fantastical city that whales made with pictures of sound. She had thought that bringing her body with her would make being with the whales harder. Ghost whales swam with the pod so that hundreds of orcas plied the water together. Ghost salmon flew into the ghost orcas' teeth, singing as they went, and babies played.

She grew lost. Time pulled like her mother's taffy.

She grew lightheaded and opened her mouth to breathe, and one of the males nosed her in the stomach so she could only breathe out air she did not have. It carried her to the top. Paulette dug her out of the water and pushed the sea from her lungs and told her to find another way.

The orcas came the next morning and as they showed her pictures of vast watery places she had never seen, she understood they were leaving for the winter.

Since she was beginning to run out of money, Annalee took a job in an ice cream store where she worked two afternoons a week to let the owner off. The children loved her so much with her odd coloring and her wistful smile that the owner kept her on for the spring, filling in every weekend until the summer children came back from University to scoop blueberry and vanilla and cookie dough ice cream for tourists.

Thus, her time was free again when the whales came back up from the mouth of the Columbia River and called to her from the water. She wept when she learned that the cow who had birthed the baby had died in a fishing net over the winter. She had saved the ice cream money she and Paulette did not need for food to buy a battered red sea-kayak which she rowed to the lighthouse every day.

She sat sadly on the shore, often licking an ice cream, and listened as the whales ate too little and the boats chased them, the children on the boats exclaiming joyfully when they saw the orcas.

One hot day almost a year after she came home, she parked her kayak in a float of seaweed and let the waves rock her to sleep sitting up. The fish were plentiful that day, and the orcas fed. The youngest females were beginning to fatten up.

A sharp high sound split the water. Fish and whales thrashed and raced away. Without thinking very hard about it, Annalee pushed back at the sound, hard, all of her anger and despair rejecting its right to reshape the underwater world.

The motor went silent.

The normal world re-filled, the sonic hologram of the sea reforming, the world come to rights.

Annalee felt the rough deck-ropes of her kayak under one hand and the hard plastic of the seat and bob of her boat in the kelp. She opened her eyes to see two men in a nearby boat standing and staring at their engine, perplexed. Half an hour later, the Coast Guard came and towed them home.

This is how Annalee learned to silence engines near the beach near the lighthouse on San Juan Island. The people who lived there year-round began to bring her ice cream and tacos and homemade-cookies to keep her strength up. On cool misty mornings she huddled under a blanket on the point, and swam in the sea, both at once, and silenced the sounds of engines. On warm days she rested in the seaweed in her kayak and silenced the sound of engines.

One enterprising whale watching crew member told his captain about her, and she told the other captains, and Annalee was taken away and thrown into jail for loitering on the sea cliff. The whales were not seen around the islands or in the straights until the Mayor freed her with an apology.

Annalee still sits there now, every day of every season, and she still scoops ice cream on cold winter weekends. The whale watch captains call her the black witch of the orca, but they do not lock her up anymore. They do always know where she is. No one knows who she is, except perhaps for the orcas and for Annalee herself. Her hair has grown half-white. Fat orca babies swim in the sea in front of her, although it is still true that only one of every two babies lives to be a year old. She is home and they are home and there are fish.

THE SEVENTH FEELING

Juice and I, and our dog Shadow, sit in silence at the metal table outside of the CoffeeSpot. We listen. Fog envelopes us. The steam of the coffee joins it, vapor to vapor. Daylight struggles to be noticed. Puget Sound and San Juan Island and the CoffeeSpot cling to the quiet crack between night and morning. I am completely calm, but this day will bring many feelings. Juice is normally quiet, but this morning her painted red fingernails dig into her palms. I find everything about her interesting, and wonder why she seems a bit nervous.

Shadow hears them first, like always, his black muzzle lifting and his ears swiveling toward soft voices and barely audible footsteps. Juice hears them next. "There." Her whisper is soft, with the faintest smile in it. Her face and eyes are round, so she often looks a little surprised. The tiny fog droplets coating her short dark hair make her look even more like an anime character than usual.

The soft whuff of electric boat engines springing to life tells us the ecowarriors are leaving. Each day, they fight other boats in the sound. This is what we poor scientists have been waiting for; our chances are better if we're behind them than if they come up on us. They are more friend than enemy in principle, but they will not hesitate to board us or to throw our instruments into the sea.

We three hold our silence until their engines fade entirely and all we hear is the call of seabirds and the soft slaps of tiny morning waves. I re-fill my coffee and then hold my hand out for Juice's empty cup, but she shakes her head. I cock an eyebrow at the unusual refusal, but she has already turned away and started for the boat, Shadow an inch behind her. By the time we have walked the length of the dock, the waters of the sound are accepting light even though the horizon is not yet a line between sea and sky. Shadow is as quiet as we are, our footsteps and his movements like a little dance. It feels like magic.

Juice's steps are precise and small. She climbs daintily into the boat. Shadow hops in after her, taking his usual position straddle-legged on the bow. He wears a bright red coat so we can find him if he falls in; it contrasts with his short dark fur. I untie the lines and hand them to Juice. She coils the fat white ropes expertly and piles them inside the cabin. We're near the end of the dock, and I push us off with one foot as I hop on, and we glide silently through water.

A harbor seal comes up to the side of the boat as we drift out with the current. It raises its nose, examines us, appears to nod, and swims off. Shadow watches it in silence, and it is my turn to whisper. "Maybe it will be a good day."

"Maybe." She says it with a little smirk that makes me think she knows something I don't, but it's time to turn on the engine, so I do. It hums to life, a soft electric purr that is easy to talk over. The sunlit fog vanishes into a crisp October morning. San Juan Island is behind us now, and I pull out my phone and call up my monitoring app. The whale's signals are all blocked now, by law, but I can see the ecowarriors lining Haro straight, "Let's go toward Lopez Island."

It's not the most likely place to find the pods, but it could happen. We might be the last scientists still doing fieldwork about the orcas. This could be as much because—for whatever the reason—the ecowarriors have not chosen to stop us. Elaine and Elizabeth were sunk last week, and when they came back, they bought us all a round of drinks and left the Island. A month before that, Paul had his canoe holed. He hasn't taken it out since. It's dangerous to be a scientist in these times. You'd think we caused the planet's near-collapse rather than merely reported it.

Shadow lies down. Juice and I sit on the bench in the cabin, hips touching. She's tense, the muscles that tie her neck to her shoulder raised and defined. I sip my cooling coffee and remember her refusal. "No cup this morning?"

"I'm only supposed to have one now."

"Is this a game of riddles?"

She smiles and then the secret I sensed earlier spills from her lips. "I'm three months pregnant."

Shadow must feel my shocked silence since he stands up and regards us curiously.

The first feeling that waves through me is betrayal. We had agreed not to do this. Damnit. This is no world for a child. No world. "How?"

She watches me closely, her expression flat, her feelings hidden. "Not on purpose."

I look away for a moment, biting my lip. The water is a dark late-morning blue now, and we are somewhat free of all of the islands, but close enough that a gull flies over, squawking. The air is salt and fresh, bracing. I turn back to Juice and touch her cheek. We make love every night. It has been three years and we've only missed a night or two when one of us was too sick, and then we held each other. It cannot be her fault; she is precise and perfect and careful at all moments except when I strip that from her with my tongue. We're starved for each other, and in this moment I want to strip her shirt and touch her bright small breasts, to turn my tongue around them as they harden. This heat is the second feeling after betrayal.

She sees it and touches my lips. This is not the place, of course. Not the time. But the heat and scent of her tells me she shares my sudden heat. I swallow, regaining control. "This will be a tough world to raise a baby in."

She hears the acceptance, the choice to keep it, and I can see her shoulders let go, see several small lines on her face relax.

That's how long it has taken to go from one state of being to another. I have gone from dismay to tender lust to acceptance on a single cup of coffee.

Shadow turns his attention back to the sea, which is still morning-calm and easy to glide across.

There isn't anything else to say, not quite yet. I look out over the water. Juice gets out the minimum of gear for the day; our best binoculars, the zoom camera, the poop collection kit, which can verify that a cow is pregnant. She sets them all out neatly on a fiberglass shelf with a lip that will keep them from falling if we hit a wake or an unexpected wave.

We travel for an hour, all three of us silent and companionable. Four of us? I marvel.

The water changes shades of blue, the wind smells of sea salt and kelp. This is my place, this swelling and sinking world of long horizons and low camel-humps of islands. We only see two other boats, a sloop with its sails furled and its motor humming and a low fishing boat that doesn't show up on my phone app.

Shadow senses the whales first, of course. He stands, and lifts one front leg, pointing. I can't tell whether he smells them or hears them. He has over three hundred million olfactory sensors in his nose, and can hear a range of frequencies four times as wide as I can hear. And of course, orcas can hear each other hundreds of miles away.

We are weak by comparison to either. Weak and pregnant. I pull Juice a little closer for a long moment before we turn ten degrees' port to line up with Shadow's nose. Juice is better than me at identifying the pods. "It's K." She sounds a little disappointed.

There are three pods. Juice was hoping for L—the biggest remaining Southern Resident pod, and the only one that has a female capable of reproducing. K is now officially a zombie pod; every remaining whale is too old to have a baby. J is probably the same, but it hasn't been confirmed. The pods don't interbreed. "No babies today."

She nods, a frisson of disappointment on her face.

"Except ours."

Her right hand flutters to her stomach, and I realize she has been doing this for a few days. "How long have you known?"

She brings the binoculars back up, covering her face. "Two weeks."

Why didn't she tell me?

She smiles. "The whales are still fat."

They are getting fatter since they have been so fiercely protected and since the dams came down. The salmon runs are up this year despite the summer of storms. The last dead whale—K13—had fewer toxins in her blubber than the previous one—a male from J. Still way too many. At this point we pull hope from any positive trajectory. Some things get better, others worse. Time continues. We scientists report. I find voice for my earlier question. "Why didn't you tell me?"

"I didn't know what I wanted to do."

Whatever her decision, she would have told me. "Why did you decide to raise it?"

"Because of what I just said. The whales look better than they've looked in years."

"At least one—and maybe two, and maybe all three—are dead pods. They'll be around to see until the last one dies alone, and that's that. What if our baby dies alone?"

"What if we die alone?" she said.

I can't answer. I threw my cup away, still thinking, still in shock. That is the fourth emotion. Shock.

"Don't you want the whales to have babies?"

"Of course."

She let me work that through in my mind. "I'll tell grandma. She'll be happy."

Juice smiled. She had met grandma once. She had really liked her. "Is she still on the farm?"

"Yes. Just her and Rocket." I glance at Shadow, and at Juice. "Rocket will care for her, but I wish she had human company as well."

Juice keeps watching the whales, pulling her pad and paper off the shelf by feel. "You're a lot like her."

"I hope so."

In front of us, a whale breaches, coming almost all the way clear of the water, flippers extended. It looks sleek and well fed, and the sun makes diamonds of the spray that flashes up as it falls back into the water.

A soft beeping turns my attention to my phone. One of the ecowarriors. I tense. The baby. "We're being followed."

Juice doesn't say a thing, just slides the binoculars and cameras and our poop collection kit under her seat and sits on it, legs crossed. Just a family out for a Thursday morning drive in the boat. Really.

They're faster than we are, so we don't bother to speed up. We turn away from the whales, but they follow.

They're like that sometimes. Hard to find when you need them, hard to get rid of when you don't.

It takes fifteen minutes for the ecowarrior boat to come up beside us. We wave, recognizing each other by look if not name. This happens a lot; sometimes we even drink in the same bars. Island living is like that, and even more so since the ferries quit and the tourist industry shrank to people with their own boats. I'm far tenser than usual, even protective. Protective does not go over well with Juice. Even though this is the fifth feeling, I suppress it. I love Juice for her fierce, centered heat. She neither needs nor wants a protector. Even now.

The ecowarrior boat is called the *Anderson Favor*, a nod to one of the men who first funded the group. He had always liked warriors, even though he fought his battles with words. My father had known him.

Maybe that is a good sign.

There are two of them in the boat, a burly black man wearing a ragged tee and no coat, and a smaller white man wearing a bright bicycle-yellow windbreaker. The smaller one cups his hand and yells at us. "We're coming aboard." He opens his yellow jacket so we can see his shoulder holster and the gleaming metal butt hanging in it.

I'm watching Shadow. He's doing what he was told. Sitting. Watching. But he's tense.

We have chosen never to carry arms ourselves. Juice stands in his way.

He stops close to her, inside her personal bubble. "You aren't allowed to be so close to whales."

"They are following us," she says.

"You shouldn't be out here with them."

"Boating's still legal. We're locals."

"I know."

The big man slows their boat a little, so Juice slides past the smaller man and he has room to step on board. I'm afraid she will push him, afraid he will hurt her and the baby—the baby!—but he just walks around her and sits on the cushion she was sitting on, squatting on our instruments, if you will. He rolls her voice from his mouth in a deep tone that demands attention. "Juice Johnson." He glances at me. "Edwin Smith." He waits.

Neither of us says a thing. The whales are still nearby, fins rising and falling. One comes close and spyhops, using its tail to shove it out of the water as if it were trying to see what is going on in the boat. "You are in violation of our rules."

"There's no law," she says.

The big man guns his motor, which is a barely audible whine on an electric engine. The whales remain. Shadow watches us. His hackles are up, but he doesn't growl. The first wind of the morning blows across the boat, a gentle whuff at odds with my stiffened spine and quickened breath. The bigger man calls, "Hurry. Don't drag it out."

I tense.

Neither of them touches their weapon.

Juice points. "It's L pod."

I look. She's right, they are joining up. A conclave. It happens. Maybe we drifted into a whale party.

The man holds his hand out to Juice and then me. When it's my turn, his hand is dry and strong. "We want you to join us."

Juice cocks her head, looking for all the world like grandma's border collie. I wish I could read her thoughts. "Why?" she asks.

"None of us are biologists."

No, I think, *You're thugs*. But they *are* the reason the salmon are back. They bombed out three dams on the lower Snake in 2036, and the fish run has been increasing ever since. They enforce a ban on whale-watching everywhere except right in the main part of Haro Strait, and they limit that to three boats a day, two from Vancouver and one from Seattle. They collect a toll, and they use that to buy their gas. They're still thugs, but they're effective. "What do you need a biologist for?" I ask.

"Protection." He looks down at his phone screen, and then he smiles and lifts his head.

He points.

Juice and I turn around.

Both pods are there. Maybe all three. I start trying to count.

An exclamation of pure delight escapes Juice, and her face blooms with happiness.

I missed it. I try to look the direction she's looking, and just as she utters the word I see it.

"Baby."

It can't be more than a few days old. It's close to its mother, behind her dorsal fin. Its two- or three-times Rocket's size, but next to its mother it looks tiny.

I have never seen a calf. Just pictures and video, but not in the water, breathing. Not in real time. I have been looking for one for years. Maybe for all of my life. It a mirage; it can't be real. It becomes a sixth emotion—sheer unadulterated awe. It's like a winter sunset or the northern lights or a hard November meteor shower.

"Is it a boy or a girl?" Juice asks.

"How would I know?" the man says. "But we need someone we trust so we can protect it. It's important."

Like we don't know that? We both go quiet. Surely she won't want to do this, surely we won't do this.

Shadow whines and comes to stand between us, staring the man down.

"Your university can keep paying you, your grants. You can work for us, too."

I swallow. Juice looks at me, her eyes wide. I can't quite read her, but I think she may want to do this. We would have protectors instead of enemies. But if we got caught . . .

"But you can't tell anyone you saw the baby. You can't take pictures. You can't tell your best friend or your best graduate student. Eventually it will get out, but if it gets out from you, we will destroy you."

Juice nods. The world rocks again. All day has been a sea of changes, a slow erosion of my direction. I pull her close to me and look down at her. I'm a head taller, and so I can see her whole face from this angle. Awe is sliding to something else.

She moves her lips—not even a whisper, but assent. *Yes.*

I look at the thug. He looks earnest now. He's done the hard thing and memorized and delivered his message. "Will you protect us?"

"Yes."

"Yes."

I catch another glimpse of the baby orca, and I smile, and Juice smiles, and both men smile. Shadow goes back to watch the whales.

I know what the seventh feeling is. It's good fear. It's the fear of warriors defending the ones they love, mothers defending cubs, of anyone defending family. It frightens me. I stand in the gently rolling boat and move as the water moves, watching the horizons and the orcas and the way Juice's dark eyelashes look against her skin.

MAYBE THE MONARCHS

I remember painting the fence. Twice. The first time, I followed my grandfather, holding a heavy paintbrush while he tugged a red wagon with an open paint can in it. He let me paint all of the bottom boards. I helped him re-paint it after I graduated from college, my ears covered with high-end headphones and filled with Lady Gaga music.

It's my fence now, but I haven't looked at it for years. Layers of white and yellowed-white and even older gone-to-gray white curl from the edges of the boards, and here and there, boards are splintered or have fallen. It will come down soon.

The sullen afternoon light fits my mood, even though my hands smell like apples cut for pie, like cinnamon, and nutmeg.

I use my shovel as a walking stick, the newly sharpened edge the same color as the barrel of the gun I carry in my pack, a heavy thing with no automatic locks on it. I do not expect to use it today, but these are times for carrying weapons. I have a single companion. Rocket. Her one blue eye—the right one—has gone blind, and she limps, keeping most of her weight off of her right front leg. I talk to her—I have always talked to her, and today I need to talk to her more than ever.

"I used to walk this fence with my grandfather. We planted milkweed here and there for the butterflies."

Rocket cocks her head in that ever-so-human way of herding dogs, as if to assure me that she understands. She doesn't of course. There is no way to explain to a dog why I have never brought my grandchildren or my great-grandchildren out here.

But it is my habit to talk to Rocket, and her habit to listen, and it makes us both happy.

"We saw monarchs a few times when I was little. We even saw one chrysalis. It was so pretty I wrote a song about it, although now I've forgotten the words. I think I was eight, or maybe nine, and it's one of the few things I remember from that year." I can still see it, glistening in this very fence, in danger from the horse's warm breath, from birds, from a hard wind. The fence had been true-white then, the tiny pod that held the butterfly a shock of green against it. I tell Rocket, "They were orange, with black edges on their wings, and white spots."

Rocket's uneven gait barely keeps pace, and the awkwardness of it tears at me. I am not too old to do this, I tell myself, not yet. I am not city-weak.

I kept looking for milkweed and butterflies long after I knew they couldn't be here. The last monarch anyone saw in Pennsylvania was in 2032. I remember, since it was my fiftieth birthday. It wasn't me who saw it.

The walk to the far pasture seems longer than ever.

Rocket agrees. She whines at me, stopping to sit on her haunches from time to time.

"I'd carry you if I could." I try to move faster so the pie will have time to cool before my family arrives, but my dog can't go any faster, so I don't either.

Rocket's spine sticks up like a mountain ridge. Her skin folds in between every rib. Her face is thin at the muzzle and gone all to gray.

Since the path goes slightly uphill, my breath presses against my chest and I wish for a breeze. We make it to the far fence. The land beyond it has gone to dandelions and crabgrass and foxtails, and here and there, an alder. Weedy plants, hardy like Rocket and me. The old oak lies on its side, partially rotted. The year I saw the chrysalis, a white swing hung from a low branch. I used to try to circle the branch, but I was too light and every time, gravity grabbed me with a stomach-dropping lurch just as I came even with it.

We pass through the broken-hinged gate and into the clod-ded-earth of the empty pasture, and I watch where I put my feet. No boots fit any more; I'm sporting ugly black shoes with rocker bottoms that leave a fat tread-mark. I remind Rocket about the last horse she knew. "Remember Ginger?"

Rocket stops for a moment, staring at a fat rabbit. Her ears swivel forward and she lets out a low growl. Then she puts her head back down, giving up before the chase starts. I try to distract her with a story.

"Edna offered us another horse, one that her cousin has over in Crawford County, a twenty-year-old bay that hurt its stifle and needs a pasture, but I told her no. I said it was our time to go."

The old border collie offers no response.

"My children's children have no idea how to clean hooves or what do about yellow bot-fly eggs." I sniff and pull out a tissue, dabbing at my face and thinking of the old mare. She lies un-der the fallen oak. Ginger. She'd been swaybacked and thin in her last year, in spite of my vet floating her teeth twice. After I had to shoot her, a neighbor—Ed, who died of cancer three months later—oiled up his old backhoe and split a whole day between repairs for the old tractor and digging Ginger's grave.

A light wind blows the dry summer air over us, smelling of fields with no crops except grass, of air with no butterflies.

I need to focus. My grand-daughter's car will bring her chil-dren by for dinner around dusk, and the pie I made is from the first of the season's apples sent in from Washington State. I haven't put it in the oven yet.

"Do you remember Ed?" I ask Rocket.

She glances up at me with her one unseeing eye and her one filmed-over eye that the vet had told me might not see much either, but then she stumbles a little. Border collies don't stumble. Except Rocket, these last of her days. She looks surprised, but gathers her-self, only looking back at me when she has full control again.

She stood beside Ed and me at the grave. I threw the first handful of dirt and Rocket stayed close enough to me to touch. She whimpered, low and soft, the whole time: a dog-song full of longing and loss. The memory drives a shiver through my bones.

"What about Ginger? Do you remember Ginger?"

We near the fallen oak; Ginger lies under the tree, surely bones now. Rocket stops and splays her front legs and ducks her head as if addressing sheep. She whines again. I figure she does remember. It wouldn't be too hard; she remembers every person who comes to the farm. Why not Ginger? It had been seven years, but Rocket recognizes all of the neighbors, even Ellie who only met her once, and that when she was still a pup.

I gesture for Rocket to sit, and she lies down and watches me walk around the tree, looking for a place. Rivers of small brown ants run in the cracks in the bark along the dead trunk. At least five rabbits freeze as I approach and then bound away, all bobbing white tails and feet. The old oak is far enough up the slow rise I can see horizon in three directions, all of it the same: dry earth and dry trees and high clouds set to refuse us water all day. I try to remember the cornfields that used to wave away from here, soft and soughing in summer winds. The cicadas. Now it's all flies and ants and pincer bugs and a billion, billion rabbits. Sometimes crows, sometimes raptors.

That woman who started the environmental movement had been wrong. There are still birds. Carson. Rachel Carson. Here, the deer went before the songbirds and after the wolves and somewhere in the middle, the last monarch chrysalis opened and disgorged its gleaming butterfly. I hear there are still deer in Canada, even a lot of deer.

I am trying not to find a spot.

Finally, I start digging. The dirt is dust on top and hard underneath, and rocky. It takes two hours and two breaks, and Rocket stays awake and watches me the whole time. No matter how blind Rocket is or isn't, she follows every move I make with her head. Halfway through, I stop for a break.

"It will be easy Rocket. Fast."

Her mouth is open a little, her tongue sticking out as she pants. I share some water from my pack with her. It feels companionable to sit by her, full of sadness but also full of rightness, replete with time. The pain is a pillowy thing, only a little heavier than other things that have to be done like laundry or giving the farm up to the law that said I could have it until I die or forfeit, and that then it would go into the great taking and become wilderness.

It will be re-wilded, unfenced, decomposed, the house torn down, the driveway jackhammered out by some great brute of a robot. This is hope for us now, this pending deconstruction.

They say they can make monarchs in a test tube.

Some day.

I've been using Rocket for an excuse. The old girl loves her farm.

I finish digging. I pile the dirt in one place, so I can use it for a chair. Even though it will be hard to get up, I sit down and call Rocket to me. She puts her head between my knees and stands with her tail twitching. I kiss her forehead, feeling the small hairs brush against my lips and cheek.

"This will be easy," I tell her. "You have been the best dog ever." I pull out the syringes the vet gave me yesterday morning. The first injector is marked with green. I lift up the fur on her neck and slide it in. She stands for it, trusting.

Her eyes close and she falls a little more into me.

The second injector has a thicker, more wicked needle, but Rocket is warm and asleep, her breath soft against my pant leg. I sit, one hand petting her, the other holding the needle until it feels like time. I lift the ruff at the back of her neck and the needle balks for a moment and then punctures her skin and I depress the plunger quickly.

I leave my left hand on her chest until I felt her heart stop.

A few sunspots shine through the empty, dull clouds, making golden circles on the hills in the distance.

"There's another rabbit," I tell her. "And another. And there's a crow." I look for a butterfly, but there have been no miracles for years. "Way off, there's still a few horses in Edna's pasture, and I know she still keeps three goats."

I watch as a big bird—I am no good at telling them apart, but a hawk of some kind—swoops down and lifts a rabbit from the field. It screams and struggles hard enough to fall, but the fall is after the hawk has pulled it high enough that the drop stuns it. The bird comes down after it, and struggles as it lifts it, but nonetheless it flies into the afternoon sun, its wing limned with gold, the rabbit's fur touched with a sudden flash of light. Perhaps it has a nest of fledging chicks.

"All right girl." She is light and thin with age. Still, it is awkward to get up and I feel a soft pull in a hip muscle. Not bad. I lean over the hole and bend my knees very slowly, keeping my back straight, but she tumbles a bit.

"Sorry, baby girl." I lie with my stomach on the ground to straighten her. The dirt smells of dust, empty of all of the richness that once made it soil. It puffs up as I throw the first clod in. Dust stings my eyes as I shovel the dirt I'd been sitting on into the hole, and some of it sticks to the damp spots beneath my eyes so I have to stop and wipe it away. I take out her collar and leash and put them down on top of the hole, covering them with rocks. If there are coydogs left I don't want them to disturb her.

"You were the best," I tell her. "You were never a weed, not like me or the rabbits. You were noble." My voice catches, choking on her absence.

I use the shovel to lever myself back up and lean on it as I walk back. I don't hesitate at the fence line, don't look back. Ahead, in front of me, the pie is waiting for the oven. The car is probably already leaving my granddaughter's house with my great-grandchildren. I will leave with them tonight. The fence and the house will come down tomorrow. Or soon. Perhaps the robot is already on the way, just like my grandchildren.

I will dream of the monarchs and the tumbled fence.

BIOLOGY AT THE END OF THE WORLD

Sumot's red coat flashed **brightly** in the artificial sun, a beacon that showed my trajectory down the zip chair from the observation cliff to the landing platform. A flock of parrots rose screeching in affront at the brightly colored humans penetrating their forest, a riotous dance of glittering color and noise. The audacity of the birds clawed an unseemly screech of pleasure from my throat. The tops of trees closed over me, hiding the parrots and displaying a riot of life in a multitude of greens and browns.

It looked as beautiful as the advertisements, like a perfect place for space eco-tourists. Maybe too perfect, since our bosses had sent us here.

I landed behind Sumot with a thump as the mag locks in my boots recognized the platform and stuck me to it. I began a short orgy of unclipping and tying and hanging and neatening my hair with my fingers. I pulled my uniform shirt tight through the strap of my waist-pack, trying to look professional in spite of the sticky air. I glanced at Sumot in hopes of an approving look, but she faced away from me, looking down. On her back, the words, *Resist, Remember, and Respect* were embroidered in a neat line, a bright yellow against the red of her shirt. I whispered them to myself. *Resist. Remember. Respect.*

We resisted the temptation to change the world via genetic engineering, we remembered the mistakes humans made in the past, we respected life in its natural form. We were the barrier between greed and life, between hunger for profit and love of nature, between destruction and salvation.

This was my third inspection. The first two had turned up clean. With luck, this one would be clean, too.

A vertical ladder connected the landing platform to the biome floor. At the bottom of the ladder, the Rising Jungle biome's principle manager, Dr. Harv Ling, waited patiently in a clearing under a shefflera tree. Parrots still screeched far above us. Closer, finches twittered and called. Damp, earthy, scents filled the air, sweet and full of life.

Dr. Ling's handshake felt firm and his words sounded welcoming in spite of his wary eyes. "Good to see you, Inspectors." He nodded at Sumot. "Dr. Sumot Kundi," and then blinked and pulled my name from memory as well. "Candidate doctor Paulette Rain."

Since Sumot had both a decade and two ranks on me, she returned his greeting in the polite, formal language of the Bureau of Diversity Protection. "Hello, Dr. Ling. Thank you for the tour. We appreciate the opportunity to see so much of your excellent work."

"Follow me?" His features failed to hide how unwelcome we were. We were taught how to notice the feelings that people want to bury, the fear under formality, the disdain under bright smiles. This man wished we were on the far side of the solar system.

We followed him along a raised pathway, armed with scissors and collection bags. I carefully clipped and labeled leaves, lured insects into cups, held tiny tree frogs in my loose fist and tipped them into boxes, and captured a spider as big as my palm in a sealed bag. Sumot took photographs and video and asked piercing questions which Dr. Ling answered smoothly.

Everything looked healthy and natural. Thus, it took me by surprise when Sumot interrupted the tour at an intersection between the raised walkway and a faint path in the forest. "Please take us north a klick."

He glared at her, and for a second I saw refusal in his eyes. But we were tracked and recorded and recording, and our minders, Alin and Suzanne, watched over us from our ship. He had no choice. As we left the main path the jungle closed around us, leaves brushed our shoulders and hair and roots threatened to trip our feet. Bromeliads clung to tree trunks, displaying bright curtains of yellow and red flowers.

The trail thinned into a whisper. "Further," Sumot told him.

"We might damage the soil," he said, his face a mask.

"We might," she said, and walked ahead of him, perhaps following some clue from one of our watchers. She stopped in a small clearing full of flowers and butterflies, the soil damp and mossy. She whispered to me. "Look up."

A profusion of bright orchids hung in the canopy, some with flowers so big they set off red flags in my brain. Were they different because the biome was in orbit, or were they gene-modded? Whatever, the flowers screamed money.

Crime almost always screamed money.

As Sumot flew one of our three precious drones up to collect a flower, I watched over Dr. Ling, recording his body language for later analysis and court evidence, should we need it. I kept my own expressions as neutral as possible, but I didn't expect we'd need analysis to confirm his guilt. I may have only been an inspector for a year, but my training was impeccable.

Back aboard the UN biodiversity protection ship Orion 8, we plugged the samples we had into analysis machines. I cupped the harvested orchid in my gloved hand and admired the petals, thinking that the magenta and yellow flower would cover my whole face if I held it up in front of me. In the folded center of the flower, pale white and pink led to yellow, which drew my gaze back to a red the color of a beating heart. Still, I steeled myself and crushed it down into the metal jaws of the machine.

"It's hard to imagine," Sumot mused, "That something so beautiful can represent evil."

My job as a hero protecting the Earth's natural biodiversity included murdering anything that had been changed by more than about five percent.

Until now, destroying entire biomes had been a theoretical part of my job.

The flower almost certainly wouldn't pass, and while one simple thing of beauty was barely worth mourning, the entire biome would be cleansed of the flower. Seed, root, stem, samples, and digital data would all die. DNA signatures would enter our multiply locked databases of forbidden life. If we found more, the entire biome would need to be destroyed. I knew why—we'd lost the Congo to biohackers, and my father had lost his father in the three-days biohacker war that followed. I had not been part of a destruction order yet, and I thought of the parrots and let a small prayer for clean genetics escape my lips.

Sumot brushed her long dark hair back over her shoulders and focused on an incoming message. Her eyes went soft-focus and her lips twitched as she looked up and through her lenses at a message her glasses obscured from me; something with high security. When she refocused, she said, "Let's go. We have a whistleblower."

I glanced out of the window at the Rising Jungle, which still held our ship in the embrace of its largest docking arms. "More samples?"

"Not from here."

I expected her to say more. She didn't.

I followed her to our ship's bay and found a tall, slim man already suited and waiting for us, his helmet clutched under his arm. His thin face looked even more wary than Dr. Lang's had appeared when we stood right under the red orchids. Under his mistrust of us, I felt a sadness that seemed to infect every muscle, every movement, and every sound. And as if wary fear and sadness were not enough, I also sensed guilt.

The guilt ran so deep that he might be hiding it from himself.

Sumot nodded at him, but didn't say anything, so I followed her lead and suited up in silence.

On the other side of the lock, we headed for the second meeting ship. Sumot had started the testing process before we got there, and the ship recorded only one bug found, a surprising slice of pretty code that had come in with a repair tech and lived in the water monitoring system. Sumot and I shared this data in silence and only with each other. I watched her face as she destroyed the bug, noting the triumph in her eyes as she verified it had been eradicated.

She released the docking mechanisms and the ship flowed out through the bay doors using only the tiniest of thrusters to keep us safe from the edges. We floated free, surrounded by stars on three sides. The station bulked above us, turning the tiny meeting-ship into an ant.

Once we were safely away from ship and station, we stripped off our helmets. The man's largish brown eyes looked from place to place quickly, never settling long on anything. His voice sounded breathy. "Is this safe?" he asked.

Sumot, as always, chose her words carefully. "It tests clear. We cannot ever know."

His head bobbed up and down and he swallowed. "Call me Joe."

"Okay." Sumot did not offer our names. He knew them or he didn't need to know them.

"You know about the smaller research stations?" he said. "The academics?"

Sumot inclined her head, her severe ponytail bobbing with the motion. "We inspect them."

"You miss the University stations." He licked his lips. "The ones from private institutions. The ones that the billionaires invest in but never talk about."

Sumot's lip's thinned, a sign of her frustration with the man's indirectness. "You came to tell us about something that disturbs you."

"Something that frightens me."

Sumot didn't respond, and he seemed to be trying to draw up courage. He chewed on his lower lip. A man whose mouth gave away his feelings. His eyes settled on Sumot, and he said, "There is a whole made ecosystem in a university station. Chai Agriculture's third station."

I almost blurted out that he was lying. Sumot remained calm, professional enough to clarify. "Made and not simply changed?"

He nodded. Then he said it, as if it needed to be said again. "Made. Yes, Made."

"All of it?"

He nodded again. Then hesitated. "Most. There's a veneer of clean experiments that hides the real work."

"Why?" Sumot asked, a slight tremble staining her voice.

He nodded a third time, swallowed. Tears glistened in the edges of his eyes. "To save the world."

Sumot questioned him for some time. I took careful hand notes that could not be copied easily once we left the meeting ship. He nearly cried his way through it, and yet he seemed unaccustomed to so much emotion. I found it hard to sympathize with him, or to believe him. The tale he spun sounded like something from a science fiction novel. Not that life could be made; we have known how to create life for a long time. But a complex ecosystem with *all* of it made? Even higher order animals?

The fear of such an abomination made me cold and shaky. This same fear drove funding for DNASec and the Bureau of Diversity Protection and the Biodiversity Police. This fear created us, and the man had the fear, and I had the fear, and Sumot sat there in silence and didn't show it, but I knew she had the fear, too.

Fear drove Joe to betray friends and maybe a dream he had once dreamed. He didn't say so directly but it felt like that. The organisms he referenced were the fairy dreams of techno-society: floating water cleaners capable of breathing life into the dead zones on the ocean, coral designed to survive heat and recover from the pounding of storm-driven waves, whales who could live with the myriad noises of humanity and still talk to their own tribes.

By the time the last story and the last details had been wrung from Joe, exhaustion had stolen most of my energy. My hand hurt from the unfamiliar activity of writing so long on paper with a pen. He looked tired and lost, as if the yielding of each secret had taken a part of his heart. I had witnessed two other whistleblower conversations. In one, the teller grew more buoyant as their great secrets lifted from their shoulders to ours. In the other, there had been a great relief, a sagging and a sense of rest. Joe's face displayed deep failure.

Sumot showed no outward emotion at all, but I read the set of her jaw and the tightness in her shoulders as controlled anger and determination. I expected that we would leave immediately, or set up a different meeting ship to pass the information we had gained to our superiors.

Instead, we returned to the station and Sumot took my notes from me and locked them into a cabinet that only she could open. "Do not speak of this," she said.

The next morning, the machines spit out their answers as Sumot and I sat in her office sharing morning coffee. Sumot summed them up. "The orchids were just the showiest sin. They've also changed the *banisteriopsis caapi* vine to make it tell you deeper dreams. They're selling it through a black-market operation known as Vision Squared, they say it's a way to escape to a new world without machines or electronics, and they promise the spirits of plants will cleanse your soul." She sounded slightly bitter about that one. But then she believed in the ability of plants to save the world, but only if they were completely unaltered by humans. I agreed, although I wasn't out to undo every rose graft that had ever been done.

"How did you find that link?"

"I didn't. The machines sent drones out as soon as they had results, and we did the *caapi* vine first."

More came over the next few days, subtle but undeniable. The parrots were made to be brighter and ever-so-slightly smarter. I cursed the moment I learned that.

Sumot and I sat together in the ship's bar after a grueling day. "Will you give them a stay?"

"No. I did that once before, and it gave the people so much hope. It makes it worse to stay an execution, like the silliness that is death row. We do not do that up here."

"I can see how it's cruel in some ways. But what if we need more time?" The parrots. I had become fixated on the parrots and on wanting to save them, even though I hadn't opened my mouth about it and told her. She would merely laugh at me and tell me to toughen up.

"We know there is bioengineering here. We don't need more time." She looked totally resolved, totally sure of herself.

I didn't feel that way. I felt hesitant, a little affronted. Surely, I would learn how to be like my mentor. I sat behind her as reporters from major stations and from the biggest metroplexes left on Earth grilled her. Sumot always kept her facts straight. She refused reporter-bait. Somehow, the very flat surety of her delivery, and the fact that every part of her agreed—that her feelings were completely clear—made the report even more chilling.

This third expedition meant that I was no longer a candidate Doctor of Biodiversity. I had passed. That had transformed into a full-fledged investigative biodiversity policewoman, but the title acknowledged my skills in biology as well. Sumot held a party in my honor in her rooms, and toasted me. When I raised my glass, and she smiled at me, her face full of unabashed approval, I felt good. That was the only good moment during the Rising Jungle assignment.

Two days later, DNAsec agents took the humans off of the biome station. They sent the tourists and simple employees like housekeepers home and threw everyone else into custody. On their way out, uniformed men and women turned off every system that powered life on the ship.

We stayed to witness the death. Cameras detailed the last flight of the parrots, and even the slightly slower death of the great rooted trees and the wilting of the beautiful red flowers. They left a stew of robots and nanotechnology behind. These opened the biome to space, dismantled and destroyed the mechanical systems, harvested the entire operation for metals and recyclables, and turned what had once been carbon-based life into fuel.

One night, Sumot stood close to me and said, "You know that we must be ruthless."

I nodded and kept my face schooled in obedient neatness. I remembered one class in my senior year. We had a heated debate about invasives. I had gone all righteous about the historic morality of hunting barred owls to "save" spotted owls. The real-life experiment had failed completely. Barred owls had evolved better

skills for northwest forests than the native owls they were replac-
ing, and murdering one species did not help the other thrive. Of
course, humans had not created barred or spotted owls, but had
simply tried to choose between them.

If we hadn't been able to choose wisely a mere hundred years
ago, how would we choose now with a far more tender ecosystem?

Sumot interrupted my thinking. "We have orders to go find
some college agristations."

I had wondered if we would go and find this greatest sin ourselves, or if she would call in bigger guns. I already felt unsteady
from sleepless nights when I dreamed of bludgeoning parrots and
crying as they fell. Her announcement drove me to the bathroom
to empty my stomach. After, I rose, trembling, looking into the
mirror. In college, I had known I was choosing a hard career.

We flew into a constellation of habitats and ships that served
the community college as labs and classrooms, living space and
gardens. Sumot chose to dock the Orion 8 at the university's main
station and take one of our flitters to the agristation: *Chai 3 Tea*.
We had no external DNAsec support with us, which implied Sumot hadn't told her superiors everything the whistleblower had
said. We did have our own security to camp on our ship at the
main station. Alin and Suzanne would be wired in to us through
tiny speakers and microphones in our ears, but they weren't in
any way equivalent to a DNAsec Special Forces team. Neither of
then looked particularly worried.

As we left, our guards looked up from their 3D chess game
and wished us both luck, Alin smiling as he said, "I'll watch
your back."

The call and answer routine that served as password to dock
at the agristation seemed unusually long and complex, and once
we passed into the stations airspace a woman's voice called out,
"Sorry for the tough entry. Students, you know. Worst security
violators in the world."

A student met us, fresh-faced and long-legged and enthusiastic. She reminded me of myself two years ago, all energy and hope. I tried hard to stay stern with her. After all, if "Joe" had been correct, she might be skipping the real world in favor of jail. I took the girl's offered hand. "Zoka," she said. "I'm Zoka, and I'm first gen space."

Meaning she had been born in space. "I'm Paulette Rain. I came up eight years ago."

"What a lovely name." She led us to separate but connected quarters. A bottle of wine waited in our shared galley, as well as enough VR tools for us to disappear into a game world or have a virtual orgy or ten. Beside the wine, a note from the chief scientist, Dr. Tollingson, rested against a fragrant bouquet of real lilacs. She promised to greet us in the morning. Sumot inspected the lilacs carefully before she sat down with a huff.

We had only spoken of this one other time, taking a meeting ship out to do so. We had shared our research, which had been carefully done since our records were open. The *Chai 3 Tea* was almost invisible on the nets. What little we found intimated that the station served as a lab for students, and primarily tested automated pollinators. After we caught up, and refreshed ourselves on the notes, I had asked Sumot about our boss's reaction, "What did Henri say when you briefed him?"

"Henri thinks Joe must to be lying. That nothing so advanced could be hidden." Her words were choppy. "He said we could go look, and report back. He's assigned a search-web of bots to look at papers coming from Chai and analyze them for hidden connections, but he's not sending a ship."

"Even if they find something?"

She shrugged. "Maybe then." Her guard was down further than usual, and a flash of pain touched her face before she banished it with a tightening of her jaws. "I am not Henri's favorite."

Sumot had never shown any sign of weakness, any opening at all. I tried to handle it tenderly. "Maybe the search-web will help us."

"Maybe the search-web will scare Henri as much as Joe scared us."

Sumot sounded frightened. Deeply frightened. She hardly felt like herself. Her fears weighed on me.

We didn't speak of it again; nothing that happened on our own ship could be kept secret from history.

We would not speak of it tonight, nor would we touch the gossamer VR gloves or the carbon glasses. Good tech, but undoubtedly a stew of viruses waiting to infect us. Sumot pulled out a deck of old-fashioned cards and dealt me a hand of gin. I found the simple game soothing. Even so, my hands shook enough that Sumot noticed and frowned at me. She herself looked like steel in every part of her demeanor.

I had worked with this woman for a year and couldn't decide if I loved her or if I hated her. Either way, I wanted to have her undivided certainty.

The next morning at 08:00, Zoka came and offered us a tour. Sumot requested a full set of schematics instead. Zoka looked slightly affronted, but said, "I'll order them up. Can I at least show you the areas adjacent to your suite?"

"Sure," I said, before Sumot could refuse again.

Zoka narrated smoothly, although she never took her eyes completely off of me and Sumot, and seemed stressed whenever she couldn't see us both at once.

I had expected something more like my own school, worn with touches of opulence marred only by plaques that identified the donors of the wood bannisters or plush study areas. But the interior looked more like a space ship than a station. Every surface gleamed. The metal handholds and rails looked like installation crews had just finished tightening the last screws, and even the occasional bot that slid quietly past us moved without a single jerk. The air smelled pure with only the slightest spicing of industrial cleaners.

If a place could have micro-expressions, this one would be screaming at me. It would say *listen to my quiet halls, look at how neat and empty I am. I am not a normal University lab. I am not.*

Back in our rooms, the schematics had indeed been delivered—on paper. The letter of the law and not the spirit. Sumot frowned at the huge bound book that covered the entire kitchen table. I expected her to demand that they take away the offending material and send electronic copies, but she merely smiled at Zoka. "Please send Dr. Tollingson to me at 13:00. We would like to tour three of your biomes this afternoon and inspect the associated labs."

Zoka would have been no good at poker; she flinched. "I'll deliver your message."

After she left, I looked over at Sumot. "I think you hurt her feelings."

Sumot frowned at me. "They assigned her to us because she doesn't have a brain in her head. She can't slip up and tell us things she doesn't even know."

"All right. But let's be nice to her anyway. I like the kid."

"It's best not to get attached to your captors." Sumot paused and raised an eyebrow, clearly trying for a joke. "Stockholm syndrome and all that."

"She's not my captor."

"So let's see that she doesn't become one. I'll look through the plans. Can you take fourteen random pages and compare them to the electronic plans you found online."

"Those are twenty years old."

"They're better than nothing," she said.

"How am I going to do that while you're using the book?"

"Tear them out."

At least since my promotion she'd started asking me to do things instead of just ordering me around. The paper felt as fine as the station looked clean, smooth under my fingers. Ripping pages loose felt almost as bad as pushing the orchid into the machine. Comparing a projected schematic to a paper one demanded complete attention, and after three hours my eyes stung. "Zip," I reported. "Did you find anything?"

"A pattern. Come here and tell me what you see."

I leaned over her shoulder and watched her flip pages. Her hands were moving in quiet sign. I wasn't fast at reading Sumot's own invented language, and she had to repeat three gestures before I understood her statement that the schematics were correct but incomplete.

I gestured back *How will we find a secret here?*

She shrugged.

Dr. Tollingson showed up right on time at 13:00. She had bend down to fit through the door to our room. Her cropped black hair and black eyes were embedded in skin that looked like it had never breathed an ounce of sunshine. Her energy filled the room. At once, she seemed warm and driven, attractive and curious.

Some people exude leadership.

Zoka trailed Dr. Tollingson, who had the student explain each room we passed through. Zoka had delivered a practiced, smooth tour yesterday; today she stumbled over words and blushed under Dr. Tollingson's watchful gaze.

Sumot paced through each lab, watching closely. I followed, asking questions about the active experiments. About an hour into the tour, Zoka led us to a long room full of bright light and orderly rows of young tomato plants in full yellow flower.

Joe had told us to find a room like this. Maybe this one, maybe another. This wasn't the danger; it led to the danger. I walked up to the closest raised bed. A brief shine caught my eye: three bright robots striped in the yellow-brown of honeybees flit between flowers, each no bigger than the tip of my little finger. From a distance they looked and sounded like bees from my grandmother's farm. The background hum and bright natural light reminded me of late summer.

Zoka pointed at a fine mesh that separated the beds. "The mesh keeps the populations separate," she explained. "Each set of beds is the same. We're testing which machines are better pollinators."

I bent down and looked closely at a bee that had stopped to touch its metal forelegs to a flower. "Why does it have a stinger?"

"If they ever get used in a real ecosystem, they'll need to protect themselves."

"Meaning birds could eat them?"

She laughed nervously. "Birds aren't that stupid. But humans might want to play with them, or even hurt them."

"Is there poison in the stingers?"

She shook her head. "There could be. But we don't load any of the bees while we're testing."

"Are they used on Earth?" I asked her. I knew the big details of Earth farming, and that mechanicals were legal for pollination. A deal with the devil that was better than pollinating by hand or starving, but barely. Extremists hunted the mech bees as if they were real insects that could be exterminated instead of re-printable devices.

"We wouldn't eat farmed food without them. Not in space. There are a few natural pollinators left on Earth, but there are the only space bees out here. After all, we don't have bats or birds, or even rodents."

"Are they your work?"

Zoka glanced briefly at Dr. Tollingson. "I didn't create them. But I tweaked them so they aren't as likely to shred the flowers they take the pollen from." She looked quite proud. Once more, I remembered a time when I thought I would save the world all by myself.

Sumot had been staring at the ceiling. "Where do you get your power?" she asked.

Dr. Tollingson replied, "From the sun, of course. Every light you see is solar-powered. The station is a net-producer, of course, and we charge up research ships that dock here for free."

Sumot pointed at the ceiling. "What's above this?"

"Above this?"

"Above this." Sumot's gaze was direct and unyielding. I tried to imitate it

Zoka looked confused. "Shielding?"

Sumot walked along the outer wall, glancing at the plants and the bees from time to time. She led us to a series of pale and artsy renditions of the letter 'Z' which created diagonals to grab onto and two flat surfaces each to stand on. They made a recognizable ladder if you stood directly in front of them. Joe had told us to look for these. Until we stood in front of them, I hadn't understood his description. "Have you been up there?" Sumot asked Zoka.

"Up where?" Zoka truly looked puzzled.

Sumot sidled next to the wall and pointed up. Zoka and I followed, and craning our necks, a door became obvious. "No."

Dr. Tollingson said nothing.

Sumot started up the wall. Zoka reached for a handhold. Dr. Tollingson jostled her away gently, as if the graceful doctor had taken a misstep. "After you," she nodded at me. Her demeanor screamed danger from tiny clues I couldn't quite put together.

Sumot began climbing the wall, counting on me to protect her if she needed it.

I swallowed, thoughts mixed and fast in my head. If I didn't follow, we'd draw attention. It might create a visible rift between us. Sumot might come down and we might miss whatever we were about to see. But if I followed, we'd be side by side in a vulnerable position.

The tiny jostle decided me. We were in danger whether we climbed the wall or not, so why not climb?

I started up. Three steps into the wall, I glanced down just in time to see a moment of change in Dr. Tollingson's eyes. They started bland and cloaked, and as if a switch turned, they went dark and full of resolve. Her shoulder twitched in response to some movement of her hands behind her back. She smiled, her whole face animated. She sent Zoka up after us, forcing me up.

Sumot had nearly reached the door.

An alarm screeched in my ear, followed by a whisper from Alin. "We're being boarded."

Had Dr. Tollingson given that order?

Mechanical bees flew up past me, near me. One bumped my leg and I thought of stingers and nearly lost my footing. I felt the feather-touch of another. Above me, I watched in horror as one turned its thorax and thrust a slender needle Sumot's calf.

I barely managed not to call out.

The door above Sumot opened. Gloved hands reached through.

Zoka hissed, "What's happening?"

I glanced down. Two burly guards had appeared at the bottom of the steps. Dr. Tollingson surrounded Zoka with her body, her feet just a step below the student's feet. She held a weapon in her hand, pointed up, directed precisely at Sumot.

"We're overwhelmed." Alin's voice in my ear stuttered and went silent.

Adrenaline raced through me so fast my thoughts jumbled around Alin and danger and Sumot and duty and the outright certainty I'd made a dreadful mistake taking this wall.

Sumot's feet disappeared.

"Up." Dr. Tollingson gestured with her hand. Zoka's face looked tight with fear, her eyebrows raised, eyes wide.

Three mechanical bees flew around her face. She swatted at one. It fell, but another stung her cheek.

I took another step, another. Something stung my calf. My foot slipped, but my hands clutched the metal rung, forearms straining as I kicked for purchase. Strange hands leaned through the door and grabbed me, hoisting as if I weighed nothing. My thighs rubbed against a hard, bruising surface and my face impacted cold metal. Rolling over, I looked up at a seamless metal ceiling in room dominated by two doors.

I had failed to protect Sumot. She lay beside me, Zoka on the other side. The exotic doctor Tollingson stood, looking down, her face a slightly fuzzy oval. It made her look more comic. I laughed at her.

A man in a mask leaned over Sumot, his thin-gloved fingers fumbling with the zipper on her uniform shirt. Someone removed one of my shoes.

Flesh and white suits and silver walls all blurred together in a dull fog.

The room seemed off-kilter, like a funhouse, and I slid through fuzzy details that should have outraged me and then fell into a dream of mechanical bees and mechanical flowers and clowns.

*

I woke slowly, my head thick and my thoughts like mist, sensation coming drop by drop. A hard mattress. A thin sheet. Tiny pricks of pain drove into my dry eyes as I rubbed clumsy fingers across them.

A voice. Zoka. "Sumot? Paulette?"

"Yes," I croaked, my voice thick. I could see by then, even push up into a sitting position. My uniform had been replaced by a white paper suit. To my surprise, I wasn't bound in any way. The room was a song of metal and white, with white charts pinned to a silver board on the wall and a single blue and colored thing. An aquarium.

The faint scent of living water suggested a real aquarium.

None of our captors were in the room.

Sumot hadn't moved at all. I whispered. "Sumot."

Nothing.

"Sumot." Then louder. "Sumot!"

She turned her head and groaned. Dried mucus glued her eyes shut.

"Sumot. Please wake up."

She relapsed into deep, loud snores.

I turned to Zoka. "Will she be okay?"

She turned her face toward me, eyes still wide. "I don't know. I didn't know the bees were armed."

"Well," I thought out loud. "Well, we're okay. Do you know where we are?"

"No," she whispered. "I've never been here."

"Do you have any ideas?"

"There's rumors down in the dorms."

"Rumors about?"

"Labs where they hide what they're doing. I didn't think they were real. I mean, it was too fantastical." She paused. "There were clues."

Bright blue fish with yellow-edged fins and doleful eyes swam languidly in the aquarium. "What clues?"

"Two students disappeared at the end of last semester, Eliezer and Edie. My roomie sorts the mail. She got a package for Eliezer. The package disappeared." Her voice sounded soft and a little shaken. "But that's not much. I thought they'd just dropped out."

I counted seven of the fish, all as big as my hand or bigger.

The door flew open and fresh air rushed in, cooling my cheeks. Three robot nurses bustled in, fleshy bodies with white lab coats and fake hair pulled back into tight buns. The one coming toward me smiled. "How do you feel?"

"Okay."

"I'm going to run a few tests."

"What are you looking for?"

"Weapons."

Wow. I didn't ask what weapons; I didn't have any except my mind and training. But it suggested a level of paranoia on the part of whoever ran this place.

Sumot muttered something nasty to the bot working on her.

After a few moments of poking and prodding with various instruments, the robot stopped and said, "The doctor will be right in."

All three robots left the room and I finally got a look at Sumot. I recognized fear under her fury, saw the whites of her upper eye and the way her brow wrinkled for just a moment. The tall doctor strode in, looking severe and followed by two new robots. At first I felt afraid, but then my reasoning mind suggested they didn't need to see us to harm us. They wanted something.

Dr. Tollingson said, "We estimate there will be three days before DNAsec arrives to investigate. We will use those days to give you your inspection. We were almost ready to report on our work anyway. You've pressed our hand, but only by a few months. All we ask is that you keep an open mind."

Sumot spoke through the thin line of her lips. "You know what we are and what we do. I will not betray that."

The doctor's face softened for a moment. "We both care deeply about the same things. That's what I need to show you. You came here to investigate. Are you still curious?"

After a pause, Sumot nodded. She was probably curious about

what she'd find to destroy this station with. The thought shifted me into looking at Dr. Tollingson and Zoka as people about to lose their future. If we did our job, the fish were going to die. It knotted me up, made me remember the parrots.

Resist, resist, resist.

"You will not be able to say anything to anyone until whenever DNAsec gets here." Dr. Tollingson turned her gaze to me. "Will you keep an open mind?"

"I will do my job."

Sumot showed neither approval nor disapproval. Dr. Tollingson glanced at Zoka. "You will be reassigned here. Consider the tour your introduction to your next graduate work."

Zoka looked as frightened as she did pleased. Funny, how often we have contradictory emotional reactions.

"Let's begin the tour."

For the first few steps, my legs were heavy and stiff, but they relaxed with motion. I felt strong and alert, as if I had caught up on sleep for the first time in years. The bees had put us to sleep. Maybe it had been for longer than I thought.

The good doctor, the three of us, two robot minders, and a young man who Zoka seemed to recognize filled the hallway, a small river of movement flowing a few hundred feet and turning right into a room so full of aquaria it stunned me. I had never seen so much captured water in one place. Ballast, balance, shielding, reservoir, gardening, a million uses for water on stations and ships. But here we were surrounded. Water above and below and to both side. No walls, no floor. Only water and life. I spun around, enchanted and suspicious. Even the trained can't avoid contradictory emotions.

Sumot crossed her arms and squinted at the fish, looking more like an inquisitor than a captive.

Dr. Tollingson nodded at the young man. "Eliezer. Please explain."

He was tall and swarthy, with intelligent, piercing eyes the same shade of washed-out blue as the water we stood on. "Your agency has stopped the re-seeding of the oceans with animals that can thrive. Instead, you demand life built for the past, designed only by nature, and certain to die in a world that nature no longer controls."

Sumot stiffened.

"Without a healthy ocean, the forests and savannahs and even the deserts are dying. You know this, but because of a few early mistakes, you don't allow anyone to engineer success."

He spoke as if Sumot and I had come from some ancient species that stopped all progress in the world. But I had seen the fire-ravaged Congo after the carbon mechs were burned out of the trees. A whole jungle, miles and miles and miles of life turned to ash and bone. I remembered what the white bones sounded like when I stepped on them, the way the fire and rockets had burned all of the color from the forest, and trying to walk in the slurry of wet ash that had once been trees.

Resist. Remember. Respect. The mantra of my profession. Eliezer probably hadn't gone into the real world yet. He didn't understand that idealism was hope and not strategy.

Resist. Remember. Respect.

"But it can be done." He brought his hands up gracefully, like a dancer's, ending with his arms outstretched and his cupped hands facing up. "Look around you. Everything in these walls, this floor, all of it, had been created from raw materials. Yes, even the water. This is a vast experiment, which has succeeded beyond our founding team's imagination."

The big tank glowed with color and life. Fish schooled in rainbows of silver, orange, aquamarine, gold, and ochre. Plants grew in orange and yellow, in multiple shades of green never seen on land, and in bright brown. It looked like a video from geography class or a retro-screen saver my college roomie had used as the alarm on her video wall.

Eliezer's voice had dropped to a low cadence, to the soft moment in a poetry reading. "Water and fish, weed and shell, sand and shark, coral and crustacean. It was created."

Sumot, arms still crossed, interrupted Eliezer's poetic recitation. "Prove it isn't a hologram."

Zoka moved her hand toward a tank and blue striped fish that looked like it belonged in the angel family darted off, followed by three others like it. Then a huge orange fish with red lips approached Zoka's pointing finger, which hung in the hair near the wall, shaking, almost touching. Zoka looked at Eliezer with shiny eyes. "You must have used real DNA."

"Real." Dr. Tollingson looked proud. "But not original. We created this entire ecosystem instead of starting with code stolen from the Earth's seas and changing it. We studied and mapped mutations in our original fish for two generations, but *we built everything you see from scratch.* We improved." She paused. When she started again she looked past us, toward some magical future. "Everything in these tanks can interact with what lives in the sea, and some can interbreed . . ."

Sumot's intake of breath sounded blade-sharp.

". . . and all of it can survive continued changes in pH and toxicity better than Earth-evolved animals. Changes in either direction—as the world gets better, they'll survive that. But this is only the beginning. This is the repopulation. This is the future of the sea, but not the repair of it."

Resist meant resist the lure of humanity as god, *resist* meant resist change, *resist* stories that have no meaning. *Resist* the lure of technology-based solutions to biological problems. As we followed Eliezer and Dr. Tollingson down the long corridor, we walked on water.

Technology amazed me and pressed in on me, technology tempted me and tortured me.

Twice, when I glanced at Sumot, her eyes were closed. Once, the look she gave me suggested that whatever she saw in my face was as anathema to her as the darting, schooling fish beneath my feet.

Eliezer and Dr. Tollingson had fallen silent. They walked quietly, their feet slipping easily across the floor. Our paper shoes were noisier, and behind us, Zoka's paper-clad feet rasped along the surface. The two robots made almost no sound at all.

We walked for more time and through more space than

should have been possible. The schematics they gave us must have been very, very faked. I figured we were on the outside of the regular living quarters and labs and classrooms, in areas that were almost always used for water engineering.

If the life here were dumped—right now—into the oceans of Earth, it would die. And if it didn't, if by some strange miracle of engineering it survived, it would almost surely add new damage to the oceans. Key species we'd been nursing would be destroyed, ecological niches overrun.

I shivered, cold and frightened and angry. A shadow caused me to look up. A shark. Menacing and beautiful, meant to kill. On my left, a large water-blue fish with iridescent scales opened its mouth and scooped up two smaller fish that failed to flash free of the bigger fish's jaw.

I took a deep breath, kept my eyes open, and swore to remain more alert than the small fish had.

Zoka broke her long silence. "This is the most beautiful thing I have ever seen. This is what a world should be like. I *want* to study here."

Eliezer turned and smiled at her before he glanced at us. "It could be dangerous. Wait until we finish the tour and we see how our judges decide to evaluate us."

"This is the most dangerous thing I ever seen," Sumot said, her certainty a match for Zoka's.

Everything about this station frightened me. The beauty and health of it, the audacity. The resources that had been spent here. They could have gone into restoration.

Dr. Tollingson glanced momentarily at each of us, trapping us, making sure we saw her look; a teacher's practiced demand for attention. "Now we'll go to the beginning. But first, a break and some food." After a short stop at a restroom, she offered water and crackers and fresh peaches on a plate. Sumot only took the water, but I ate a peach, savoring the sweet sticky juice in spite of my nagging guilt.

The doctor led us to a room where a huge video wall dwarfed three rows of comfortable chairs. No fish. Only dead wall, a bare and slight light giving away that it could be brought to life. We were seated with the doctor and the robots between us, Sumot and I as far from each other as possible.

Dr. Tollingson stood in front of us, right at the door we had come though. "This will take three hours. It is important that you pay attention. We'll start with a real reef off of Belize, a part of the barrier reef system. Our heritage was an early and failed attempt to save the reef you are about to see."

The overhead lights dimmed as the walls brightened, and the doctor's voice started into what sounded like a beloved and practiced lecture. Grainy footing showed healthy corals, sponges, and parrotfish. "We begin with a photo. The seas off of the coast of Belize were once bright and beautiful, but beginning in the early 2000's, they were slowly and inexorably damaged by storms . . ." The coral that surrounded us on the wall lost its color slowly. The number of species thinned, and then they disappeared one by one, until only a handful of fish could be seen. At first the changes were stutters as one photo gave way to another, one video to another, and then they became a more seamless record during the thirties, when the endless recording of all things started. The doctor's narration continued. ". . . by changes in the composition of the seas, by tourists, by sedimentation, and by efforts meant to save them."

She fell silent. We watched the coral whiten to bones and slump to an unrecognizable slurry covered over by slick green/ brown algae. The last frame didn't show any life. The dull, lifeless colors seemed ineffably sad.

"This is the reef today. It has looked like that for years. We take new pictures every day, and every day we are reminded of what we are doing, and why. We brought up DNA from the damaged corals, and even samples, all taken with grants and permission. We used it to re-create the conditions of a dead reef."

"A fake version," Sumot said. "A lie."

"Perhaps," the doctor conceded. "But as far from a lie as we could make it. It took twenty years. A team of three scientists worked tirelessly to bring the coral to life and then to destroy it, and we know from their writings that it nearly broke their hearts."

"Can we talk to that team?" I asked.

The light from the screens behind her made her a silhouette. She cleared her throat, and sadness infused her words. "They have been dead for decades. An alternate reaction to same misguided and unfortunate events that created DNAsec." She took in a breath. Two. "We placed hope in innovation."

DNAsec celebrated it fiftieth anniversary the year I signed up. Seven years ago. Five years in training, one in an internship, and now almost one with Sumot. A career that had suddenly turned into a thriller movie, missing only bonds on our arms as we sat and watched the enemy try to explain why they should be our friend.

The university's hubris sank slowly into my awareness. Fifty years. Fifty years of secrets, including secret funding. From billionaires. Fifty years of hiding from us.

The screen still showed the quiet of a dead reef, with small currents occasionally teasing bits of decay up from the ocean floor so that they danced like macabre brown and white ghosts.

The image shifted, but only to another view of another spot on the melted reef.

Dr. Tollingson spoke again. "We created what you see in front of you in a secret place. We built it to mirror the destroyed reefs. It is unchanged DNA, imported and grown and created in such a way that it would pass a DNAsec inspection." She passed, perhaps making sure we heard the derision that spiced her voice. Or perhaps to put off one emotion and take another, since she changed to a more coherent and passionate tone. "Now, watch. The next hour will show you restoration. You will see it in time-lapse, but the video spans five years. During the video, you will see some things that were not in the aquarium you just walked through. They are not part of our final vision. Tools." Inexplicably, her next words were, "You might be horrified by these."

At first, nothing happened. Zoka's breath stayed calm, Sumot's sounded labored and laced with anger. I couldn't hear Eliezer's breath. A glance at him revealed a bowed head, like a monk in prayer.

A long thin worm-like being slithered onto the screen. Something like—but far bigger than—a jellyfish floated through, pulsing, pulling water through its body as a way of moving, and maybe of eating. Two more followed, slightly different. The water slowly cleared. More worms littered the floor of the sea, brown and ugly, and ever more visible as sand began to appear beneath them, clear and clean and as inviting as a handmade beach in a Hawaiian resort.

The worms split open, skin peeling back and curling away from their slick, slimed insides, color blooming from their blood.

New corals?

Fish came. Small fish at first, gray and green and eventually silver and gold. Blues and greens and yellows and rainbows followed, a few colors I have never seen in nature and hadn't even noticed in our aquarium walk. Teals and brilliant purples.

Scarps and rocks appeared in the distance as the water cleared. A small shark swam in front of the camera. A ray undulated in the far distance, and then another joined it. The picture froze on a sea full of creatures and ablaze with color. The world we had been given, and had destroyed.

Zoka spoke my question. "It is beautiful. But it looks like the old reefs. Why not create something completely different?"

Surely they knew their chances of succeeding with something that looked completely different were zero. Their chances with this were barely more than that. I waited to see how they would answer. Dr. Tollingson said, "This is what we set out to do."

Beside me, Eliezer shook himself, as if waking from a trance. "We aren't smart enough yet. We will be, some day. Even though we created it all, we based it on a success, or a framework if you prefer. Maybe we can do something entirely new next, but if we can, we'll do it somewhere beside Earth." He nodded at the screen, where fish darted and schooled and anemone's waved clear and colored arms, where coral glowed in rainbow colors and sponges opened gaping and beautiful maws to a clear and crystal sea. "Your bees are not longer, or stronger, than Earth bees. They *are* more resilient."

"My bees are robots," she said. "Those aren't robots," Zoka said. "Of course not. But the design considerations aren't wholly different." He stood, waving his arms again, talking with his whole body. "This is moral, and right, and real. This is life."

Sumot said, "It is a plague of impurity."

"It is built from what we know and *made better*. The way we have made transportation and flight and living in space better. The way we have improved our own lives to give us each over a hundred years. This is only a beginning." He knelt then, knelt in front on Sumot like a supplicant. "We started with the ocean, because it is the closest ecosystem to a death spiral, and because it feeds all other ecosystems. If the ocean dies, humans die, at least on Earth." Pure belief filled his face; so pure it might be called faith. "Dr. Tollingson. Can you start the next video?" He glanced over his shoulder to see the screen turn back to the original browns and whites of death. Nodded. "This is a simulation of what happens on our current path."

Nothing for a while. More decay, until no sign of the coral remained, until the seafloor looked as flat and empty as an abandoned highway. Small animals began to shiver in the muddy, silty ocean bottom, and then a few larger ones wandered into view. They looked reminiscent of lobsters, but with more legs and odd-shaped heads. Over time, the screens in front of us populated with beings far more different from us than the fish and corals of the created life.

"This is one simulation," Dr. Tollingson said. "Here are two more."

In one, the ocean froze, in another the fish all looked like eels, long and sonorous and eventually bright and with many tiny jointed hands. These were as removed from us as we were from the Tyrannosaurus Rex.

"All of these are possible," Eliezer said. "No simulation that destroys what was our ecosystem recreates it. All are different. Some are strangely beautiful." A picture flashed behind us, land this time, everything long-legged and insect-like. Another one of huge animals, and another of what I could only call evolved cockroaches.

The screen returned to the existing reef off of Belize, the one true picture we had seen all day. "This is already dead," Eliezer said. "We can re-create something close to what we had, or we can stay up here in space and evolve ourselves while the Earth chooses a path, and hope that it is a path we can live inside of. Today's initial conditions could also create surfaces much like Venus or Mars."

Resist. Resist. I closed my eyes, and behind them, pictures of colorful fish and the tiny waving arms of corals lay in wait.

Dr. Tollingson grew wide-eyed. "We've been boarded."

"Good," Sumot said.

Henri must have been closer than I thought.

Eliezer glanced around as if evil DNAsec agents were about to leap through the door. If they did, I wondered if they'd recognize us in our paper suits.

"They will find us," Sumot said.

Zoka said, "But it will take time, right? What else were you going to show us?"

Eliezer looked at Sumot and then at me. "Did you hear us? The sea we know is already dead. Every trajectory, every model, results in a version we won't recognize. Which means every ecosystem we know is dead. Humans are dancing on a grave, arguing for nothing, and pointing weapons at us. At us. The very people who might yet save the patient."

He was so earnest, so certain of himself. *Resist*, I thought, *Resist.* Although the word stayed small inside of me, thin, maybe even foggy. *Resist . . .*

Sumot didn't seem to have any trouble resisting their imagery. "When they find us we will tell them to destroy all that you have."

"This is one of many locations." Dr. Tollingson said. She waved toward the screens. "The Earth. That is everything in one basket. We learned from that mistake."

Meaning they had hidden even more than this from us? More aquariums, or more projects? Or was she bluffing?

The two robots took Sumot and I by the arms, and led us from the room. At the first possible choice, they took Sumot one way and I another. Eliezer and Zoka went with me and Dr. Tollingson stayed with Sumot and her handler.

As we walked down the corridor, Eliezer asked, "Is it better to let the destruction we've started take its course than to fix it?"

I swallowed. My training screamed at me. Yes, yes, yes. "Humans aren't smart enough to fix nature, we have to step back."

He kept going, his whispers hot in my right ear, the robot cold on my left side, holding me next to it oh-so-firmly. "We are nature's only hope. We caused this; we have to fix it. If we don't act, who will? If no one acts, we all die. Maybe not humans, since we can carry our destructive selves to the stars."

I didn't answer him. I was thinking too hard, trying to be like Sumot. Trying to resist.

Zoka spoke up, awe and discovery in her voice. "If we learn to fix the earth, then maybe we won't do damage in other places."

Eliezer went on, "If we can demonstrate our capability here, we can be responsible there. For example, if we could bring this knowledge, this ability to Mars, we could accelerate its livability by decades. In a hundred years, it could be lush."

The robot led us to a small room, and I prepared to be left there, locked in. Being alone and away from Eliezer's questions would feel good. I had so much to think about, to decide. To feel.

Eliezer went to the closet and pulled out my uniform, and the clothes Zoka had been wearing when they captured us. "Put these on," he said.

Getting out of the uncomfortably noisy paper suit sounded almost as good as being left alone. I changed. Zoka did, too, and we both brushed our teeth and hair and washed our faces. She smiled at me, her eyes alight with excitement. "Isn't this wonderful? All this work. Being here. It's got to be historic."

I had to take a deep breath to keep from following her down that particular rabbit hole. We left our paper suits and paper shoes in the room. I felt better. Being clean helped, and wearing my own uniform helped even more. The motto embroidered on my back and the UN Biodiversity Protector logo on my pocket felt like shields.

As we walked, I listened to Eliezer and Zoka talk between themselves, like little gods. I'd never heard such enthusiastic arrogance.

The image of the healthy sea had been so beautiful I finally understood Joe's tears. But I didn't understand his choice yet. Had he sounded like these people? Had he been one of them?

He chose to betray this work, but why? I didn't know how to find out; we were sworn to protect our whistleblowers. Joe probably wasn't his name anyway. And I didn't have any contact information.

Eliezer was telling Zoka, ". . . the hardest part is the cleanup. We had to make species that would die naturally. We didn't want to have to kill them, because, well, we'd miss some. Eradication programs don't work reliably anyway. Better to build in their death from the beginning."

I asked him, "Isn't that still playing god?"

He hesitated, went serious. "There's ruthlessness in restoration as well as destruction. You of all people should know that."

When we stood over the dying parrots, Sumot told me to be ruthless. To kill them all, since they were all tainted. She had told me not to feel guilty, but I had cried myself to sleep for all of the nights between the destruct order and the day we flew away. Even now my mind skittered away from thoughts about the Rising Jungle biome, from its gaudy advertisements and its ecotourism and its efficient, ruthless death at our hands. At my hand. The blood of parrots stained my soul.

I expected to be handed over to Henri in a corridor. Instead, they led me to a bright room full of lights and reporters, full of conversation, movement, and energy. Micro-cameras hovered near my face, and I waved them away. They moved back, but just out of easy range.

I searched for Sumot.

No sign of her. But in the back of the room, Henri. Sumot had said he did not like her. And now he was here, and I was here, and she wasn't.

Dr. Tollingson was here too, beads of sweat on her forehead

and her jaw so tight that it twitched. Her face transformed with a broad welcoming smile when she saw me. She gestured me toward a chair that would make me the center of attention.

I walked up to her, looked up into her dark eyes, and demanded, "Where is Sumot?"

She glanced at Henri. "She went back to her keepers. You'll join her soon enough. But first, we have a press conference."

A jolt of anger braced me. How dare they? We controlled the press on investigations! I thought of Alin. "Where are our guards? From our ship?"

"Safe. They have been detained in comfort." She glanced at the chair. "Sit down. We want you to talk to the reporters, and your boss has said that you can take that role now."

I stared at Henri, who was too far away for me to ask him a direct question. He nodded. Only the barest of movements, but I had been taught to read micro-expressions. I nodded back, maybe an inch of brief acknowledgment.

My mouth gaped wide enough that I may have looked like one of the fish in the aquarium corridor for a moment. I caught myself, breathed deep, and looked back at Dr. Tollingson.

"We have given the reporters the tour that we gave you."

My thoughts raced, confused. "When?"

"We just finished. They saw the movies and the simulations on the way in, and now they've seen the fish and the sharks and the anemones, and they understand how they were made, and why."

We were in space. Not next door to anything or anyone. The timing couldn't be accidental. No more accidental than Henri's arrival, anyway.

I sat, struggling to do away with my anger. I was on duty, and my anger anathema to the calm needed to make good choices. I drew in deep belly breaths with my eyes closed and started over. I needed to be an investigator. Not a ball of confused anger. *Respect. Remember.* If Sumot wasn't here, I had to be Sumot.

There were about twenty humans in the room. Five robots were probably guards. Two were badged as reporters. I recognized a tall, gray-haired man from the press conference after the

Rising Jungle, when I had sat in the back and listened to Sumot answer questions. He was from one of the liberal presses that adored us and our mission. He was also by himself, with no one to talk to. Which implied the other reporters might not be on our side.

I identified three factions, which I suspected were for us, against us, and militantly against us. Names and faces floated back up from briefings.

A man from the back took his hat off, and I recognized Joe. Our whistleblower.

Dr. Tollingson stood up, and the room slowly quieted.

"You asked to see the inspectors. We have brought you one. Please welcome Doctor Paulette Rain. She has been on the same tour that you were just on, and she watched the same videos you saw see on the way in."

My hands shook. They must have called the reporters in right when the inspection was ordered.

Hands shot up. Dr. Tollingson picked a tall red-headed woman who had been mildly against our mission in the past. "What do you think of a wholly created ecosystem?"

I hadn't had time to think about it. "It's illegal," I said. "It's what we were created to protect against."

"That's not news," the reporter said. "But what if they're right? What if they know how to save the world now, after we've destroyed it?"

"It's not dead yet," I snapped, trying to buy time. Maybe trying to buy the Earth time.

The reporter kept going, her face eager for a killing question. "*You* haven't saved the world yet. All of the protection in the world hasn't saved anything but the bald eagle and a few frogs. It's not enough."

It wasn't a question so I didn't answer. Advice from Sumot. Let them state whatever they want—their statements wouldn't end up in the news.

Dr. Tollingson allowed another reporter. "If you could destroy all of this, would you?"

I felt the question hit my gut. "The UN Biodiversity Protection rules demand it."

"Rules can be changed," the reporter said. "That wasn't my question, anyway. Is it your decision, and what will you do?"

I didn't know enough to answer. I glanced from Dr. Tollingson to Eliezer, to Joe.

Joe smiled sadly, but didn't offer any words.

The reporter pressed. "They've sent their research to us. They asked us to pick it apart. In general, we couldn't, not enough to argue with their primary conclusions that we act now or we fail to save the Earth. If it is your choice, what will you do?"

I remembered my dreams of parrots, and Sumot's straight back, and her words about ruthlessness. I remembered that she didn't have any trouble sleeping. I wanted to please her, to be like her. I respected what I had signed up to do, and I needed to say the words that would make Sumot proud of me.

But I could not pull this trigger. The colorful anemones, the blue angelfish, the fish with the orange mouth that had gaped at Zoka. The shark. The reef before humans melted it. I took the microphone and sent a question back, looking directly at Joe as I spoke. "Why should we trust our technology when it damaged or destroyed so much?"

I was pleased to see Joe stand up. I wasn't ceding my decision to him, or anyone. But he had started us on this path, and here he stood at the end.

Tiny flying mics hovered just in front of and below his mouth. He didn't look at me, but at Dr. Tollingson. "I ran from here because you frightened me, and I frightened me. I'd been working as if I were a god for years, for almost all of my life. But then I made some mistakes and I lied about them. I realized how frail I am. I am not a god. So I left and came to you."

Beside me, Dr. Tollingson gasped.

Joe went on. "I watched the Rising Jungle die. I knew I could kill this work. I thought I wanted to."

"And now?" Dr Tollingson demanded. "Do you still want it all to die? How can you?"

Tears fell down Joe's face. "I went home." He kept his hands at his side, making no move to wipe the tears away. "Now I know that's another way to play god. Now I know that destruction is worse than creation."

"I would like you to answer my question," the reporter insisted.

I remembered the proud look on Sumot's face when they promoted me. I couldn't change the rules of the UN. That took a vote of nations.

Dr. Tollingson looked at me. The tiny lines around her eyes gave away her need, and the stillness in her face. A forced stillness, a personality that couldn't quite put her fate in my hands. "You are in a position to stay judgment."

I had asked Sumot the same question about the Rising Jungle. *Could I buy time?* I took a deep breath and closed my eyes and searched for the images that came up. Schools of fish and Sumot's fear. She would let fear make her destroy all of this, like an avenging goddess of the government. She would have no regrets.

But I remembered the brilliant parrots rising away from us, the screech of the voices, the life in them.

I glanced at Henri, but he didn't move or offer any help. Coward.

I looked straight into the cameras. "I request that my superiors at the United Nations Bio-diversity Protection Force allow a three-month stay of execution for the beings here. This will buy time to explore this solution."

I didn't need to read any micro-expressions to see the effect of my words. Joe's shoulders relaxed as he smiled. Dr. Tollingson continued to look neutral, although she couldn't quite keep the edges of her lips down. Eliezer looked so relieved you'd think I'd saved his life. Zoka screamed in happiness and hugged me, planting a kiss on my cheek. Her voice sounded like the screech of a happy parrot.

HER GRANDDAUGHTER'S TEACHERS

Sun dappled the thin path as Anya followed Marti through the Silver Creek forest. The air smelled clean, washed in morning fog that also dampened their footsteps. The day felt perfect. Except for one thing. Her patrol partner walked as if someone had filled her pockets with stones. Anya spoke to the Forest Guard symbol on Marti's back, a gold flame with a red diagonal stripe across it. "What happened? Talk to me."

"My grandson came home for spring break."

"And?" They crested a ridge. Anya's eyes swept the succession of additional ridges in front them. Douglas fir and oak, periodically sharpened with the red bark of madrona. Tall, conical redwoods clinging to the side of gullies. No smoke. There hadn't been any visible smoke for three years. But then, the edges of this forests were fenced and guarded. It would be hard for humans to sneak in, and neither coyotes nor robots set fires. Only people and lightening. "It's clear. We're good for a while. Tell me what happened."

"Jakob chose to be the last of his line."

Anya's breath hiccupped in her chest. "They sterilized him?"

"Of course not. *They* aren't allowed to perform sterilizations." Anger, maybe even hatred, thickened Marti's voice. "The Health Clinic did the deed, the day he turned sixteen. But *they* talked him into it."

Anya walked up a rise, using half-buried granite boulders to steady herself. "Sixteen is too young."

"Any age is too young."

Anya smothered a sigh. If Marti would turn around, she'd be able to tell whether or not tears streaked her cheeks. They had patrolled Silver Creek together for thirteen years, and Anya knew Marti was either crying, almost crying, or furious. Maybe all three.

Marti's next words were clipped, sharp with anger. "He told me the law says he can choose his gender at sixteen. So why the hell not, he said, couldn't he choose whether or not to be a parent at the same age?"

"And you bit your tongue?" Marti didn't support gender choice that early, even though Anya did. They'd argued about it twice.

"So hard it hurt."

Anya ducked under a low-hanging branch. "Jakob is choosing to stay male?"

"So far. But he's the third boy in his class to request sterilization. Damned robots." Marti's jaw clenched and she muttered the words again. "Damned robots."

Anya took a deep breath and let a half mile go by while she thought. Sterilization couldn't be reversed. Law, or course, not science. It was medically possible. She couldn't remember why, just like she would never know why humans still burned carbon fuels, or abandoned puppies. She shook her head, breathed deep, let the forest in to calm her. Above them, warblers called zee zee zee, and a gray squirrel twisted around a trunk, over and over, maybe just to show them it could. Silly thing. "Stop in Devil's Hollow?" It was another half a mile on, and maybe Marti would calm by then.

Early leaves fell around them as they traversed the switchbacks down. Devil's Hollow was marshy meadow, a stream, and tangled tree trunks sprouting seedlings. A welcome early fall rainstorm had temporarily freshened the shallow streambed that bisected the meadow. Anya pulled her boots off and dipped her feet into the cool water.

Marti sat stiffly beside her, shoulders back, head up.

Sure enough—tear tracks. "I'm sorry," Anya told her.

"Damned robots."

A sudden fear rose in Anya's chest. "Hsu will turn sixteen next year."

"Your granddaughter, right?"

A lump clogged Anya's throat as she nodded. "Damned robots."

Marti laughed, and Anya joined her, both of their tones bitter.

Two nearly-sleepless nights later, Anya struggled to keep her eyes open as she drowsed on a rock, waiting for a cab. She startled when it thrummed up, purring more like a refrigerator than a car. She leaned in and told it "Find my daughter," as she thumbed the cab the necessary information from her phone.

It paused for a moment and then said, "Yes" in a silvery voice.

She told the cab, "Set up for sleep."

With a light whir, the seats lay down. She folded the blanket the way she liked it on the bed, crumpled her coat under her head as a pillow, and prepared to stare at the roof. "Wake me an hour before we arrive," she commanded.

Surprisingly, she slept instantly and deeply, dreaming of forests and fires. Maybe sleep came to those who acted.

The cab sang her awake at a rest stop outside the city. After using the facilities, she perched in the newly-configured seat. The city unfurled around her. Autocars of all types twisted and darted as they negotiated for places in traffic. She had to clutch the handhold in front of her twice to avoid pitching left as the cab jigged right. The sidewalks were emptier than she remembered. No homeless. No obvious police presence or poverty. Sterile to the point of oppressive. From time to time, she asked the car to tell her about buildings she didn't recognize, or parks that looked newly sprung from whole city blocks. It answered politely and quickly, its voice threaded with silk and seduction. It dropped her near Golden Gate Park, the city's heat slapping her face and drawing beads of sweat immediately to her cheeks and brow. The car reminded her, "Please take your belongings."

Anya reached for her coat, waited for the cab to open its hatch so she could grab her backpack. "Thank you."

"You are welcome. Stace is likely to walk by the Rideout fountain in ten minutes."

"Thank you," she repeated.

The park was crowded. Maybe a third were single people walking dogs, another third people walking with friends or carebots, and the other third striding alone.

Stace would be walking alone. Or at least, she'd look that way.

Anya perched on the edge of the fountain, her mouth dry as a dead leaf, her stomach in tatters. She shouldn't have come. She didn't care, damnit. Shouldn't care anyway. She was sixty-one, born in 1990, and she didn't understand cities or kids or any of it anymore. The fountain felt like a fitting location, its central sculpture a tiger fighting a snake. She felt like the tiger sometimes, spending her years holding off fires in dry, brittle woods, trying like hell to save something for Hsu's generation. The tiger on the fountain looked certain to lose. Surely it was exhausted after decades spent holding the snake at arm's length.

Anya recognized Stace's walk. Her daughter had long green hair and wore a white jumpsuit with lace at the calves and arms and chest, and a goddamned cape. A cape. Blue. Her glasses glowed red on the edges, a sign that she didn't want real-world disturbance. A sign she was fine striding powerfully inside whatever fantasy world she inhabited at this moment. She could be spaceship crew, an alien visitor, or any of a thousand heroes or heroines. There would be a map of the real world as well, integrated to whatever story she lived. Given the outfit, maybe she was an exotic dancer. Anya took a deep breath, telling herself to be charitable. Stace was beautiful and weird, and it was perfectly fine that she'd hate being interrupted in the middle of whatever game her glasses were feeding her.

As Stace strode toward her, time stuttered. So many days when she had seen Stace like this, so many ways she had tried to change every choice her daughter had made. So many failures.

Unexpected nerves meant Anya wanted to lean down and retch into the fountain. Except that would produce a robot cop or a rent-a-cop or a drone with a fine for her. Probably a drone. She had lost track of all the ways the city herded its people.

She swallowed the rise from her sour stomach and forced herself to stand, to match strides with her daughter, to put a hand on Stace's lace-clad left forearm.

Stace flicked her arm sideways, as if she were dumping a moth that had landed there back into the sky.

Anya clamped her fingers around Stace's hand, kept her pace matched, and waited.

A hundred feet further along the path, past the fountain and almost to the Rose garden, Stace reached her right hand up and removed her glasses. "Whoever you—" She blinked. "Mom! I told you never to surprise me."

"I'm sorry. But it's important."

"Are you okay?"

"I am."

Stace's blue eyes narrowed. "Did your trees die?"

"No. The forest is fine. The wolves are coming back and we have two mountain lions."

"That's good, Mom." She sighed, slid her glasses back on, and mumbled something into them. She jerked them back off and spoke in a clipped voice. "I've just paid a sub for half an hour. Hopefully she won't fuck up my rankings."

Anya winced.

Stace, on the other hand, blinked rapidly and shook her head, finally falling out of whatever augmented reality she had been playing in. "I'm sorry. I know you came a long way."

"I did." Now the trick was to get Stace into a good mood. "Where were you? What game or place?"

"Never mind."

"How are you? How is your life."

Stace's words were clipped. "I'm fine. I'm just fine."

"How is Hsu doing?"

Stace's eyes narrowed. "Let's sit. Hsu is fine." She led Anya to an unoccupied bench.

The stone bench's heat forced Anya to sit up as tried again. "I'm glad you're okay."

Stace stared toward a copse of pleasantly droopy eucalyptus. "I'm perfect. I'm busy."

The words sounded defensive. But then Stace had been defensive since she was two. "How is the city doing?"

"The city is just fine. Busy."

Anya wondered what it was busy at. A lot of people still worked, but since the free dole started, no one had to. Anya had worked since she was Hsu's age, starting with walking dogs in an animal shelter. The dole was voluntary; Anya had never accepted a penny of it. Stace had worked herself off of it early, something to do with being good at leading people through virtual worlds.

The awkward silence stretched thin. "When did you see Hsu last?"

Stace lifted her wrist, narrowed her eyes. "A week ago. She's fine. She likes her school. The bots have them all agog about space. She thinks she might like to go."

"To one of the stations?"

"Maybe a science hub in one of the hotels."

A place with no forests, no deer. "I heard some of them are closing."

Stace reached toward her glasses reflexively, stopped herself, spoke to her wrist, which chirped, "The third of four SpaceTown Suites stations shut down last week. The remaining hotel has pledged to stay open through the end of the decade to serve its long-term residents and elite guests."

Stace didn't show one bit of remorse for missing what had been the big news story of the previous week. "Well, maybe she'll have to go to a science station."

"I think they're struggling, too."

"Look, Mom. I don't care what she does as long as she's happy. Isn't that what you always told me? Do whatever I want?"

Anya bit back words about how big a mistake that had been. "There aren't as many options as there used to be."

"As long as she's happy, why do I care?"

Anya temporarily changed the subject. "Do you know how many babies were born in San Francisco last year?"

Stace stared at her wrist but didn't ask it anything. "No."

"I checked on my way here. Three hundred and two."

"Is that a lot?"

Anya gripped the bench hard, keeping the stress out of her voice. This was always the way between her and Stace. Stace wasn't stupid. She earned a phenomenal amount of money doing whatever gaming and influence thing she did. She just seemed so out of it when came down to real things. Anya worked for a casual tone. "It used to be around 8,000 babies a year in this city. So, three hundred and two is what—five percent of normal? Close enough. There were one thousand, three hundred and seventy-two the year before last. That's less than a quarter of normal. It's been like that for three years, the number of babies falling like a stone into a lake."

Stace's eyes narrowed, making the beginnings of wrinkles in the creases of her face stand out. "Well, wasn't there a low birth year while ago? Maybe this is an echo."

Anya sighed. "No. The trend line bends almost straight down."

Stace drummed her fingers on her slender wrist, the pale lace bouncing. "Know why? We're no good for the planet anyway. You've told me that a hundred times. We destroy everything. Maybe if we're not here, your wolves and deer will thrive." She stood and looked down an Anya. "I don't care about any of this."

The words drove Anya to take another deep breath. "Okay. I know. Will you put me on the list to visit Hsu?"

Stace glanced at her wrist. "If you go now."

Anya turned her head, blinked back a tear. "I will. Tell her I'll be there in half an hour."

Stace's eyes widened in surprise. "Is that what this was about? You just wanted to see Hsu? Not me?"

Now Stace looked like she wanted to cry. What was it with everyone these days? Years of climate and poverty and fighting. But she could share. "My best friend's son got sterilized this week. At sixteen." The puzzled look on Stace's face told Anya she shouldn't have said anything. "It made her sad. That's all."

Stace held her hand out, and in a totally uncharacteristic gesture, pulled Anya up from the bench and then close in for a hug.
Then she whispered close to Anya's ear. "Hsu can choose. I think
she already has. She doesn't need children."

Anya wrapped her arms around Stace, the unexpected embrace as beautiful as Stace's words were frightening. "I might like
a grandchild," she whispered into Stace's chest.

Her daughter said, "I'll come see you sometime," and then she
let go and backed up.

Anya gathered her things and turned to say good-bye. Stace
was already walking away, the glasses over her eyes, the red leave-
me-alone lights pulsing.

San Francisco's Academy of Distinguished Youth was a con-
verted luxury hotel most of the way across town. It took Anya two
busses and a trolley ride to work her way there. She could have
used another autobot, but she had always chosen shared public transportation when it was available. Given that everything
was electric, it didn't matter. Not really. But she needed the extra
twenty minutes to compose her thoughts. She hadn't really come
with a plan, and she'd slept away any planning time she might
have had. The last time she'd seen Hsu, a year ago, the girl had
been—at least a little—interested in Anya's work. More than Stace
had ever been.

Anya let out a sigh of relief when a human woman dressed in
a blue and beige school uniform met her at the door and led her
to a visiting room on the second floor. The room was comfortable, with four chairs, a long table, a drink dispenser, and a thick
burnt sienna rug. A window looked out over a greenspace. She
had barely had time to settle when a robot bustled in wearing the
school's green and silver uniform, leading Hsu behind it.

Hsu had grown. She wore makeup now, stylized purple curli-
cues that encased her pale green eyes and drifted toward her dark
hairline. She had her mother's slight build and casual prettiness,
but there was something more solid about her than Stace. Her

hair flowed over her shoulders, naturally dark but tipped with white and purple below her chin. The colors complimented her makeup. The girl looked more like a twenty-year-old than a fifteen-year-old. She was tall enough to meet Anya's eyes straight on, and she did. She nodded her head. Polite. Quiet. "Pleased to see you."

Anya struggled for a moment with what to say. "I've missed you. Stace—your mom, said to say hi."

"That's nice." Hsu waved the robot out of the room, and after it closed the door, she sat on the chair closest to Anya. "What can I do for you?"

Not *Hi Grandma, I missed you*. But maybe that was fair. "I just wanted to see you. You're family." She paused, struggled a little. "I should have come more often. You're taller now."

Hsu's smile was more like a thirty-year-old's, poised and utterly calm. "Are you still a Forest Guard?"

"Yes. There haven't been any fires for almost fifteen years, not near us, but we still watch. We're also rewilding the forest." A slight show of interest in Hsu's eyes convinced her to keep talking. "We have more deer now. And they are healthy. The wolves keep them that way. Remember, I showed you pictures last time? And we've kept most of the invasive species—most of the weeds out. Native species and coming back to the part of the forest my friend Marti and I keep up. Animals from before."

Hsu looked curious. "Before?"

"Before people came and brought plants that took over some of the understory. When people settled the West Coast they brought berries and other plants with them that outdid some of the native plants." She hesitated, watching Hsu closely to make sure she understood. The girl nodded, so Anya kept going. "We can't do it exactly right of course. The patches of older forests are so small. Some of the old plants can't thrive anymore." She paused for just a moment, breathing. "The woods will never be the same as they were before people came. But there are as many birds in the forest now as there should be, chickadees and warblers and a few kinds of owls."

Hsu nodded sagely, but some of the interest had started to fade from her eyes.

Anya's cheeks flushed hot. "Sorry, Hsu. I've been talking at you. And, well, you asked." She stopped, waited.

No response, although Hsu seemed full of patience rather than half-elsewhere like Stace. Very present for such a young girl, like a buddha or something. Willing to enjoy silence.

"I came to see how you are and what interests you, and if I can help you. In any way." Anya leaned forward. "Your mom said you're studying astronomy."

"I'm studying space."

"I know a little bit. What are you learning?"

"About spaceships. How to build the kind that go really far. There are some new robots now who are focused on that. They're going to take our story to other places."

Anya narrowed her eyes. That hadn't been on any news channels she'd seen. "You mean to the stations?"

"No, Grandma. The stations are dying. Everybody knows that."

Well, Stace hadn't. But Anya said, "Yes, but where? Mars?"

"No. Other star systems."

Anya sat back. "But doesn't that take lifetimes?"

Hsu looked amused. "Not for robots."

"Oh." Anya felt lighter. "You're not thinking of going?"

"Of course not. No humans will go. We couldn't anyway. Don't you know? We're married to the Earth. We need the biome here, the things in our guts that keep us well, the food from here, the right sunlight. There won't be any other place for us."

Good. The robots weren't supposed to be able to lie. "But you're still interested in the ships? Why?"

"We made the robots. So a part of us is going. I'm certain that's why we've never seen aliens." Hsu was slowly becoming animated, even moving her hands some as she talked. "If there were any aliens, they'd be robots, and they probably couldn't talk slow enough for us to hear. That's what Professor Klein says."

True enough. The cab she'd taken here had been negotiating

for spots in traffic with hundreds of other vehicles at once. Anya had an old truck at home, but no human drove in cities. Not anymore. "That makes sense. And they wouldn't have to sleep or eat."

Hsu grinned. "That's right. They wouldn't. They can just turn off and wake themselves up when they need to. They can even be part of their ships."

Anya blinked, absorbing. Hsu was as excited about this as Anya was about her forest. But surely ships she couldn't even ride in wouldn't keep Hsu from having children, or at least waiting to decide. Anya hadn't realized how far the population was falling until she'd looked up the birth numbers on the way in. Not really. World population fall had been a low-level conversation, but not really a news story, at least not out in the woods. There were no children in the Forest Guards anyway. Or in the Coast Guard. She and Marti had each seen a few kids on farms, although mostly the crops weren't harvested by people anymore. "Have they started building the spaceships yet?"

"Yes. But only just. It's going to take at least ten years. They've said I can help."

Anya was genuinely curious. "Why would you devote yourself to something you can't use? At least I walk under my redwoods every day." And talk with some of them, like old friends. But that might not be something Hsu would understand.

Hsu didn't even stumble over the question. "We all need something to do before we die. This is what I'd like to do. The math is fabulous, and it will be so much fun." She leaned in, and for the first time this visit, enthusiasm lit her eyes and widened her smile. "It's like your trees. I'll be doing something big that matters."

Anya bit her lip, took a breath. "I don't think they're the same at all. Humans need trees. We can't even use the spaceships."

Hsu tapped her foot on the floor. "Don't you see? They are our creations. The robots. Even the ships, even though we couldn't build them without the bots. But the bots were created to care for us. They'll tell our stories. There's even a plan to take human DNA, and Earth animals and plants. In case they find a planet they can build for humans. It's still all about us."

Anya felt so tense she had trouble opening her mouth. Not that she knew what to say. The kid was being brainwashed. Clearly. Machines didn't care about people. Well, they did. Because of programming. But they had no souls. Damnit. She took a deep breath. "Do you know a boy named Jakob? I don't think he goes to this school, but he's in one somewhere nearby. Jakob Mills? He's Marti's grandson."

To her surprise Hsu nodded immediately. "He's in an all-boys school, St. Michael's. They come over here for dances even though we have our own boys. He's already signed up to work on the spaceships."

Should she be direct? She didn't even know how much time she had. The little room seemed smaller and more confined than it had. Maybe the robot was listening outside the door. "Can we take a walk? I like to be outside."

Hsu looked down at her wrist. "I have class in an hour."

So little time. "Is there a pathway around the school? You could show me some of the buildings. Are the spaceships here?"

"Oh, no. They're in the desert. We're just learning about them here. Yes, there's a path. The robots turned the old parking lot into a park for us. They even planted trees. It's beautiful." She hopped up and headed toward the door.

Anya expected deeply manicured gardens, but the slight wildness surprised and pleased her. California buckeye, cypress, bay laurel, and a young willow shed lacy shade over pretty benches. Bright violas and marigolds competed for her attention in raised beds.

They walked along a rubbery feeling pathway. Hsu pointed out fountains and named flowers like a pro. She was the picture of a happy, engaged student. Anya almost hesitated. But who knew when Stace would let her see her granddaughter again? "Hsu?"

"Yes?"

"I wanted to ask you about your future. You want to work on the spaceships. That's fine. Maybe that's good. My mom didn't understand why I was passionate about saving forests, not when she wanted me to do social work. But I am worried about so many of you kids choosing not have children. We have a chance at living well here, now. We learned a lot about climate, and how to live better without being so evil. And children—children are a blessing."

"You and Mom hate each other."

Anya stopped halfway down a ramp that led to a small koi pond. She swallowed, fighting for breath. "I don't understand her. But I've loved her since the day she was born."

Hsu, now at the bottom of the ramp, looked up at Anya. "Is love all about wanting people to change?"

"Of course not." Anya forced her feet to move. "It's about wanting people to be all that they can be. And children—children teach you things you wouldn't learn otherwise. So do grandchildren."

Hsu circled the pond, looking down into its waters as if counting the bright orange and white fish that darted from side to side. "My teachers don't try to change me. They just show me interesting things. I know they're not human, but they spend their time helping me choose what I want to do, and teaching me really neat stuff. I don't want to stop learning." She glanced back toward the school. "Children would slow me down. After all, I'm here and not with Mom. You left Mom when you went to the forest." She gazed directly an Anya, her head cocked.

Anya bit back words, unwilling to defend herself. She hadn't abandoned Stace. She had stayed with her until Stace was 19 and in school. She had left then, full-time. But wasn't that the way of parenting? Hsu's question made her so dizzy; she knelt by the pond and put a hand on a rock to steady herself, looking down into the same waters Hsu did. "Do you have to decide now?"

Hsu waited a while before answering, exuding the same calm she had shown in the office. When she spoke, it sounded almost like she was addressing a child. "I'm helping to build a better future. There will be people who have children. Some." She frowned. "I don't think many though." She stared at Anya's reflection in the water, and then looked at her, drawing Anya's gaze from the fish to her granddaughter's face. "That's better for all the things you want to save. Better for the Earth, better for your forest."

Anya's breath caught. "I want to save the trees for people. For kids and grandkids and . . ."

Hsu held up a hand, her voice still calm. "Not for themselves?"

She stopped. Swayed. Swallowed. "Of course."

"Won't it be better for the trees if we are not here? Or at least, not many of us?"

Try as she might, Anya couldn't meet Hsu's calm with calm. She blurted out a question. "Racial suicide? Refusing to have children? For everyone? How could that be better?"

Hsu shrugged, as if it was a given and Anya was simply too old or too slow to understand.

Anger stained Anya's worry, making her fingers twitch. Humans had created the robots to help them. She and Marti even used some in the forest, to clear when they had to. But those were older and more physical models. Neither she nor Marti took orders from bots. They gave them. She felt dizzy, daunted. She was failing. "Can I come visit again soon?"

Hsu cocked her head. "If you want."

"I'll try to come back in a few weeks."

"Okay." Hsu leaned over and hugged Anya, still calm. The young woman felt ethereal, almost unreal. Anya felt like Hsu was blessing her and telling her it would all work out.

Anja didn't buy that, not one bit.

Three days later Anya and Marti worked side by side, finishing out checklists for the day. Anya stumbled through the story of her trip to town. Marti didn't ask a single question, although she shoved the tools away with clacks and clangs and broke the wooden haft off of a shovel. Five minutes after Anya finished, Marti spoke calmly, her voice edged with sadness. "If the kids only know what the robots tell them, and they live on campus, how would they know any better? Sure, they seem happy. Jakob seems happy. But they can't be, can they?"

"Hsu seemed weirdly spiritual. Like she had removed herself from the world. She felt like a monk or a priest."

"Do you think the robots are doing something to them?"

"Like what? Chipping? Brainwashing?" Anya swiped the list she'd just completed closed and stood up. "I don't know. She looked and felt normal. I mean, other than being too calm and happy for a fifteen-year-old girl. And too thin. But she's always been thin."

"And you're worried." Marti stood and tugged her light blue coat from the hook, opening the door for Anya.

"I'll go back and see her."

"You should. I do go see Jakob once a month." Marti's grin looked slightly evil as she shut the door behind them. "Whether he wants me to or not." She pulled her old scratched-up red mountain bike out, shoved her empty lunch sack and water bottle in the saddlebags, and climbed on. Marti biked any time of the year, even nights like this when it was damp and barely fifty degrees.

Anya had driven her old truck to the ranger station. As she neared it, she spotted a figure leaning against the hood, almost completely still. Stace. She wasn't even wearing anything that obviously put her in some other world. No headset or glasses or anything. She wore tight jeans and a flowing shirt, with a light poncho in iridescent green. Her hair and face looked slightly less made-for-cameras than usual. "Stace? Are you okay?"

"Maybe I just wanted to see my mom."

Not true. "Hop in. You haven't seen my new place."

"Yes I have."

Anya grimaced. Virtually. It wasn't the same. "Can I make you dinner?"

"Can I spend the night?"

Anya's stomach tightened, but then a little ray of hope loosened her completely. She smiled, feeling almost giddy. "Of course." She'd have to find sheets and sweep a few boxes out of the spare room. Stace. Here. Wow. "Put on your seat belt or the truck will squeal."

Stace blinked twice. "Oh, I forgot. Sure."

Anya pushed the old truck on. Startup lights winked along the dash. She told it, "Go home." The truck was old enough that it forced her to put her hands on the wheel, although it slid through her fingers of its own accord as the truck cornered out of the parking lot. She waited, letting the silence grow a bit.

Stace eventually mumbled, "I went to visit Hsu twice since I saw you. That's twice in a week. Then she stopped taking my visits."

"Can she do that?"

"Yes. Not forever. There's a contract and I can see her at least once a week. I didn't even knew that more required her permission after she turned twelve. Who would have thought that?"

Anya suspected Stace had never tried to visit even once a week, much less more. "What are you worried about?"

"I got to thinking. I don't care what Hsu decides. I don't care what your friend's kid decides. But what if no one ever has any more kids?"

"We all die, I guess."

"Well," Stace said. "We will, anyway."

"You know what I mean."

"I have a lot of abilities. In the otherworld."

Stace's generation's term for whatever the Internet had grown into when it went more multi-dimensional. Anya had seen demonstrations, but she'd never needed that skill for what she did. Any form of not-reality made her a little sick to her stomach.

"So I went to find out. That's the kind of question you can't ask directly. How many babies are in the world? I didn't think I cared. I really didn't. I didn't think I gave a damn. But you know what? There's not many. You were right. So I set off to figure out if it was just because so many of us are happy enough in the otherworld. I mean, I never wanted Hsu. You know that. But shit happens. I kept her until she was five, but then the schools would take her and she seemed happy and I was happy. She still seems happy." Stace ran her finger along the edge of the truck's big window, her gaze on the trees rather than on Anya. "But I want you to go to town. To see her. To see if you can stop her. She won't listen to me."

"You never listened to me."

"But maybe she will. She's interested in your forest. She looked up your history, and she told me a story about how you stood off a whole brigade of ATV riders once, said they almost killed you. I didn't even know that story. Was that story true?"

Anya laughed. "I was twenty-two and stupid. It's a miracle I didn't get shot. They were tree thieves. We learned, after, that they had killed three Forest Guards in a Washington State forest."

"You stopped them?"

"Someone had to."

"You really did do that? Why didn't I know?" Before Anya could answer, Stace continued. "We're allowed to take her out. Let's go get her and bring her here. She'd like to see the trees."

When they picked Hsu up, she wore a pair of brand-new taupe boots with white laces and carried a simple white backpack. Anya and Stace let her climb in first, all long legs and fluid movement except when she swung her legs over, apparently unused to shoes the weight and heft of the boots. They followed her in, crowded together. It had been years, maybe even ten, since all three of them were in the same car. They talked hesitantly about school, and then Hsu went quiet. Anya prompted her, "Tell me more about the ships."

Hsu stared so intently out the front window Anya wasn't sure she'd heard the question. But then she said, "They have to fly for hundreds of years. Maybe more. That drives most of the design. They're lean and light, with invisible shields around them. We're building them in space, of course. I have some drawings."

She showed them pictures that looked like thin lace stretching across the dark sky. "They don't need life support," Hsu pointed out. "So they don't need spin or oxygen, or anything like we would. No food. Just repair bots and fuel and parts printers. And small ships to land on planets."

Anya's sense of disquiet grew. Surely the robots didn't need human kids to build spaceships. They had been programmed to take care of humans, to keep them happy and engaged. They weren't allowed to kill them. For that matter, they weren't allowed to genetically engineer them or to sterilize them. But they were allowed to teach them whatever they wanted to learn. And any teacher could lead a student.

She held her right hand out in front of her and stared at the wrinkled skin on the back of her palm and at the two knuckles which were far bigger than they should be. An accident chopping firewood a few years ago. She rubbed at those two fingers absently even though the pain had long since gone, the quiet musicality of Hsu's voice sending her into a near-trance. Hsu wouldn't be building anything that hurt her hands. Machines could out-engineer any human, out-build any. Hell, machines could do what she did.

After they stowed Hsu's things, Anya led her daughter and granddaughter on a walk. To her surprise, both Stace and Hsu paid some attention as she pointed out and named her favorite trees. Hsu kept her composure as they splashed across streams and got mud on her newly-printed boots. She willingly touched the rough bark of redwoods and sat more easily on granite ledges than Stace did. Stace had always been awkward in the woods.

Hsu probably wasn't awkward anywhere.

Stace asked for a break and sat on a rock staring into her glasses while Anya took Hsu a few hundred feet away to sit and look out over a clearing. They spotted a doe and two of this year's fawns, long past the all-spots-and-legs stage but still only two-thirds the size of their mother. Slanted late-afternoon sun pained them with a soft glow. "They're beautiful," Hsu whispered.

"I often like to sit out at this time of day and watch for animals. It's a little early. I wasn't sure we'd see anything." She smiled. "Maybe they came for you."

"Of course not."

Anya sighed. "You don't believe in a little magic?"

Hsu turned toward her, bathed in the same light as the deer.

"Breathe," Anya told her. "Just sit and breathe. Smell the forest."

Hsu closed her eyes and breathed deeply. "It doesn't smell like the park."

"No. It smells like wilderness."

Hsu glanced back at the deer, watching them move into the

understory. As soon as the clearing emptied, she stood. "We should check on Mom."

They found Stace where they had left her. Hsu folded into a meditative pose beside her mom and hummed.

After about three minutes, Stace quietly pulled her glasses off and blinked a bit as she adjusted to the light. "Is it time to go back?"

Anya glanced at the sun, and back towards where the deer had disappeared. "Dinner will be ready in about an hour. So, sure, we can use the time to clean up and rest."

At midmorning the next day, Anya stood between Hsu and Stace as they waited for the autocab. It felt a bittersweet to stand together, like a forbidden dessert she'd regret tomorrow, but also remember for a long time. As if in sympathy with her, the air was dry and cold, and so still they heard the autocar before it rounded the bend in front of them.

Stace climbed in first. Hsu bent down and pulled off her muddy, stained boots. "I'll leave these here, Grandma. Maybe someone else can use them."

Anya closed her eyes for just a second, blinking, then held her hands out for the boots. "Thank you. I hope you had fun. I want I see you again."

Hsu smiled. "Come visit any time."

Stace was already wrapped in the otherworld, and surely Hsu had somewhere else to go as well on the way down. Anya waved and watched until the car was out of sight, and then she threw the boots at a rock and crossed her arms over her angry stomach.

A few minutes later, Marti walked up and stood quietly beside her. "Any progress?"

"With Hsu? I don't think so. But we saw a family of deer."

Marti swallowed, and then briefly embraced Anya. At least she didn't say it would all turn out okay.

Two weeks later, on another Friday, Stace stood at the side of the truck again. Once more, she wore no obvious devices. Her hair was unbound, surprising Anya with its length.

Stace smiled. "I missed the deer last time. Can you take me to see them?"

Anya grinned. "They're wild. But yes, we can go look. We have to go soon if you want to see them tonight."

"Tomorrow."

She had washed the sheets. She glanced up. "There's a full moon tonight. If we take a night walk, we'll be able to see stars. We might hear owls."

"I'd like that." Stace reached for Anya's hand and tugged her mom close.

"Me, too," Anya whispered, eyes closing. Stace smelled like the city, but she also smelled wonderful.

CITY, INNUNDATED

Back muscles strain. Wooden oars
slip hard through black water.
I slide between ebony buildings
in an ecstasy of history, biceps
pulling me soft and curious inside
the depopulated city of Seattle
at the turn of the new century:
twenty one hundred day three.

Did the last denizens stand devoutly, watching,
perhaps performing a ritualistic
greeting of each new onslaught of wind
and wave and rushing sea, each susurration
of disaster, act on act in the play of god
or man or both?

What the fuck did they do?

Heat stings the corners of my eyes.

I round the sodden top of the Pike Place
sign and see the humped perigee of the
drowned Ferris wheel. A gondola cart
swings in a soft, slight wind. I sit in my canoe,
knees bent up, oars shipped,
wondering how our grandparents

spent the last golden days of denial.
Did they ride these sea-slimed seats and pretend
the breaking could still be fixed?
My throat constricts and I force out
benediction. *I forgive you for you knew*
not what you did.
Even though you did.

You did.
You did.

My oars slide through silent water.

You did.
You did.
You knew.
You did.

Moonlight makes a road in heavy black water and I follow
its shimmering shifting path back to the shore. Somewhere
to my right, a fish splashes through a window.

OUT OF ASH

N ew Olympia was, at best, half-birthed.

The evening after the legislative session ended, I walked her nearly empty streets in a comfortable pair of jeans and a pale pink sweatshirt. The shirt was so rugged that Susannah, my chief of staff, had tried to steal it and throw it away a week ago. But I loved it, and besides, it made me look like no one. Far easier than looking like a governor. Guards followed at a distance.

Mist gave way to soft rain, then faded back to damp cold. Stored sunlight made octagonal tiles on the path under my feet glow. I followed its light to the middle of Central Park, where dusk barely illuminated the blue and red mosaics of the town well. Volunteers had moved every piece of the well they could salvage from drowning historic Olympia to the replica in New Olympia. By car, the journey was over 65 miles. The new city perched on the lower slopes of Mount Rainier, and the water tasted as clean, although more like mountain than river. This well, like the old one, operated as a free community asset. The glowing streets, the well, and, a few blocks away, the new State Capitol all looked even more beautiful than the artist's renderings. The city ran on sunlight. Edible plants bordered parks, fed by recycled wastewater as clean as the well water. New Olympia gave as much back to the local ecosystem as it took.

I ran my fingertips over the decorative tiles on the well. I had set the first mosaic in a ceremony that had taken all of 15 minutes. Impossible to tell now which one it was, although I recalled the blue-green of a sunlit summer sea. Immediately after, I'd been rushed away to visit heartsore firefighters after flames erased over 400 homes in Wenatchee.

I had dreamed New Olympia into being, fought for her, introduced bill after bill and bared my soul at physical and holo lecterns. New Olympia. A new capitol for a new time. A place for a time when humans were finally driven halfway into one another's arms by the vast price of our sins. When I first won the governor's job, it had been partly because voters shared my vision of a new state rising from the ashes of the world we were burning with yesterday's carbon.

Tears stung my eyes. I should have paid attention. But no. I'd sold the idea and ridden it to power. Then I'd assumed New Olympia would work, or at least believed people when they told me it was working. So stupid.

All session, New Olympia had been full of lawmakers and deals, of passion and argument. Then, yesterday, cars drove themselves up from Seattle, Bellevue, Vancouver, Cle Elum, Walla Walla, and every other corner to gather the beleaguered servants of the State and their many minions and ferry them to shrinking constituencies far from here. The protesters had left with them. Also, all of the reporters except the few assigned to me. They knew what I knew.

I had failed. I had built a city, but I had not moved one. New Olympia died as soon as the lawmakers left each session. Yes, Washington's people had almost all snugged up to thriving Seattle or Bellingham, and yes, our population had shrunk for 10 years running. But there were still a lot of people in Washington State, and this beautiful place wasn't attracting them. Meant as a model community, New Olympia served as a temporary home for a desperate government twice a year.

I sat on the cold, hard bench next to the well, my hair damp, the sky low and dark. No stars. Nightbirds chattered. I'd rather hear the aggravated pleas of parents calling children in for dinner, the chatter of friends strolling and talking, the padpadpad of joggers, and the lilting notes of street buskers.

Exhaustion weighed on my bones and muscles. It felt almost

like despair, which was never, ever acceptable.

Session had been full of knives. Not the old knives of lies, but the new ones of competing realities: low birthrates, disease, food shortages, fires, sea level rise, threats from neighboring Idaho, and no help at all from the Federal government. We had succeeded at many things—because we had to—but no bills passed to *move* other cities. We had merely condemned more to die as we scraped human infrastructure from places in peril. Managed retreat rather than glorious rebuilding. Returning what we had taken to nature about to take it back anyway.

I had failed an entire state. In this, anyway. In vision. Washington's politicians and her people—both—had bought my dream and given me money.

Seawater had risen faster than the scientists predicted, and disruptions had slowed design and building. The people of Olympia had needed to move before we finished their new home, and they had gone elsewhere.

I let the water run over my hands, cool and bracing. The original well had been forced up and out by gravity and the pressure of rocks, a gift from the Earth. Here, we had to drill down and force the water up. There was meaning in that metaphor, but I was simply too tired to pull it together. I ran my wet palms over my face, turning my skin crisp and cool. I wanted to do so much more for Washington State, but first, I had to make this right. Political enemies were already making it election fodder. Washington's people had birthed this dream and fed on the hope it carried.

Mist surrounded me as I strolled back to the governor's mansion.

At home, I stared out of an ornate living room that overlooked the empty Main Street and sipped hot mint tea. After an hour, I called my harried chief of staff. "Susannah?"

Her tone was friendly and unsurprised, even after 9 p.m. Susannah had been with me for 16 years, since 2027, when I was partway through my first stint as a state congresswoman. "Louise?"

"I need help."

Tired curiosity edged her voice. "What can I do for you?"

I felt as exhausted as she sounded. Maybe more. "I need help with the city. With New Olympia."

A short silence, then questions. "An urban planner? An artist? An engineer?"

I laughed. "They did their work. I need an immigrant or two, people who will be liked."

"Two? Is that enough?" she asked.

"Two. With organizing experience. And of course not. I need 50. But let's start with a team I can hide inside my operating budget."

"Any other specifications? Immigrant is a little broad." I heard the smile in her voice. "Refugees? From a particular country?"

"They'll need to talk to residents. Bilingual." I mulled her question. "Young? Enthusiastic, anyway."

"I'll have them there by noon."

And she would. Susannah knew me well enough to read import in my tone. "Thank you. I . . . I need to fix this."

I didn't have to explain what, and even though it might be utterly unfixable, she replied, "Of course you will. We all need this damned city to thrive."

In my dreams I walked the gleaming, nearly empty city all night long.

At noon, an older woman I had seen before, but couldn't remember talking to, and a woman maybe a third of her age stood awkwardly just inside my office door. The older one shifted her burly body back and forth, one foot to the other. The younger woman's dark eyes looked eager, excited, a little apprehensive. Long black hair fell flat and perfectly manicured down her back. Her khaki pants and navy shirt were neat and practical. The older one appeared Latina and the younger East Indian. Susannah hustled them into chairs. "This is Guadalupe and Chandra."

I smiled to put them at ease while Susannah offered them peppermint tea and small chocolate cakes. As they sat, I asked them to tell me their stories.

Guadalupe had worked as an organizer on my first and second gubernatorial campaigns, primarily on the peninsula. A reminder of the thousands of people I had never met but needed, owed. Her family had come up from Nicaragua in the late 1990s and she had been born just *after* they crossed the border. A Justice Warrior now, and once, when it mattered, Antifa. Her voice rumbled through the room, deep and compelling. She would be able to convince crowds. I signaled Susannah that she was a keeper with a nod and turned my attention to Chandra's story. Her father died of heat in India. Her mother brought her from Uttar Pradesh when she was 10, taking a cruise and disembarking forever and illegally in Florida. They'd made their way west, finally finding a path to green cards here. The girl looked like she might be 20 now, although maybe a little older? In her last year at the University of Washington. Her voice sounded quiet, and so calm that it took me a while to understand that her response to her father's death was a plan to fix the entire climate and remove all the greed and meanness from humanity along the way.

I mulled that for a while. Was she too naïve for this? Too young? She showed passion. I hesitated. Eventually, I touched Susannah's arm to signal my approval for Chandra, and the four of us began to plan.

A day later, we rode one of the armored cars into Seattle. While Guadalupe seemed focused on the problem of populating New Olympia, Chandra peered out of the windows and took hand notes in a paper journal. From time to time she asked the car a question. After a while I put it into tour guide mode, so that it told her where we were and related snippets of each town's history as we passed through. Chandra's questions implied a keen interest and expertise in flood and fire scars.

The Seattle Downtown Coalition was always happy to meet with me. I wore one of my *go-ahead-underestimate-me* suits complete with purple granny glasses. I settled Guadalupe and Chandra in back to observe as I pressed a room full of CEOs and CFOs. Yes, they would move some franchises to New Olympia. *If* we subsidized them. They had, already, hadn't they? Who cared if they only stayed open half the year? Yes, the University was a draw. But it wouldn't open for two more years. If that. Hadn't the whole city been two years late? No, they wouldn't move tech jobs there. People in tech could live there if they wanted. They could live anywhere. Anyone could choose New Olympia, if I could figure out how to make it attract them. Right now it was too far away and too sterile and there was no nightlife. What would I trade for small manufacturing? Not the price they quoted me. Couldn't I just be patient? After all, they asked, why did it matter?

They concluded with a question. Hadn't they helped to clean most of the drugs and homelessness out of Seattle? Made huge investments in affordable housing?

I had to say yes to that. And thank you.

After, in my Seattle office, Guadalupe gestured and fussed over corporate greed, about the right thing being utterly unimportant. She paced. I empathized, without reminding Guadalupe we needed an economy. When the fire of her frustration burned down, she sat back and asked, "How do we teach them to give a shit?"

"Good question." I poured myself a glass of merlot.

Chandra looked up, catching me with her quiet, intense gaze. "You asked us to watch that horrid meeting just to show us that this path is dead."

I raised my glass and nodded in acknowledgment.

After the door closed behind them 10 minutes later, Susannah plopped on the couch and poured herself a glass of sauvignon blanc. She brushed long dark hair away from sky-blue eyes and sipped her wine with purpose. After a long moment, she let out a noisy sigh. "Chandra's quieter than I expected her to be. Maybe you frighten her."

I smiled. "She parcels her words out like gold. And mostly, they are."

Susannah nodded and we turned to other matters of governance. Tomorrow, I had meetings on infrastructure and safety, and Chandra and Guadalupe had an assignment. Each was to find one regular person—a laborer, a teacher, a shop owner—

willing to move to New Olympia for a year. We would subsidize moving. Only that; it was coming from my personal budget. Still, the basic state stipend would be enough to buy food and pay for housing. There were 40,000 empty dwellings out of session, 15 in. Two new residents a night was like two drops in a dry riverbed. Not a program, but a series of tests.

Sunset spilled gold and umber across the glassy surfaces of the tallest buildings before I escaped to wander the city. I wore a long blue coat and a tight black hat. Just a middle-aged blond woman out for a late-spring walk. Never mind the black-clad guards behind me with dogs and the small drones scanning the area around me.

The crowd sounded good, upbeat, chatty.

Tourists. Workers. Buskers. Families. Pike Place's iconic "Market" sign glowed primary red and the air smelled of fish and flowers.

Seattle would never retreat. We'd just keep building more sea wall. The latest iteration had added 10 feet. West Seattle, visible from here as a low-lying hump of hills that projected into the sound, had climbed up and away from its beaches. Olympia had been doomed for lack of elevation. It had no place for a wall, just a thousand inlets for the South Sound that also served as outlets for multiple river basins. Seattle had the resources and will to wall itself safe. West Seattle could climb away from drowned beaches. Olympia's two choices had been move or drown.

Downtown hummed with laughter, music, hawkers. Night-clubs, shows. Seattle was the "hot" city on the West Coast. With a little help from government. From me. But frankly, not much. The people I'd lost the arguments with the night before had earned the right to argue with me.

I climbed up University Street. High-rise on high-rise on high-rise. The occupants of a mere 10 of these buildings could fill most of New Olympia's squat five-story housing.

A rooftop bar in the Nickels Building offered a view of other rooftops spread below it. Rhodies and azaleas bloomed in pots, and rooftop gardens were dark with freshly turned soil or spring-green sprouts. Laughter still inhabited Seattle—and safety. The rich weren't going to move because I asked them to.

I hesitated, chose a black metal table by the edge of the balcony. Two of my minders took a table near the wall and watched me watch the city. Embedded communication tech would let us talk if we needed to.

A short, thin middle-aged man pulled up a chair at my table. Nondescript, with regular features and the beginnings of a bald spot, undistinguished in any particular way. "Can I buy you a drink?"

Tempting. But I wasn't stupid. I'd order my own. "No. But thank you." I pulled off my cap. Ran my fingers through my hair.

His voice sounded soft and sweet. "Do you mind company?"

"No."

He hadn't recognized me yet. After he sat, I looked directly at him.

"Do I . . . *Governor!*" He stood.

"No. Stay."

He leaned away, one step already taken, poised to flee. "I didn't vote for you."

"I don't care." I smiled my best Louise Smith smile at him. Just a public servant. Nothing to see here. "Join me."

After a minute, he sat, and after a minute more, his shoulders relaxed and he almost smiled. "Pretty night," he whispered.

"Yes."

"I didn't mean to intrude. You just looked . . . lonely."

That hit a mark I seldom noticed anymore. I flinched. "I'm thinking."

He flushed, looked down.

I spoke into the awkward void. "I'm thinking about New Olympia. How to get people to go there."

"Why?"

Wasn't that just the question? But I countered. "Why not? Would you go?"

"Me?"

I laughed. "Yes. I did after all." Not that moving the governor's mansion was anything like moving a normal person, or even a displaced family.

"I have a house. Here, in Seattle. If I sell it, I don't know if I can get back in five years if I want to."

Real estate. Seattle's golden goose and Achilles' heel. "What if you could rent your place for the cost of your mortgage?"

"I couldn't."

Because I had helped champion rent control. "What else?"

He blushed. "And I like the opera. There's no opera way out there."

"I like the opera, too."

I wore an earbud. One of my minders spoke into it. *Frank Smithson. Inherited a concrete company. Built part of the sea wall. Votes for your opponents. Two kids.*

It irritated me to know people's names before they offered them to me. I made a mental note to remind staff not to give me personal information unless someone was a threat or I asked for the data. "Thank you for saying hello. And for the honest answer."

He nodded, smiled. And fled the moment I stood up.

A woman about half my age recognized me, gestured for me to join her. I did. I'd seen her somewhere. Ebon skin with long, black hair caught in a net. She wore a trendy emerald-green pantsuit. "Kinady," she stood and offered an elegant and long-fingered hand. "I interviewed you for Seattle News Now."

I reached across the table, shook her hand. Her nails were perfect blue ovals with stars on them. We hadn't met in person, even in the interview, but I'd seen her on newsreels and in press audiences multiple times. Always stand-up-and-notice pretty. "You talked to me about the military bases we bought?"

She interpreted the question as an opening. "Yes. Do you mind if I ask a few follow-up questions?" Her smile was broad and friendly. "I'm freelancing now."

"I can schedule time with you later this week."

"I heard the Chinese . . ."

I stood. "Thank you, Kinady. Nice to see you again." I didn't want Kinady to move to New Olympia. Reporters were required for democracy, but they were also why governors couldn't ever say a single wrong word. "I will set up a time."

A signal. Staff would tell Susannah, who would set up a meeting, and I'd lose an hour for prep and 20 minutes for the interview.

I left, and before I'd had so much as a single glass of water. Back at ground level, the streets were so packed the guards walked close enough for me to hear the dogs pant.

The next morning, we met in my most impressive Seattle conference room. Chandra looked stunned by the sweeping views of downtown and peekaboo sightings of Puget Sound. Birds wheeled by the window. Guadalupe proudly showed me pictures of three families, all brown-skinned and dark-haired, with two children peering out from behind one of the men. "They will go, maybe start a restaurant." Guadalupe watched me closely, looking as much like a student who wanted a good grade as a 63-year-old woman.

"Thank you." I told her, genuinely pleased. "That's fabulous. I'll write a personal note to the families and send it when staff contact them tomorrow." Regular people like Guadalupe—well, regular activists like Guadalupe—could do so much more than I could. Why the hell did I forget that over and over?

I glanced at Chandra.

She smiled. "I found a piano teacher willing to move if we help her move her piano. I said we would do it." She projected a picture of a diminutive Asian woman with wispy white hair and deep wrinkles.

Less impressive than Guadalupe's find, especially since the piano teacher was a senior citizen. But, I thought, better than I'd done. I asked, "Chandra, why did you choose her?"

The girl offered me a wise smile. "Every city needs music, and Amelia Wu is the matriarch of a large family."

Well.

The seven days went quickly. We collected 30 people in all, which was 10 more than my budget had planned for. My efforts accounted for two.

Susannah found me a donor to cover the costs. God bless the chiefs of staff of every elected official everywhere.

We were making progress and learning lessons. But in a week, I would have to stop this foolishness and run back full tilt into campaigning and the other duties I was giving half-time to.

I gathered Chandra and Guadalupe together. "Where shall we go now?"

"Spokane?" Guadalupe suggested.

I shook my head. It was a gateway to Washington, but military intelligence suggested it would fall to Idaho soon. Not through actual war, of course, but Spokane's people (mostly) liked the Idaho ideology of every man, woman, child, wolf, and dog for themselves. "Walla Walla?" Guadalupe asked.

"No. But that's a good idea. I'll have the Border Patrol tell immigrants they let in through Walla Walla and Vancouver that we'd look kindly on them locating in New Olympia."

"Can you make them?" Guadalupe's voice fell to a mumble as she said, "I know it's not what you normally do."

"And become a dictator?" Spokane might be falling in love with a dictator in Idaho, but Washington wouldn't go there on my watch. "People need the freedom to move where they want. We'll encourage immigrants to choose New Olympia, but I won't force anyone."

Guadalupe's slight grin signaled relief. So she had become comfortable enough to test me. Good.

Chandra stood and moved to the window. "What smaller cities are being relocated? I hear there were votes about that, money given."

Her question was good. The Long Beach peninsula had been gone for 10 years, and Ocean Shores and Moclips lost as well. The tribes were taking care of themselves; gambling increased near the end of the world we used to know. The Quileute Tribe and the Lummi Nation had each moved significant parts of their reservations to safety. We had helped, a little. But the tribe had been pretty damned capable. I stood and stretched, providing a moment for my minders to catch up and whisper in my ear. *Sultan's downtown.*

I did remember. Good choice. "Sultan. On the Skykomish River. We prohibited rebuilding two years ago, and this is the year of return." Return. The law called it managed retreat, but return sang happier in my heart.

Guadalupe's eyes widened slightly. "How the hell did we lose Sultan? That's not near the sea."

Chandra spoke up. "Atmospheric rivers. The Skykomish flooded Sultan and Gold Bar badly in 2036 and again two years ago. They hadn't really finished rebuilding yet." She looked proud of herself and called up a few more facts. "One hundred seventy-two homes were destroyed, and 86 other structures. A chunk of Highway 2 as well."

I had signed a disaster resolution for that. But somehow it hadn't surfaced in my head, not really. Sultan wasn't huge, but it had been home to families and lost a historic downtown. "I'll have two days."

Susannah asked, "A formal visit?"

I didn't hesitate. "No. I'll stealth in."

"Does that work?" Guadalupe asked.

Susannah answered for me, laughing. "Sometimes."

Chandra raised her hand for attention. "Can we go next week instead? Saturday?"

"Why?" I asked.

"That's the town's *LastDay*. The burning."

I'd been to Olympia's burning. I'd hated it. But she was right. I glanced at Susannah. "Can we make that happen?"

"I have to move out some meetings on next week's agenda, and the interview you just scheduled. Kinady."

"OK."

Chandra spoke up, an unusual note of pleading in her voice. "I went to school with Kinady. Can she come?"

A reporter? Chandra had started to earn my trust, but now she wanted me to jump off a ledge. I stopped myself from saying no. "Why?"

"She sees things I don't. All of her work bends toward fixing things."

Even when she had to skewer me or one of my programs to do that? But it wasn't like I could populate New Olympia by myself, and damn it, the town needed people. I hesitated.

"Please?"

The piano matriarch had, in point of fact, already convinced two of her children to go with her. And they had children. But a reporter? A hard look at the trust and hope in Chandra's eyes convinced me to surrender. "If she'll agree not to broadcast unless I say she can."

"But you won't censor her? I mean, if you do let her do a show?"

I relented. "Very well. She can meet us there."

We rode in a line of armored trucks camouflaged with dents and scrapes and missing bumpers. I had ordered the stealthy appearance, including requiring my guards to dress in old jeans and leave the dogs in the car with a minder.

Blue sky hung over a late spring day. Sultan's streets were potholed and cracked, spalled at the edges, and in a few places missing altogether. The houses, of course, had been scraped off the selected streets by the Department of Ecology cleaning crews. Street trees and yard trees showed off their best bright new growth, the greens of katydids and not-quite-ripe limes. They would stay behind to capture carbon and retain memories until they flooded or burned away. Glass and metal would have been recycled, the best wood as well. Toxins carted away and properly disposed of. Street art re-homed. Now, a pyre of consumables built on a parking lot rose almost two full stories. Rotted but unpainted wood from fences and side yards, paper and cardboard, cotton draperies. It was deliberate. Everything could have been recycled or trashed. But every town we retreated from deserved a funeral pyre. There were at least 100 cars and trucks pulled onto the high school parking lot and field already. Residents whose homes were high enough and didn't need utilities, and thus had been allowed to stay. Former residents. Curious neighbors. Press and pseudo-press. National Guard, as well, scattered here and there in soft camo. Tables and chairs and bright canopies filled the center of the field. People grouped and mixed and mingled. Children played. Dogs barked at one another.

It was going to be hard to stay here all day. So much pain.

More people came. Families. Women holding hands and glancing at the burn pile with distrust or loathing. Children running and playing, laughing while they waited for the last town barbecue. The river that had destroyed the town ran gray-blue and fast, holding itself neatly inside its banks as if it were well behaved.

Chandra walked up to me, Kinady striding behind her. Today, Kinady's shirt was a blue brighter than the sky. Darker blue and carmine beads clattered together in her newly braided hair. She wore drones like decorations, small and expensive. A tribute to her success, even if they did look like pet insects.

Food came in on trucks labeled with the names of various climate NGOs and community groups, even Elks and Rotarians—vestiges of an old world almost lost. I pulled my hat down and went to wander through the tables and gathering crowds.

No one expected me; no one saw me.

A pair of old men commented on the size of the crowd. "Vultures coming to watch us die."

His companion answered him with a bit of a growl. "People need entertainment."

The first speaker laughed. "It's not Burning Man. Did you ever go? That was entertainment. We were making a new world. The man was 80 feet tall the year I went. What the hell do we burn the town for?"

The other man laughed. "So we know it's gone."

"I knew that when it flooded."

I passed them, lost the thread of their talk. Catharsis. Not creation. I'd been to see the man burn once, and that had been defiant and showy. City pyres were acquiescent and sad. Small, to keep the carbon cost low. A woman told two daughters, "Stay away from the fire until it starts up, burns a few minutes. Someone hid fireworks in the Ocean Shores pyre."

Guards watched this fire. Not just because of me. This day would wipe away a city founded in the 1880s. Its loss wouldn't please anyone. Generations had owned some of the houses we'd forced them out of. Nobody liked it. Return hurt. Every town fought its own demise. Not that it made a difference. Lawyers, insurance companies, and climate events were bigger than the people who lived in these places. Every adaptation stuck a knife in someone's heart.

I passed a middle-aged man sitting on a bench by himself, fiddling with a drone. He was dressed in old clothes, and a large backpack sat on the ground beside the bench. It had tools and water bottles and a red raincoat tied to it.

I picked up my pace, trying to force myself out of the morose mood squeezing my chest.

A hand on my arm. Kinady. I turned to look at her, a brightly colored dark woman in a sea of mostly white rural Washington faces, her body so full of energy that even when I stopped to give her an opening, she bounced in place. "What do you want to tell people?" I asked her.

She spoke fast, smiling and speaking with her whole body. "I found a family I want to talk about. They moved here 20 years ago, from Mexico. Fleeing Tijuana. Now they have to flee again. And the Xiangs. They came here from China. And the Paulsons, who have been here as long as they know. All of them. Not one kid moved away. Now everyone has to go. I will make their stories compelling."

I pursed my lips. Thought about the mother and the old men. "Can you make the burn pile mean something? The sacrifice?"

She nodded.

I wanted more. "Can you keep the story from being sad?"

Her smile had a sardonic edge to it. "Maybe not. Not for these people." She glanced toward the crowd continuing to gather around the food, to take plates. Kinady continued, "Chandra asked me to talk about Amelia Wu. She's already moved to New Olympia. Chandra and Susannah found her a condo on the top floor. When she practices, her music will spill out into a park."

Chandra hadn't told me that. Surely she was going to? I could see the story Kinady was putting together in her head. "So people will see that New Olympia is a valid choice?"

"One of many good choices, but yes."

Could she pull it off? She was following the rules I had lain down, asking. Legally, she didn't have to do that. I really didn't want to like a reporter. "Chandra wants you to include me in the story, right?"

Kinady smiled at me as if I were a 5-year-old who had earned a silver star. It irritated me, a little. The people from Sultan probably had places to go already. But some might not. And there were two other towns on the list for this year. Maybe no more for a few years. Maybe. If the damned disasters slowed down.

Kinady was a reporter. She'd be hard on me. "You're going to tell them how I failed."

She licked her bottom lip, hesitated, then leaned slightly toward me. "I'm going to say that it takes more than you to succeed."

I recalled the new well in New Olympia. The old well in the drowned city had given to us freely and the new one took engineering, force, and effort. Hope, and bringing a heartbeat to New Olympia, also required engineering and force. Kinady was a force of human nature. And Chandra. And me, to the extent I could get out of the way. "Go ahead. Have fun. Tell me when you need me."

She grinned. "Can *I* be the one to reveal that you're here?"

I swallowed.

"Not yet." Her eyes danced with the idea of her story. "In a little bit. In fact, I'd like it if no one knows you're here for another hour."

"I often get recognized."

"I know." She leaned toward me, as if offering a hug, but then stopped herself.

We stood self-consciously apart for a moment. Then I told her, "Thank you."

She disappeared into the crowd despite her bright colors. Maybe I would regret this. But maybe not. There would be no single answer to New Olympia's population problem, no one way to bring life and heart to the city when we politicians weren't there.

The firefighters coming to keep the last fire safe pulled up in a truck. We had robots, but I knew from briefings that we chose humans on purpose. Somehow it was far more fitting to see the

young men and women in bright yellow uniforms with white helmets and silver tape and big black boots. They looked appropri-
ately somber.

I tugged my hat further over my eyes and headed to find
Chandra and offer her a more permanent job on my staff. She
had a good eye for detail and strategy. I could use that. I'd get a
grant for Guadalupe's operation, help the people on the peninsula
who weren't going to be displaced by flood. They were threatened
by depleted fisheries, strong storms, and dry forests. Washington
needed a good leader there.

And after that, in spite of the horror of it, the sadness and
loss, a part of me was looking forward to Sultan's funeral pyre.

Out of ashes.

BLACKSTART

July 18, 2032, 11:30 PM

Katharine Wilson peered down at the lights of Phoenix through a small window. Up here in the stratosphere, in a shared observation room on the Voyager tourist balloon, the temperature hovered at about seventy degrees. Below her, even though it was almost midnight, the megacities of Phoenix and Tucson suffered through a hundred degrees, even in the dead dark of night. Brutal.

The affable pilot, Bran, smiled at her. "Your turn."

"Thanks." Finally, the view she had paid for—a chance to sit in a clear room high above the Earth. As she started down the short hallway, her wrist buzzed and she looked down to see "Happy Birthday" scrolling along her forearm. Her heart quickened for a moment, then fell again as she realized it was merely a robo-greeting from a communication company she used to run.

She had imagined something like the glass walkway above the Grand Canyon on steroids. Indeed, it was clear, but metal supports bisected the glass so often that looking down felt like seeing through a stained-glass window. Padded dots at the joints were designed to hold her weight. She crept onto them, knees and hands on the round cushions. She made out a dark wildlife corridor, a seam between the two desert cities. Rural areas lined the corridor, and lights and streets and cars marched in ever-denser and brighter lines into the two cities. The green and red lights of an airplane blinked by below her. She searched for Arizona City, where Carmen had chosen some stupid uniform job instead of following Katharine into business. Their geosynchronous position put them just south of the small town.

The least Carmen could have done was send a birthday note. Katharine did that much for Carmen every year. Ungrateful. She swallowed hard, pushing her bitter disappointment down into her belly where she couldn't taste it. She'd expected Carmen to come with her. It had taken a year to secure two slots. Carmen had turned her down just last month, muttering something about training at her job.

At least the spare slot had sold for a profit.

Katharine shook herself, took a deep breath, and braced to roll over for the real view she'd come to the stratosphere for. A friend had told her it was worth ten times the price of the ticket.

As the pilot had suggested, she felt her way through the careful turn, settled her haunches and back and head against the pillow-dots, and then opened her eyes to see the stars. Only a few struts blocked this view. Stars. More than she had imagined existed. Bright lights. The foggy river of the Milky Way. Her breath caught in her throat; she let it out slowly. As she took air back in, the stars seemed to fill her. Awe. More. Her stomach rolled and she felt like a feather loose in the universe. Dizziness took her in waves. If she weren't lying down, she'd fall. She closed her eyes again. To her surprise, they were damp.

So small.

She felt so big, so much a part of everything, and so small, the contradiction strong enough to dizzy her.

Katharine rolled over, looking down. She hadn't expected the stars to unsettle her so. Being higher than an airplane suddenly felt too high, and the struts she had hated gave her a way to feel connected to human ingenuity. She reached her hand to her throat and felt the jewel her daughter had given her. A geode, really, polished, and full of smart gear. It ran half of her personal systems. "Call Carmen," she whispered, her head still light and dizzy.

A whisper came in her ear. "Calling Carmen Wilson."

In three rings Carmen's voice cut through. "Yes, Mom. I can't talk."

"Just for a moment? It's so beautiful up here."

"Oh yeah," Carmen said. "The balloon. I forgot. Can you call after you come down next week? This is my first solo patrol and people go crazy on hot nights."

"Can't the cops deal with that?"

"Sometimes that's me. Sometimes I fight fires. Sometimes I'm a medic. I gotta go."

"Carmen?"

Nothing. Her daughter had hung up on her, on her birthday.

Movement caught her eye. Not movement. The movement of lights. No. Loss of light. It looked as if someone had flicked a switch and turned three-quarters of the lights below her off.

Her breath fled as the implications sunk in. At midnight, it was hot enough to kill people. Whole neighborhoods, maybe whole cities (who could tell from so high!) were now dark and hot, and soon would be light and searing. Self-driving cars would run without power—for a while. But not without communication. They depended utterly on the data cloud.

Carmen!

She breathed, waiting.

The lights didn't come back. She clutched her jewel.

"Katharine!"

The pilot. Bran. She took a last look at the darkened ground, at the sparseness of the points of light. Then she followed Bran's voice, climbing backward and reaching for the floor with her toes. As he took her hand to help her turn in the tight space—or maybe to comfort her—she asked, "What do you know?"

"The power is out. Worse, I can't communicate with anyone at home base. Just with the other Stratollites—they're the un-manned version of a Voyager." His face was colorless, his blue eyes wide. "Will you help calm the cabin?"

He knew she was an ex-CEO. The other eleven tourists were a mix. Five high school kids sent on a grant from the govern-ment. Two solo engineers—maybe from rival space companies.

One of them had bought Carmen's ticket. An old couple, heirs to some food fortune and likely to be of little help. A young couple from China who hadn't said a word in English, maybe didn't even speak it. She grimaced. "I'll help."

As soon as she started to gain order, Bran retreated to the cockpit.

The din of questions, squeals, and worries took a while to organize into four teams, all making notes about what they saw. Luckily, one of the students spoke Mandarin.

Almost nothing moved below. Here and there, the flash of a siren. Classic cars or maybe tractors with human controls.

From time to time, she tried calling Carmen. Nothing.

As soon as she could hand temporary control to the older couple, Katharine headed into the cockpit, where Bran labored over a screen built into a white plastic table. "What do you know?"

"It's a hack. Eco-idiots of some kind. Whole damned western grid. Texas to California. Power companies are cleaning up the hack now."

She swallowed. "They'll have to blackstart."

"Blackstart?"

"Bring it up from the outside in, one piece of the grid at a time."

The look on his face told her he still didn't get it.

"By hand. They have to bring it up by hand."

He swallowed, his thin Adam's apple bobbing. "That will take too long!"

"Yes." Days? "They'll have to get the right people to the right places."

"How are your fellow tourists?"

"I've organized teams to pinpoint lights. Where there's power, there will be cooling. One of the engineers got the nav computer to help geocode the lights. We're making a list for the people on the ground. Can you get the data to them?"

He looked pleased at her competence. "I think so. I've set up a comms relay between Stratollites. I'm talking to emergency managers in Texas."

"Do they have time for us?"

"Some. We're a priority because of the heat." He nodded toward the window. "There's a few satellite phones working down there, but regular communications channels are dead. Bring me your map data?"

She nodded. "I have to make a call first."

"I told you all communication is down."

She smiled. "I think I can figure something out." She was a communication exec, but before that she had been an engineer. Carmen had a jewel that matched hers. Katharine just needed to link the two.

July 19, 2032, 3:00 AM

Carmen walked as fast as she could manage while still looking like a real public safety officer, rather than a frightened one. Sweat ran down her back, bathed her face, and invaded the backs of her knees. It could only get worse.

The streets were full of newsbots and automated police, which was to be expected. They were also full of lost, hot families. Walking. It was hot enough for dead cars to be uncomfortable, but in two hours when the sun came up they'd turn into ovens. So people abandoned them. Families carried children and walked dogs, or carried dogs and walked children. Older people tried to help each other. The streetlights shed yellowed light on worried faces.

At least the hack had happened at midnight. It was possible no one had died because of heat. Yet.

Soon she would meet up with her boss, Ruthanna. Even though she had finished enough training to work on her own, Ruthanna had promised to check in with her at intervals. They had a planned meet-up location: a convenience store that Carmen had never imagined they'd need to use. Who expected a disaster on her first solo?

A young man carrying a toddler on his shoulders came over to her. "Miss?"

"Yes."

"Do you have water?"

"The city is working to get emergency stores to you. But I don't have distribution information available yet. Are you completely out?"

He looked resigned, and worried. "We had some in the car, but we already drank it."

"Find a place that will be shady."

"I know. But how will you find us?"

"Stay near major streets."

"I'm Bolo." He bounced so the sleepy toddler smiled. "This is Ricky."

"I'm Carmen. Good luck."

"Will we be okay?"

She couldn't tell him yes. Not with the heat that was set to lick up over the horizon. "I hope so."

He glanced up at his child. "We have to be."

She smiled at Ricky. "We'll do our best." She was supposed to help these people, but all three of her communication channels had died. The convenience store was only two blocks away. Maybe she could learn something there.

Bolo left.

"Carmen!"

She blinked. Her mom? Didn't she know there was an emergency? "Yes."

"Are you okay?"

"Sure, mom." But oh! "How did you reach me? I mean, I know, the jewel. But it's not short-range."

"I patched together a relay. We can talk to other balloons up here."

Her mom was thinking about other people? "Do you have any news?"

Carmen stopped dead, listening, as her mom told her about the hacking, and that there might be a day to get through. A day in 127-degree heat. "Is there help coming?"

"Not for hours. Not with all the dead cars blocking the roads.

But I do have a list of locations with power."

Carmen let out a long breath. "How many?"

"There are three close to you."

"What kind of power? Will it stay on all day?"

"How would I know that? I can see lights. Look, can you get a file?"

"None of my personal comms work. But I can find a way to write. Can you hold on?"

"Of course."

One block down, Carmen spotted the convenience store. She had been half-afraid of looting, even though in reality that would probably come later. But Ruthanna stood in front of the store, and she had three other officers with her.

Carmen broke into a jog.

3:30 AM

Bran gestured for Katharine back to the cockpit.

She nodded. "Just a minute." She spoke the last three GPS points she had into her comms, and after Carmen acknowledged receipt, she slid into Bran's office and closed the door behind her. "What's up?"

"Did you reach your daughter?"

"I did. I gave her every point we've recorded." She glanced out the window, wincing at the light that had started to glow along the far horizon. "We won't be able to see power via light soon."

"No. But split your team. Send half to rest. Then I want you to watch for anything moving, especially vehicles."

"We're so high!"

"Use the tourist binoculars." He smiled gently, the flashing lights of displays reflecting in his eyes. "It won't be for long. Five Stratollites designed for Earth observation are heading our way. By tomorrow, we'll be tourists again."

Hopefully she'd be sleeping by tomorrow. She'd been up twenty-one hours already, but she didn't plan to sleep while people below her fried. "What about the power? Any news?"

"They've tried three cold starts, and they're going to have to do the blackstart you mentioned."

She barely managed to refrain from saying I told you so.

"They have engineers on the way. Please watch for their copters. The local fire stations have water trucks. It's not potable, but they can use it for cooling. Those are going out. And there's three military cargo planes on the way. PHX can take them. Distribution will be hard. Tell your daughter. Does she have any on-ground comms?"

"The amateur radio networks have come up."

"Thank God for people who love the past," Bran muttered.

She shifted, slightly uncomfortable in the tight space. Small displays that might has well have been phone screens showed the Earth below them, while others displayed data about height and pressure and more she didn't immediately recognize. The magic of being up here didn't show in this room, but the engineering fascinated her. "There aren't many sets or operators anymore."

Bran tapped something on his screen. "One of the phone carriers has set up some kind of testing relay people can use with phones."

"Really?" She'd read about that for years. The companies had fought it. "Which carrier?"

"People's Radio."

It had to be the smallest. Still, she'd relay that to Carmen. Any port . . .

"Someone is also working on making a network out of the cars. They're just stopped, but most of them still have power."

Another good idea. "How long till the power's back?"

"No one knows," Bran said. "I'm going to nap for an hour. Please send in one of the engineers."

*

10:00 AM

Carmen pulled her sunglasses out of her pocket. Since she was the only one able to communicate with her mother, they'd set her up on a rooftop patio on the tallest building in town, with a walkie-talkie to the Emergency Operations Center.

Someone had used a camp stove to make instant coffee for her and the amateur radio operator that shared her table. The bitter taste helped keep her awake while she wrote notes and coordinates on her paper.

Arizona City had fallen quiet. Her pencil scraped audibly across the paper. A few generators hummed, and voices wafted up from the streets. Most people were holed up, trying not to melt.

It could only get worse.

1:00 PM

The teenagers in the main room had been excited all night, but now they were exhausted. Katharine had kept four of them awake, split the engineers between shifts, and sent all of the other adults to bed. The midday heat beat down on the desert below her. The teenagers sat spread out, looking down, watching for flashes of light that were really signals for help. It required focus, and Katharine moved from watcher to watcher, encouraging them and telling and re-telling them how important a job they were doing. At one point, one of the boys looked at her and said, "Sit down and rest. We've got this for an hour."

He reminded her of Carmen.

She sat.

From up here, mountains that she'd climbed looked like clods of dirt struck from a giant's shoes, and the houses like grains of sand. In the far north of her view, the Salt River was a thin line of silver, and directly below, the Gila River looked like a gray hair. At the farthest edges of the incredible view, water became visible again, the pathetic remains of nearly-melted glaciers sticking to the tops of mountains.

8:15 PM

The table around Carmen had filled. The cars had turned out to be an effective relay, and the amateur radio had saved countless lives. There were two operators now, chattering back and forth to each other as they accepted slips of paper with data that needed to be relayed and wrote answers. Dusk had begun to fall on the eastern side of the city, but the heat felt as unrelenting as it had an hour ago. Ruthanna came up her. "That was pretty phenomenal first solo day."

"Yeah."

"Take a break. Some of the cavalry has arrived up above, and we have communication with two other Stratollites."

"How?"

"Amateur radio."

Carmen laughed. She touched the jewel that had kept her in communication with her mom, marveling yet again that the two of them could work together. A whole day, and not one word about how stupid it was to want to help the poor, or how she should accept her inheritance and become rich and powerful.

9:00 PM

Freed of her duties by the second shift, Katharine headed back into the observation bubble. The bright pink and orange sunset had finished falling off the edge of the earth, and the streets below her were dark again. Maybe even darker—some of the emergency power had spent its batteries or gas or whatever it had been running on. It probably wouldn't cool for a while. Bran had told her power would return soon, and she had chosen this place to watch.

Time passed. An hour. Two.

Light bloomed along the horizons. It spread toward the cities below her from two directions, then three, then from everywhere.

Katharine touched her jewelry, asked it to call Carmen. It took a moment to connect. "Do you see it?"

"Yes."

"You did great."

The line went quiet for a long moment, and then Carmen said, "You never told me that before."

Of course she had. Hadn't she? "I'm sorry."

"Happy birthday."

Katharine smiled. "Thanks." She rolled over, and this time when she looked up at the stars she didn't feel nauseous at all. She felt connected. Starlight fell through the balloon, through her, and all the way to the ground below.

FOR THE SNAKE OF POWER

Rosa rubbed at her eyes, trying in vain to focus on the map in front of her. The electronic image of the great—and greatly damaged—solar snake that covered the canals of Phoenix swam in her vision. The snake had been bruised, battered, and in a few places, actually broken by the huge dust storm that had enveloped the city three days ago. A haboob. Uncountable motes of dust carried in on a scorching wind and left behind to dim solar panels, catch in the wires that held them together, and clog the maintenance robots. Such tiny things to have done such damage. Forty-three deaths. Trees knocked down and signs ripped from the ground and hundred-year-old saguaros laid flat. But those weren't her problem. Power was.

The snake had been overengineered on purpose, built to supply the future. She'd been working with the snake's maintenance AI, HANNA, for two years now, and even with the dust and the damage, the vast, beautiful array should create enough power.

"HANNA?" Rosa addressed the AI, which listened through a button-sized speaker on her desk. "Have you figured out why the power drawdown keeps getting worse?"

Rosa had chosen an old woman's voice for the AI. It sounded calm as it said, "Not yet. I will keep looking."

A stray thought made Rosa tell it, "Look beyond the engineering. If you haven't seen a problem there, then the problem is somewhere else. Power storage? Legal?"

"Is that permission?" HANNA asked.

Rosa hesitated. But HANNA wouldn't ask if Rosa couldn't

give it permission. "Yes."

"Logged."

"I'm walking down to the closest break."

"You have worked 14 hours today."

The machine wasn't responsible for maintenance on *her*.

"Maybe if I see for myself, I'll understand. Goodnight."

"Goodnight, Rosa."

Rosa left the building, still wearing her blue Salt River Project work shirt. A hot, dry wind created a small cloud of dust that tickled her ankles. After half an hour, Rosa spotted the snake's glow from a block away. Its pale blue and yellow lights looked brighter than usual with the streetlights dimmed to half power.

As she stepped under the arch and onto the pathway, she startled as a maintenance robot scuttled overhead, a tiny broom stuck to one "arm" and an air puffer clenched in the other. It reminded her of a fantastical creature from fiction, half squirrel and half Swiss-army knife.

The path was busy. Two young women wearing roller skates and pushing children in carriages slowed her. Hoverboards and bicycles sped in both directions.

Her earpod pinged softly and she touched it. A newsnote, read in a flat masculine voice. "The Association of Solar Power raised rates yet again, citing a deficit of power. Brownouts are scheduled to begin at noon tomorrow. Schedules will be posted at 7:00 a.m."

In summer, brownouts killed. She clenched her fists.

As she neared the break, the walls separating the neighborhoods from the canal looked haphazard. A bit of chain link, a makeshift wooden fence, a neat brick section, an adobe segment with the shards of glass embedded in its top glittering softly in the snake's light. Her old home. She had been gone six years. She didn't recognize the people lounging against the walls, sharing beer and listening to music. Two young men stared at her, and suddenly she wished she had changed out of her SRP shirt.

As she passed, conversations lowered or changed tenor, although no one approached.

She reached the break and stopped under it, staring up. The snake undulated throughout the city, sometimes only 20 feet above the canals and sometimes the height of a tall building, the design part art and all function. The taller loops reached for sun that buildings or bridges would block. This break was near where a segment began to rise. Three supports had come down. Solar scales had shattered on the pathway and, almost certainly, into nearby backyards. A few still dangled, askew, edges connected to the wire scaffolding that managed the panel's tilt.

The breach was serious, but a hundred yards beyond it the snake continued up toward the top of this curve, lights on, clearly working. Every two or three poles carried power and optics into underground conduits. Any break could only affect the area of the break plus two segments at worst. The snake had lost four segments of power here, but there were thousands. HANNA reported 153 segments out, which was less than 10 percent.

Tonight's low was expected to be 95, and next day's high 121. The rich often had their own systems. If not, they had cool places to go, and transportation to power if they needed it for oxygen tanks or powered wheelchairs. The poor wouldn't even be able to run a fan.

Rosa had held her grandmother's hand when she died of heat in the power wars of '32. She had been just seven years old, sweating and miserable, her head afire with heat and dehydration, singing to her grandmother. She'd felt her grandmother's hand go limp, had seen the life fade from her smile, her cheeks, her eyes. Rosa had cried, hot and miserable, and slept with her head on her dead grandmother's chest until her father found her there an hour later.

She swallowed, able as always to feel the slip of that hand into death. Some memories burned themselves into your soul.

Steps from behind drew her out of her reverie.

"Rosa. That you? That really you?"

Although she hadn't heard it for five years, the voice was family. Home. Rosa turned and smiled. "Inez."

"You work for power now? For SR f'ing P?"

Rosa took a step back, slightly put off by the sheer press of Inez's voice, and of her body, which was bigger than she remembered, broader and more muscular. The light from the snake and the path lights combined to paint Inez's face a dull blue. "Yes."

"You going to fix this?"

"SRP is doing everything possible to restore power . . ." The look on Inez's face made Rosa hear the corpspeak she was spilling out, and she stopped. Took a breath. Looked right at Inez. "If I can."

The two women stood quiet long enough for Rosa to wonder if Inez was as unsure of what to say as she was, then Inez said, "I knew you'd do okay. I'm sorry. I just didn't . . . expect . . . I didn't think you'd become . . ."

"The enemy?" Rosa smiled. "I'm not."

Inez merely stared.

They had been good friends once. Done homework together. Skipped school together. Yet Rosa felt a distance from Inez that bothered her. "Are you okay?"

"I got two kids. Mom's sick. Dad died."

"I'm sorry. About the sickness. Congratulations on the kids." She was stuttering. Was Inez married? She didn't remember. "Sorry about your dad."

"He was a bastard." Inez's shoulders relaxed a tiny bit and she smiled. "The kids are great. Lonny's five and likes to cause trouble. His little brother, José, he's small and smart."

"And your mom? I remember she used to make me chipotle and chicken soup when I had a cold." Inez's mom, Maria, had smiled whenever Rosa ate her soup, and Rosa had felt better whenever Maria smiled. "What's wrong with her?"

"She's been wishing to die since dad left us. But I don't want her to die."

"I understand. Remember my grandmother?"

"Yes." Inez swallowed and shifted her weight. "I came to tell you to be careful. There's people who don't care for SRP here. And you just raised the rates again."

"I didn't. Besides, SRP doesn't set rates anymore. That's the governor's Association of Solar Power. The ASP. A committee."

Inez narrowed her eyes. "People still hate SRP."

Rosa nodded. After her grandmother died, she'd hated SRP. She'd hated them until they championed the snake. Then she'd loved them. The snake was supposed to make power available for everyone, rich or not, as long as they wanted it. Since the rich had their own systems, the snake was a public work for the poor. The cheap power and net connectivity that ran down the snake had helped her compete in high school, helped her get grants for college, helped her with everything for five years. Now all that was threatened, and for no reason Rosa understood.

"You should go," Inez said.

Rosa nodded, glancing once more at the destroyed sections of the solar array. "I'm tired. I've been working all day."

"Killed a boy when that came down. Nine months old."

Rosa swallowed. "I'm sorry." That hadn't been in the regular news. But she'd be able to find the information if she looked. This neighborhood had its own news sources that flowed through the knots of idle poor like water running downhill.

"Come back on a better day," Inez's smile was faint, but genuine. "I want to know how you are."

Rosa thought about leaning in for a hug, but extended her hand instead. Inez took it, her grip strong. She repeated her request. "Come back."

"Soon." It felt like an empty promise and she wondered at that, unhappy with herself. What right did she have to ignore this place she'd come from?

The next morning, she arrived an hour early for her shift. As she threw her lunch into the crowded fridge, she said, "HANNA. Good morning. Anything?"

As always, HANNA was right there. "I found three large contributing factors. We have been working on the tracking system failures."

They had. For a year. "And there are still no parts. Go on."

"Weather."

Rosa sat down and began turning up her systems. "Like the dust storm from hell."

"And the one before that? No. It's an average of three degrees warmer so far this summer."

"I know that," Rosa replied.

"People have used seven percent more air conditioning."

She hadn't known that. The SRP staff infoweb loaded up on her screen.

"And power is leaving the system."

"I know." She scanned the web. The brownout schedule would post in 15 minutes. Call-takers had been pulled in early. The Emergency Operations Center would stay activated. A hot wind would come today. No storm. She blinked. "How much power? More than usual?"

"The usual amount. Twenty percent."

She frowned. HANNA was feeding her data slowly, making her think. One of its described duties was staff training, but she'd thought she was beyond most of that. "So it's 20 percent of power, no matter how much we generate?"

HANNA said, "It's a fixed amount equal to 20 percent of full capacity."

Rosa stopped moving. "That amount doesn't get reduced in an emergency?"

"No."

Her screen filled with snippets of contracts. She had interned with the law department; she could parse the language. As she reviewed the clauses HANNA sent, a deep revulsion rose in her.

The governor had signed away 20 percent of their power.

The SRP power grid was the snake, and it was meant for Arizona's poor and middle classes. Not for the cooler north. She poured a cup of coffee, took a deep breath, and went to find her boss.

Susannah Smith was in her office, drumming her fine, thin fingers on the table. Her usually curled hair hung around her shoulders, still damp, and she looked as tired as Rosa felt. Nevertheless, she glanced up and smiled as Rosa entered. "Did you sleep last night?"

"Not well."

"Is everything OK?" Susannah turned her attention back to her computer. "The lists just posted. I hope you brought a lunch. We may not get out today."

"I have a question."

"Ask away."

"The governor sold our power. Did you know that?"

Susannah turned back around. "We've always sold off our excess power."

"This isn't excess. Chicago and Salt Lake have first dibs. That's new."

For a brief moment, surprise flashed across Susannah's face, and her lips opened to speak, but she clamped them into a frown. She shrugged. "This is not our problem. We support maintenance, not contracts."

"But surely in an emergency . . ."

Susannah's glare was uncompromising. "We can't fix it."

Why did Susannah look so angry? "Why not?"

"Not you and I. And not today." Susannah stood up, which made her a few inches taller than Rosa. "Can I help you prioritize your work?"

Rosa wasn't ready to give up. "Who can change it?"

"The ASP." Susannah took a step toward her, not menacing, but pressing. "Go on. We've all got full plates today, and long days."

True enough. "I can't—"

"Go."

Susannah had never used that tone of voice with her. Rosa went, angry tears stinging the corners of her eyes and nails digging into her palm.

Back in her office, HANNA swept her into work and she spent the morning cataloguing the missing solar panels, checking HANNA's designs, and approving orders for materials and for the maintenance bots. At least they didn't need to worry about the price of replacement panels. The governor had managed to get an emergency declaration and FEMA would pay.

Every way she could think of to fix this was constrained by the governor's bad contract, or slowed to idiocy by the multitudes of safety mechanisms that threaded throughout SRP—half of them relics from the days when power ran on high-voltage lines and touching it killed.

Right before lunch, Rosa sent a note to Callie, who had been her formal mentor when she started this job, and who had continued to help her. Callie could get anything through the stifling bureaucracy. She agreed to meet in Rosa's office for lunch.

Callie plunked her huge frame in the chair and threw her head back, almost dislodging the big, messy bun of gray hair that crowned her head. "Are you as tired as I am? The phones are crazed, and there's three old women with protest signs out front. Hard to spin this."

Rosa told Callie what she'd learned, and shared her conversation with Susannah.

Callie frowned. "That's way upstream. There's nothing we can do."

The word we gave Rosa hope. "Are you sure?" She glanced at her computer. "It's 118 degrees already." Her voice rose. "People will die, to give power to Chicago, where's it's only 92 degrees. There's nothing fair about that!"

Callie shook her head and popped open a coffee bulb. "No. But you and I can't change it. Policy. I can get stuff done, but only to support SRP or the workers." She sipped her coffee, brows furrowed. "You mess with this, you might get fired."

"I told Susannah. She was surprised. I could see that in her eyes. But she sent me away."

"Susannah's been here long enough to know what's what. Some things." Callie rolled her eyes and held out a coffee bulb. "Have one of these."

So Callie wasn't going to help her either? Rosa took the coffee, and drank so fast she burned her tongue.

During her next break, she used her personal phone to try calling the governor. The lines were busy.

Every little thing she did to help fix the snake felt like pulling a single needle out of a ball of cactus. This shouldn't be an emergency, and they shouldn't be using workarounds and running bots past their maintenance cycles. They should have time to be careful.

She ran into Callie on the way out of the door. "This is still wrong," she told her. "Three people died already. Old people. In one day of brownouts. It will get worse."

"The city is opening cooling shelters."

"For how many people?"

The look on Callie's face told her it wasn't enough, and she didn't even answer the question. She just said, "You're doing your best."

"It's not good enough."

"All you can do is your best."

Rosa stared into Callie's eyes. "Maybe I can do better."

It was already bedtime when she finished wading through the heat to her one-room apartment. Someone had posted the brownout schedule on her door, and a list of power conservation tips. She glanced at it, realized she had two more hours of cooling, and passed out on the bed in her uniform.

When she woke near dawn, her limbs were heavy with a dark anger she couldn't put any images to. Sweat beaded her brow and clung to her hair. As she stared out the window at the whitening sky, the anger pushed her out of bed and into a clean uniform. She ate a handful of berries and two pieces of toast, then plaited her hair into long braids that would be cool.

She stepped outside and started toward work, then she stopped. If she went in this morning, the anger would consume her. She had felt pride in her work until yesterday. Not now. She worked for the power company, and she knew what it was to die from lack of power. Her hands shook, so she clenched her fists. She turned and walked fast back toward her old home. She could lose her dream, her job. But if she could save a grandmother somewhere . . .

Usually, the long canal soothed her. But this morning, the whole thing—the wide canal, the arching snake of power, the graffiti on one wall, the elegant natural art on the bridges—all of it felt like separation.

Inez was easy to find; her mother and sister still lived in the same old, faded green house. While the sister told Rosa where to find Inez, she kept glancing warily toward the SRP logo on her shirt. But she asked no questions.

Inez sat on the front stoop of a pop-up brick house, small and square and exactly like the three next to it except for a mural of a donkey on the side wall. Inez's children were both slender and dark-haired and shy. After introductions, Rosa asked, "Who matters here now? Who tells the neighborhood things?"

Inez stood, the boys behind her, the taller one peering out and the shorter one hiding behind Inez's ample right thigh. "What news do you have?"

Rosa told her about the contracts.

Inez looked more angry than surprised. After a few moments, she asked, "Do you remember Penélope López? She was two years behind us in school."

"Maybe." A thin girl with short dark curls who liked high-heeled boots, even in summer?

"She's got a local show. Regular dissenter, that one. A good girl." Inez picked both boys up, balancing one on each hip. She pounded on her neighbor's door and shoved the boys inside, then led Rosa to Penélope, who still wore high-heeled boots, but was taller now, and angry. Rosa told her story and Penélope wrote.

As she talked, Rosa's stomach burned. She was an hour late to work, and she was wearing an SRP uniform and telling tales on the most powerful public company in Phoenix.

Next, Inez took her to Jack, a tall black man in dreads with a soft smile. He had read Penélope's post. "I love what you said. Truth to Power." His smile widened. "May I? It will be live. It will be now."

Rosa swallowed. "Who will see it?"

"Everybody."

Rose hesitated.

Inez watched her.

Jack smiled, full of patience.

Rosa nodded.

Jack handed Inez a camera so small Rosa kept losing sight of it. She was careful only to say what she knew, to use facts, and Jack asked her hard questions. When she refused to answer some, he said, "That's okay. You can refuse. That tells us as much as an answer."

That made her stop and breathe, and worry, but she kept going. She was saving a grandmother.

Jack held out a hand, leaned in, and hugged her, smelling faintly of smoke and apples. "You're brave," he whispered. He led her to the canal, and they stood near the break where the hanging wires showed. He asked her some of the same questions again while Inez zoomed in on her shirt and her brown face and long braids.

Rosa leaned into her words. It was hers now, her choice, her story, her anger.

An old woman who carried herself like a turtle came up and hugged her. She turned to Jack, who interviewed the old woman while she called for everyone to come and protest, to stand under the shade of the snake and be heard.

Penélope called Inez, and said she, too, would call for a protest.

Over the next hour, the paths under the snake began to fill. People brought water and food, chairs and signs. They also brought anger, children, dogs, and music.

Rosa did three more interviews.

By the time the Phoenix news channels showed up, the paths were full, and rumors that other neighborhoods had joined reached her. Even middle-class neighborhoods, ones that had their own power. A news program let her read their signs, which had been crafted with glue and glitter and fancier markers than the ones near Rosa. But they said the same things.

POWER TO PHOENIX

THE SNAKE IS OURS

POWER FOR ALL

As the day wore on, the signs grew angrier and more clever.

THE SNAKE FEEDS US ALL

GET THE SNAKE OUT OF OFFICE

FOR THE SNAKE OF POWER

A college-age couple resting on a bench shaped like a rock with thornless cactus arms recognized Rosa and stood up together, gesturing for her to sit. She blinked at them for a moment, but when the woman inclined her head and quietly said, "Thank you," Inez sat and pulled Rosa down next to her and the couple melted into the crowd.

Despite the snake's shade over the bench and the water flowing five feet from them, the heat punished. Protestors clumped together under the solar panels, and Rosa swiped sweat from her brow. Young men worked the crowd, selling metered pours of water from great sacs they rolled in front of them on red wagons. Newscams hovered in the air, some clearly violating the rules about proximity to people.

Felipe, who Rosa had burned for in eighth grade, came and shook her hand. His warm, sweaty touch drew a nervous smile and Rosa momentarily felt like her younger self even though Felipe dangled a girl of three or four on his hip.

An international news channel came by and interviewed her in horrible Spanish, and she managed not to laugh while she repeated her simple litany of facts. The reporter's camera zoomed in on the logo on her shirt. "You are a whistleblower?" he asked.

She shook her head. "I love my job, and SRP. But people had to know about the contracts. Three people died from heat already today. More will."

Voices rose. A water seller who had stopped near them after selling out climbed up on his wagon and called out, "Police!" He turned and faced Rosa. "They come for you! Go."

Rosa stood, confused. People bunched in front of her, some chanting *Save the Snake!* or *Power to the People!*

Inez climbed up on the back of the bench. Her eyes widened. "Riot gear."

In spite of the wilting heat, of a hot wind, of the sun now high overhead and unrelenting, in spite of all that, the crowd continued to bunch. Inez said, "They're blocking the police."

The water seller, peering back and forth like a crow from his vantage a foot or two higher than her, said, "Not for long."

A hand fell hard on Rosa's shoulder. "There you are."

Rosa turned to find Callie staring at her. She'd stripped off her uniform and wore a hat that *might* hide her face in such a large crowd. "Susannah locked you out of the building."

It didn't surprise Rosa, but it hurt.

Callie offered an unexpected smile and said, "I told this to the *Arizona Republic.*" She looked like she had just won the lottery, her eyes glittering with energy.

Rosa stuttered. "You . . . you did? Couldn't you get fired, too?"

"No. I retired before I talked to the paper. I came because of you. What you said to me, that we had to care, you made me ashamed."

"So you're safe?"

"Yes. I think so. But you're not."

"I don't mind." Rosa leaned in to hug Callie. "Thank you."

"I came to thank you. For saying you could do better. I decided I could, too."

Rosa smiled.

The water seller called, "Something's happening!"

Rosa glanced at him, but Callie said, "Wait."

When Rosa turned back, Callie told her, "HANNA and I did something before I lost access."

Inez, still balancing on the back of the bench, called out, "They're coming closer. We can move faster than they can. We should go."

Callie shook her head. "No need. HANNA helped me turn off the transmission."

Rosa blinked. "What transmission?

"The lines going to Chicago. I know someone with a backdoor to HANNA, and he helped me. It's enough. Just the protests might have done it. But you made me want to help. The governor will announce soon."

Rosa stared at her mentor, blinking back tears and sweat. Callie had always loved her job, always defended it. She had hated much of the process, but never the real work. And now she had been this insubordinate? "Will they arrest you?"

Callie was still grinning. "And admit their own AI helped?" She shook her head. "There will be a press conference. The governor will say she was going to use the money to repair the snake."

"Was she?" Rosa asked.

Callie shrugged. "Who cares? We win. People don't die."

The water seller said, "You should go."

Rosa looked at Callie. "Other money can pay for repairs."

Callie glanced at her watch. "It might already be over."

A roar from the crowd was hard to interpret, a wave of tired whoops and louder calls, a few whistles. The water seller said it first. "The brownouts are cancelled."

Rosa and Callie shared a long smile. In spite of the heat, Callie folded Rosa in her arms. She whispered, "I'll find you."

Rosa turned to help Inez down. By the time she looked for Callie again, she was gone.

"You did this," Inez said.

"I had help."

"This wouldn't have happened without you."

The water seller hopped off of his wagon. "The police are almost here." He began to move away, and Inez pulled Rosa after him, and in a moment the crowds had enfolded them both, pushing them down the river of people under the snake.

She had done better. She would find a way to bear the price. It felt good to be home.

HEROES

The distance between a mother and daughter can feel like an ocean. The morning after the Russians overran Vancouver, Canada, my daughter Lucienne and I sat side by side on a hard wooden booth in the Sacred Brew Coffeehouse, my coffee cup and her hot chocolate both empty. Across from us, Juliette twisted her empty cup in her hand and looked like she wanted to be anywhere else. Her lashes curled dark against her coppery skin, her gray-green eyes looked past us both. Lucienne fidgeted, glanced furtively at each of us, looking by turn angry with me and like Juliette was a goddess.

Juliette and I had already said the things we needed to. It felt awkward but sweet, like the mornings after she and I dumped our fear and stress in long, sweet lovemaking. I had used her to feel touched and noticed. She had enjoyed it. It had been release, never forever. One knows. We even said so. But in that moment the pending loss of her made me soft and frightened. I reached over and took her hand. "Stay safe," I said for the third time, as if I could charm the words.

"You, too." She took Lucienne's hand in her free hand. "Keep your mom safe."

"I will." My daughter's eyes were wide and wet, her lips tight.

The pending war intensified our basic natures. Lucienne became angry, and serious, and deeply thoughtful. I worried. I forgot where I put things and slept badly. Keeping my emotions in check became hard.

Juliette became brave.

Now, the threat bore down so hard my focus felt as sharp as a hawk's talon and I quivered with the need to flee. The border between Canada and us had never been defensive. It started as a quiet nod to neighbors who liked each other. It gained some teeth in the early terrorist years, and it still had those teeth. But there was nothing about that thin line between big countries that would stand up to a wall of robotic tanks or waves of battle drones.

Our packs were ready, locked in the trunk of the car. Extra clothes and toys and oddments of food from our nearly bare cupboards had been stuffed in nooks and crannies between the swivel seats. The parade of cars on the street outside the shop moved slowly, constrained by city rules, most of them overfull with two to three people in single vehicles. Every moment we waited crawled up my nerves. Lucienne looked at Juliette and the street but didn't let her gaze near mine. I set my empty cup down. "Now."

Lucienne held her slender wrist up and touched her wristlet to Juliette's, her eyes staring at her as if she could change the world with the force of her gaze. "Stay connected. Promise?"

"Yes." Juliette's voice sounded thick with unsaid words. She stood and came around the table, standing behind us. She kissed us Lucienne on her upturned cheeks, and brushed my lips with hers, hard and fast. A goodbye. She left, dropping her cup and ours in the bus bin just before she closed the back door quietly.

She had chosen to stay, picked a job as a sentinel and a relay. She had spent nights away at classes and acquired a few knives and found unseen places to strap them. Pointless against a war of machinery.

Lucienne and I weren't hers to protect. But Lucienne was mine, and we were leaving.

Outside, the sky a tapestry in shades of gray, some parts light with sun and others pregnant with rain. Right after we climbed into the car and doors closed, Lucienne said, "I hate you."

"All twelve-year-olds hate their mothers."

"I hate you more than anyone."

"I know."

The car lurched forward. We settled into silence and devices, as if this were any trip to school or work in spite of the fact that emergency supplies and far too many pre-teen sized clothes filled every spot in the car that we didn't.

To my surprise the car was able to cross Lake Washington on the 520 bridge and catch side streets to interstate 90. National Guardsmen in bright orange vests with guns and knives waived cars forward and forward and forward again in spurts, letting new vehicles in from the side roads and the onramps in clumps and then letting the main group of us inch forward again. They appeared to be getting silent instructions from the same emergency traffic control that fed the cars. Perhaps they were as extraneous as Juliette would surely be.

American military vehicles rumbled past from time to time, some in camouflage colors like the gray sky above, and sometimes Army green. It was hard to see the soldier's faces, but they stood or sat stiffly.

I had stayed too long. My company had paid me a generous bonus to stay, and Lucienne had been working on a final school project. Juliette held me every night, warm and alive and sweet.

Besides, the Russians hadn't seemed real.

Lucienne alternated between glaring at me, fiddling with her wristlet, sleeping, and talking to her friends. Most of them had already left. Only two remained in Seattle: Lisa on a houseboat in Lake Union and Scott in a warehouse near the docks.

From time-to-time Lucienne narrated the news for me, and all of it seemed to be about numbers. Her voice came out flat and calm. "Forty thousand people have left the city this morning. All lanes of I5 southbound are stopped. Two northbound lanes have been opened for southbound traffic." A few moments later. "Thirty-two hundred people in Vancouver, British Colombia are reported dead."

While I gasped at that, Lucienne did not. She might as well have been playing a video game. "You know this is real?" I asked in spite of my better judgment.

She rolled her eyes.

Just after we crested the pass and started heading down toward Cle Elum, she gave a little gasp. "Juliette saw one. She sent me a picture."

The car braked and we swayed and then it started more slowly. I peered out, but there was nothing to see but lines of cars with dimmed lights and tall trees and stars. "Saw what?"

"A Russian tank. With robots. On the freeway. She sent me a picture."

"Can I see?"

She held her wrist up. The image had been taken at an odd angle, with a street light askew so it looked like it was about to fall down. The tank was light gray against a dark gray sky, all hard angles and sharp lines looming over the optically tilted light pole. It struck me hard, but I swallowed and squinted at it, trying not to be frightened. "I don't see the robot drivers."

"They don't look like people." She stared out the window, lying down so her view had to be mostly sky and the occasional tree. "We could walk faster than the car is going."

"We can't leave the car. We need it to sleep in."

"I don't want to live in the car."

I pointed at the mounds of stuff all around us. "Do you want to carry all this?"

She dug a piece of paper and a pencil out of her backpack, changed her seat so she sat up straighter, and started writing things down.

"Is that a list?"

"Hmmmhmmm." Her head bobbed up and down, her soft red curls catching a ray of afternoon sun. As usual, the weather had changed when we crossed the spine of the Cascades. Here, the sky was a dusty blue just darkening toward the gray-blue of dusk. The sun, behind us, would fall over the mountains soon.

"What is it a list of?"

"Everyone back home."

"We should start looking forward."

She practically snarled at me. "Isn't it bad enough that we left?"

I grit my teeth, clamping down on my anger. After I had taken enough breaths to feel back in control, I changed the subject. "Is the *Times* broadcasting anything?"

"Bellingham surrendered."

Such a strange phrase. It stuck in my heart, making me heavy with something deeper than fear. Dread? Bellingham was closer to Vancouver than Seattle, a medium-sized town known for artists and tourists and expensive houses. Seattle would not surrender so easily, but what had Bellingham faced to force that?

"There's fighting in Lynwood."

Even closer to Seattle. We had a friend in Martha Lake, which was near Lynwood. But she had left three months ago, urging us to go. I had wanted to wait for Lucienne to get out of junior high. Better to move between high schools. I laughed, bitter. Better to pretend everything was fine. Until you couldn't anymore.

The traffic in front of us stopped.

A woman in an orange vest rapped on the window.

I opened it a sliver, peering out at her. She was my age, or maybe older, with a grim smile. "Are you two okay?"

I nodded.

"Do you have food?"

Again, I nodded. Lucienne watched us quietly.

"Get off at the next exit."

"There's nothing there." I knew that. We needed to go one more exit to get to the stores or restaurants in Cle Elum. It was downhill. But I nodded, fully intending to ignore her.

"We're pulling everyone who is okay off the road to let babies and sick and the like have a head start. Take the opportunity to sleep." She rattled a can and an orange spot appeared on my windshield, some of the spray coming back to dust the edge of one of the other windows. "Hey!" I yelled at her.

She ignored me.

I watched her back, fuming, then leaned back in my seat. "We should have left a week ago."

"We shouldn't have left at all," Lucienne snapped. She pointed at the other side of the highway. It periodically filled with military trucks, but I hadn't seen any cars on it for hours. "We could go back home. That way is clear."

I'd read analysis that suggested if the Russians controlled Vancouver and Seattle, they could run the whole Northwest. "We have to go east."

Lucienne's anger filled the small car, washing against me, tempting me to rise to it and say something I'd regret later. I fought to stay silent, watching the sky roll by.

After a while she said, "Juliette is fighting. She has a gun. I didn't know she had a gun."

"How do you know?"

"We're friends. When her friends post a picture of her, I see it."

"What about your friends in Boulder?" That's where we were going. I had social media friends there. One had said he'd take us in for a few weeks. It was something. "Are they on your list?"

"They're not in any danger."

"Neither are we."

"That's the problem."

I sighed. It wasn't, not to me. Lucienne hadn't lost anyone close to her. Death was movies and a video games and books, but it wasn't real.

She pointed up. "Planes."

"Maybe you shouldn't look at pictures of Juliette. Not if she's fighting." Did I have to tell Lucienne she might see Juliette die? Did I have to spell the risk out as if she were two?

"The planes are going into Seattle."

"What direction are they flying?"

"They're coming from the south."

Ours. Thank god.

The lines of cars started moving again. A blond teen girl in an orange vest made everyone with orange paint on their cars get off the highway. We were in an abandoned ski area lot, the pavement overgrown with weeds but serviceable enough. The car followed directions, and parked us in a mob, with just enough room between cars for doors to open. It felt like concert parking. The concert of war, maybe.

We slid out of the car and followed the pointing finger of an old woman with shocking green-gold eyes who said, "Don't leave your car for more than an hour. Be back in your car before first light. We don't guarantee your safety or anyone else's. Anything you have could get stolen." It sounded like a chore for her to say all those things, like she'd repeated it so often she was running out of voice.

"Is there a bathroom?" I asked.

"Latrine—that way."

Guardsmen kept people from leaving the line to pee in the bushes. Two days ago, I had sat in front of a computer screen helping people who wanted to have their dogs walked while they were at work. The deluded helping the deluded, the last ones out of Seattle except the fighters. Lucienne stared at her wristlet, making sure to keep at least three feet from me. I poked at mine from time to time, but I was not good with it. Not really. I could get the headlines but not read the stories.

The latrine stank so badly we walked away fast after we used it. As it grew dark, we huddled in the car, packs for pillows, jackets for blankets. Even after the seats folded themselves away there wasn't much room. We ate food bars and nuts. Lucienne let out a small squeak and then said, "Mom?"

"Yes?"

"Lisa's boat just blew up."

I closed my eyes, seeing a girl just Lucienne's age, with dark hair and eyes and a propensity for wearing yellow. She'd come to our house for dinner once. Last year. "Is she okay?"

"She's running through the streets. There's no one with her. I don't see anyone, anyway. All I have is her stream and her track."

That would be a live stream of shots taken every few seconds and discarded, and a bunch of orange points that looked like video game trails showing where Lisa was and had been. She would have it; they were friends. I wouldn't.

I hadn't even location-friended Juliette. I didn't want to see her die.

Lucienne, her eyes fixed and wide, watched Lisa run for her life, staring at a screen that was two inches wide and one inch high. Her lips were a thin line. Her pinky shook so hard it made her screen quiver. She grabbed her hand with her other hand and stilled it.

I wanted to hold her. She'd stopped even letting me touch her a year ago.

I whispered. "Is Lisa okay?"

She nodded.

I watched her, afraid for her friends, afraid for her. In what world was the United States attacked?

"Her light stopped."

"Maybe she's catching her breath."

Lucienne shook her wrist. "Maybe she ran out of battery."

"I hope so, honey."

"We should be there." She turned away from me, staring at the wall, and after a while her breath stilled into sleep.

Even though they were bulletproof, the windows were made to hear things through. An owl hooted somewhere outside and two men talked nearby, their words too thin for me to make out meaning. I wanted to stay awake, but I had barely slept the night before, and I drifted off into strange dreams.

I woke to find Lucienne gone.

No note. No nothing. One of the packs was gone as well.

The car had grown cold. "Car," I commanded it, "Let me out."

I checked my wristlet. I had location-friended my daughter. Clearly she had blocked me.

I raced through the cars toward the latrine, watching for her. She wasn't in line. I had a flashlight in my pocket, but no coat, no pack. I went back and gathered those things, left her a note that I'd gone to find her. Told her I'd be back at the car in an hour.

She wouldn't try to walk back to Seattle.

More cars drove in along the long road, passing us, going who knew how far. Everywhere that I saw people out and about, standing between cars and talking, I asked after Lucienne. "Have you seen a twelve-year-old? Red hair. Black shirt. A little skinny?"

They all shook their heads.

Three men agreed to help me, and then a woman. Soon there

were ten or more people fanned out in the dark, calling her name. My breath was fast and hard, my heart racing. I thought about texting Juliette, but surely she had other things on her mind. The hour passed, with nothing. My helpers agreed to keep looking and I made my way back to our parking place, eyeing the barely lightening sky. We were supposed to be ready at dawn.

Lucienne wasn't at the car. Of course she wasn't. My hands shook with panic as I added to my note. When I went to stand, my legs refused to support me and fell back into the open car door. Tears fell onto my hands.

Maybe she was texting Juliette. I texted her. <*Lucienne missing*> <*Have U heard from her?*>

God, I sounded cold. No intro. Just the fact's ma'am. I added <how are you?>

Nothing. I used my arms to force myself up, and started looking again, glancing at my wrist from time to time.

Light spilled into the darkness. Birds sang.

I hadn't seen my daughter for six hours. When did she leave? Where was she?

What could I have said differently?

Was she safe?

I found a thin, stooped man wearing the ubiquitous orange vest. "Have you seen a child?"

"How old?"

"Twelve."

"Do you have a picture?"

"Of course." I sent him one. He futzed with his wristlet, then looked up and said, "Go back to your car."

"I'm not leaving her."

He spoke slowly, as if I were hard of hearing. "You need to be in your car for it to get out of the lot."

"Other cars can go around it."

"Go to your car. We'll find you."

"Okay." I didn't. I jogged between rows of cars, watching people wake up. People in orange started yelling at everyone to get in their cars, and I waved at them. Sure. Sure. I was going.

Where was she?

Engines began to turn on.

Cars pulled out, a slow, depressing line. Our still and silent car probably slowed them down some, but I couldn't tell.

A drone flew over. News drone? Battle drone?

As the cars near me started, lights flipped on, and soft engine noise declared life. I jogged between them, heading for the front of the lot, suddenly afraid she'd be in someone's car. She was a beautiful little girl, angry but ripe for the right predator. I wanted to watch every car to be sure Lucienne wasn't trapped in any of them.

Another drone came. They dipped and dove and shot at nothing and no one shot at them. But people everywhere watched them, sitting up straight and leaning out windows and taking pictures with wrists and other small cameras. The drones were eerily silent, as were the cars, everything so electric and quiet the sound of birds singing came through the morning clearly.

A hand landed on my shoulder when I wasn't expecting it, and I jumped. A tall man in an orange vest striped with safety yellow. His sunglasses—pushed on top of his head—matched. I hadn't seen such a full beard in years, brown but starting to grow in gray. "Go to your car."

"I have to find my daughter."

"They found her."

"Who?"

"A friend. Up the road. In a tow truck. He's bringing her back."

"Up the road? Where?"

"She was on her way to Seattle. She was almost at the crest." He looked violently disapproving, as if I'd lost her on purpose.

Shame and anger and relief warred inside me. I bit them back and said, "Thank you."

"Wait in your car."

I didn't want to comply. I compromised by heading toward the car and hovering within a few hundred feet of it.

Juliette didn't text me back. I tried not to think about that, but it was like not thinking about pink elephants. I kept imagining her falling, her hurt, her alone and dying.

Lucienne didn't turn on her location beacons, so I couldn't tell how long it would take for her to get back to me. I fought for calm. I had to be calm. I could keep her safe if I could stay calm.

The lot was almost empty, even the drones gone. A bald eagle rode a thermal above the lot. I periodically read headlines. Russians pouring down I5. Missiles hitting downtown. Fires. People fleeing from Tacoma. A truck had taken down a bridge, snarling traffic. Russians starting down two more border points, one in Montana and one in North Dakota. They hadn't yet captured anything in Eastern Canada, and our troops were helping the Canadians as well as fighting for us. People were rushing to join, and I thought of Juliette again, and wondered where she was. Almost everyone else I knew had left Seattle before we did.

When the bearded man brought Lucienne back, her face was so white I wondered what he had said to her, and my anger fled into some other protective state. "Are you okay?" I asked as soon as he had gone.

She swallowed. "Lisa's dead."

"Do you know that?"

She stared at the ground and mumbled. "Someone else is using her wristlet. Someone who speaks another language."

"Is that all you know?"

"Yes."

"Is that why you left?"

She toed the ground. "I wanted to help her."

There was still a chasm between us. I could feel it, and I made myself stand still and not reach for her no matter how much I wanted to. "I'm sorry."

"I haven't heard from Juliette. I don't know if she's okay, either."

"I texted her when you were missing."

"I don't want to leave home," she said. "I can't help anyone from here. I can't do anything useful." Her voice started to rise. "I can't be a hero."

Was that what this was about? "Of course you can. Give it a little time."

"I want to be a hero now." She was almost shouting, my little serious child who almost always followed directions.

My voice rose in return, matching hers, rising above it. "Like what? A comic book hero?"

She simply stared at me, as if the question had shocked her still.

I stepped toward her. "Is Lisa a hero?"

Silence.

Anger licked through my bones, burning away any self-control I had left. "Does dying make you a hero? We could arrange that." I sounded snappy, even to myself. Mean. Horrible. Noisy. I can only imagine what I sounded like to her. "We are family. We need to keep each other alive. There will be more chance to die in your life. You'll have them. Plenty of them. But you have to learn more before you can be a hero." I took a deep heaving breath.

Lucienne eyes widened. I never yelled.

Except now. I kept my voice high, piling my fear for her into it. "Lisa is no hero. She's just dead. Or not. You don't know. But if she died, it didn't do any good. Death doesn't do anyone any good."

Lucienne said nothing, merely stared.

"It's true. You can choose to die any day. Any day. But you can also choose to live. We're going to live."

"I want to fight."

"You have to live to fight!"

My wrist buzzed, interrupted my tirade. Juliette. <Did you find her?>

I felt parts of me relax, breathe out. <Yes>

<I'm OK. Sleeping now. Love you. Text you tomorrow. Keep her safe.>

This time all I felt was relief. No warring emotions. Just relief. I showed Lucienne the texts. "She's fighting to keep you and I safe. We should go."

A tear streaked down her face.

I couldn't help myself. I reached out and plucked the tear from her cheek.

She stepped into me for the first time in two years, and her arms curled around me.

"I love you," I whispered. "I need for you to be safe."

"I never hated you."

My whole body shook. "I know." I felt no distance between us, just her heart beating against my own chest.

THE ROAD TO NORMAL
IS CLOSED

My seatbelt clicks under a sky charred with russet,
gray, and sepia specks. These were oak leaves, aspens
beside creeks, and red cedar that stood on ridges
for a thousand years. Greens and golds and yellows have
been transformed by Washington fires with names
like Evans Canyon, Pearl Hills, Downey Creek, and
Big Hollow. The names memorialize places humans have
loved and ruined by oil, by disbelief, by casual mistakes.

In Montana, the big sky is stained by Bridger Foothills,
State Creek, Cinnabar and the Drumming Fire. Smoke has
swept to sea from California and back to this place from
the Bullfrog Fire, Fork Fire, Creek Fire, Doe Fire, Shackleford Fire,
El Dorado Fire, Rattlesnake Fire, Apple Fire, Lake Fire, and the Feather
Fire as if the deer and frog and snake and the shade that covered streams
gurgling down the middle of canyons hovers in the sky, heading
for whatever heaven blameless wild birds might fly into.

In Utah, pale blue appears above, the sky turned almost to
itself, the sides of the road lush with willow and untroubled
cattle farms. The road pulls up to Salt Lake and down to Grand
Staircase Escalante and then to more red rock near Lake Powell.
Dropping through clipped, hairpin turns near Oak Creek,
signs tell me sirens will cry if any flames lick at the parched
trees on either side of the canyon. After I hike Little Horse trail in
Sedona, the sun sets over a slightly sullen horizon, and I taste ash.

ACKNOWLEDGEMENTS

A collection comes to be because of many supporting hands. Initial thanks, of course, goes to people to read my work.

My wife, Toni, puts up with me stealing away to write at odd hours or for long weekends or at retreats. It does cost us time, and I am every so grateful for her patience, support, and grace.

Thanks to Patrick Swenson of Fairwood Press for supporting this, for helping to get it out by Worldcon, and for being such a lovely human, writer, and publisher!

Thank you to my writing group: Darragh Metzger (who may have read every story I've published), Kathy Klein, Maura Glynn-Thami, and Janka Hobbs.

Many publishers originally bought these stories. Thanks to all of them of course, with particular thanks to Ed Finn and Joey Eschrich from the Center for Science and the Imagination at Arizona State University. They were responsible for three of the stories: "Out of Ash," "Blackstart," and "For the Snake of Power." "Blackstart" and "For the Snake of Power" came out of wonderful in-person workshops at ASU where writers, illustrators, and engineers and/or scientists shared knowledge and ideas.

ABOUT THE AUTHOR

BRENDA COOPER is a writer, a technology professional, and a futurist. Two of her novels, *The Silver Ship and the Sea* and *Edge of Dark*, have won the Endeavour Award for the best science fiction or fantasy book written by a Pacific Northwest. Brenda's most recent novels include a climate fiction duology set in the Pacific Northwest (*Wilders* and *Keepers*) and the tenth-anniversary re-drafted release of her Fremont's Children series. Her love of technology, science, and science fiction drives her interest in the future. She is particularly interested in robotics, climate change, and the social change that must go hand in hand with fixing the human relationship to the natural world. Brenda lives in Washington State with her wife, Toni, and their multiple border collies, some of whom actually get to herd sheep. She loves to exercise, garden, read, and talk with friends.

PUBLICATION HISTORY

"Solastalgia Meets the Alps" originally appeared in *Anthropocene Magazine*, December 2022 | "In Their Garden" originally appeared in *Asimov's Science Fiction*, September 2009; reprinted in *Years Best SF 15* edited by Kathryn Cramer and David G. Hartwell, Eos/HarperCollins, June 2010; podcast in *Starship Sofa* #264, November 2012; reprinted in *Surviving Tomorrow*, edited by Bryan Thomas Schmidt, Aeristic Press, June 2010 | "Callme and Mink" originally appeared in *Clarkesworld*, October 2020; reprinted in *The Year's Top Robot and AI Stories: Second Annual Collection*, edited by Allan Kaster, Infinivox, November 2021 | "Elephant Angels," originally appeared in *Hieroglyph: Stories and Visions for a Better Future*, edited by Kathryn Cramer and Ed Finn, William Morrow/HarperCollins, 2014 | "When Mothers Dream" appears here for the first time | "Southern Residents" originally appeared in *Current Futures: A Sci-fi Ocean Anthology*, edited by Ann Vandermeer, XPRIZE Foundation, June 2019 | "Annalee of the Orcas" appears here for the first time | "Maybe the Monarchs" originally appeared in *After the Orange: Ruin and Recovery*, edited by Manny Frishberg, B-Cubed Press, 2018 | "The Seventh Feeling" appears here for the first time | "Biology at the End of the World" originally appeared in *Asimov's Science Fiction*, September 2015 | "Her Granddaughter's Teachers" appears here for the first time | "Out of Ash" originally appeared in *Slate Magazine*, May 2022; reprinted in *Forever*, edited by Neil Clarke, Wyrm Publishing, February 2024. | "Blackstart" originally appeared in *Overview: Stories of the Stratosphere*, edited by Michael G. Bennett, Joey Eschrich, and Ed Finn, Arizona State University Center for Science and the Imagination, 2017 | "For the Snake of Power" originally appeared in *The Weight of Light: A Collection of Solar Futures*, edited by Joey Eschrich and Clark A. Miller, Arizona State University, 2018; reprinted in *Navigated Narratives: A Thematic Reader*, by Hawkes Learning, 2022; reprinted in *Beyond and Within Solar Punk: Short Stories from Many Futures*, edited by Francesco Verso, FlameTree Publishing, October 2024 | "Heroes" originally appeared in *Children of a Different Sky*, edited by Alma Alexander, Kos Books, November 2017

All poems are original to this collection: "An Ice Free Future," "Tahlequah," "Zombies," "City Inundated," "Curse of the Orcas," and "The Road to Normal is Closed"

OTHER TITLES FROM FAIRWOOD PRESS

*Obviously I Love You
But If I Were a Bird*
by Patrick O'Leary
small paperback $11.00
ISBN: 978-1-958880-37-1

Space Trucker Jess
by Matthew Kressel
trade paper $20.95
ISBN: 978-1-958880-27-2

Shifter and Shadow
by Sharon Shinn
trade paper $16.99
ISBN: 978-1-958880-36-4

*A Catalog of Storms:
Collected Short Fiction*
by Fran Wilde
trade paper $18.99
ISBN: 978-1-958880-31-9

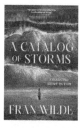

*Better Dreams, Fallen Seeds
and Other Handfuls of Hope*
by Ken Scholes
paperback $19.99
ISBN: 978-1-958880-32-6

Changelog: Collected Fiction
by Rich Larson
trade paper $20.95
ISBN: 978-1-958880-33-3

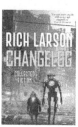

Black Hole Heart and Other Stories
by K.A. Teryna
trade paper $18.99
ISBN: 978-1-958880-29-6

One Last Game
by T.A. Chan
trade paper $15.99
ISBN: 978-1-958880-34-0

Find us at:
www.fairwoodpress.com
Bonney Lake, Washington

www.ingramcontent.com/pod-product-compliance
Lightning Source LLC
LaVergne TN
LVHW042358060925
820333LV00003B/127